THE WOODHOUSE PENDANT

Neil Cawtheray

Grosvenor House
Publishing Limited

This book is published by
Grosvenor House Publishing Ltd
Link House
140 The Broadway, Tolworth, Surrey, KT6 7HT.
www.grosvenorhousepublishing.co.uk

This book is a work of fiction. Any resemblance to
people or events, past or present, is purely coincidental.

A CIP record for this book
is available from the British Library

ISBN 978-1-78623-245-8

I dedicate this book to all my new friends
from St. John's Church at Farsley,
who between them have created
such a warm community spirit that
I have not experienced elsewhere.

I also dedicate it to Mrs. Irene McDonald
because I know that's what Barry would
have wanted me to do.

My heartfelt thanks, as always,
go to my dear wife Jennifer,
whose love and affection over the years
has always meant so much to me.

CHAPTER ONE

"That girl there," boomed Mr. Rawcliffe, the head-master of Woodhouse Junior School, his words being directed towards Eva Bentley who was attempting to engage the pupil sitting next to her in conversation. If he was ever displeased about something, which was frequently, he always addressed his pupils in this fashion even though he knew the name of every child under his care. "I'd like you to tell me everything you know about apostrophes, if it's not too much trouble."

"I beg your pardon, sir?" said his victim in a subdued voice.

"I want you tell me everything you know on the subject of 'Apostrophes', Miss Bentley," he repeated.

"Wasn't he that Greek philosopher, sir?" she suggested, hopefully.

"What is the title of this afternoon's lesson, young lady?"

"The title, sir?"

"Yes, you silly girl, what is it about?"

"English grammar, sir."

"Then perhaps you can explain to me why I should be asking a question about ancient Greece in an English grammar lesson."

"No, sir, sorry, sir."

There was much laughter at our fellow pupil's discomfort and, shamefully, I was one of the main ones involved. I think it was probably because we were all elated that we were coming to the end of term. After this day we had only two more school attendances to make before we broke up for Easter on the Tuesday following.

"Now, I'd like you all to listen, and you in particular Miss Bentley, to what I have to say concerning apostrophes," went on the headmaster. "I was looking at a composition handed in by one boy, who shall remain nameless, and I had to stare really hard before deciding that it did not, after all, contain dozens of tiny black insects crawling all over it."

There was much laughter again from his audience.

"It's all very well to laugh," he went on, "But it is very important to know when to use an apostrophe and when not as it can change the whole meaning of a sentence, as I shall shortly demonstrate. I no longer want to see any pupil of this school inserting an apostrophe simply because a word ends with the letter 'S'. Apostrophes are only used to indicate either omission or possession." He picked up a piece of chalk and began to write on the blackboard. "Now here are two examples of how the meaning of a sentence can be changed." He wrote ROSES ARE RED. VIOLETS ARE BLUE. "There you have two simple statements concerning the colour of two individual species of flower." He picked up the chalk again and wrote ROSE'S ARE RED. VIOLET'S ARE BLUE. "Write it in this second way and you are immediately transported to the rather mysterious world of ladies' underwear"

There was a baffled silence among my fellow pupils for several seconds before the penny dropped and the silence was broken by howls of laughter. It was noticeable, however, that one class member did not seem amused by the headmaster's remark as Violet Pemberton blushed crimson, put her head in her hands and slumped forward onto the desk. It was most unusual for Mr. Rawcliffe to inject any form of humour into his lessons and I can only assume that it was the prospect of the Easter break looming on the horizon that was responsible for this change of mood.

The remainder of the lesson, however, took on a more serious note and by the time the bell sounded to signal the end of the school week there was a hurried scramble for the door. When the state of the weather became apparent to all, however, our hitherto overwhelming desire to make haste was seriously diminished. The rain was so intense and the force of the wind was causing it to blow almost horizontally. Before long a bottleneck formed with everyone being reluctant to step outside to face the elements; that is until Tucker Lane forced his way to the front. It was not surprising that he chose to be the first to step outside while chiding everyone else for being such wimps. He had long been regarded as the school champion and liked nothing more than a good scrap in the schoolyard whenever the opportunity arose and if, on occasions, it did not arise then he was more than capable of initiating such a situation. His position as school champion was rarely challenged, but it had been recently enhanced when he was victorious in an epic bout with an obnoxious newcomer who wanted to be known by the name of Krusher Kershaw, a battle which was already gaining legendary status among the pupils of Woodhouse Junior School. The fact that his opponent had been universally detested resulted in his victory being immensely popular.

Eventually, a few of the others began to trickle out but whereas Tucker was strolling manfully along Jubilee Terrace towards Woodhouse Street, those who followed broke into a run while emitting shrieks and howls of protest. Billy and I decided that ten minutes of voluntary detention was quite sufficient and ventured out to face the harsh conditions which had in no way abated. We began running as fast as we could but we pulled up sharply within the first few yards as we were greeted by the sound of an almighty crash.

"Crikey! Look at that, Neil," yelled Billy striving to be heard above the sound of the wind.

We both watched in awe as about seventy per cent of the scaffolding surrounding the roof of the Electra Picture House came crashing to the ground. We ignored the extreme weather conditions and contemplated the scene before us, as there was no way that we could get any wetter than we already were.

"That's going to set them back a bit, Billy," I said.

It was only recently that work had begun on repairing the roof of our local cinema after it had recently been damaged during a substantial storm. This had occurred on a Friday evening, which was always one of the Electra's busiest nights, and had caused much consternation among the patrons. We decided not to hang about and hurried to cover the few remaining yards to the shelter of our respective houses which were three doors apart.

"What was that awful clatter?" was my mother's greeting.

4

Nell, a scruffy-looking mongrel who, in the absence of a more affluent family at her time of need, which was more than five years previously, had reluctantly decided to accept us as the guardians of her canine welfare. She now observed the soaking wet, dishevelled apparition that had just intruded into her comfort zone and no doubt wondered, as she had been forced to do on several earlier occasions, whether her decision had been a wise one. She gave me a look of disgust and moved closer to the coal fire and resettled herself on the clip rug.

"All the scaffolding round the Electra has blown down, mam" I said, in answer to her question;" Well nearly all of it, anyway."

"That's a pity," she responded. "It was due to reopen soon. If the weather stays as bad as this for a day or two it's certainly going to delay things."

"I know, mam. I can't wait for it to open again."

"Well, I'll tell you one thing for sure. You're certainly not going to the Astra or the Royal tonight; not in this weather."

My mother was well aware that Billy and I used to like going to the pictures on a Friday evening whenever possible, and it was only recently that I had been given permission to visit the only other two cinemas in what she considered a reasonable distance, one of which was in Woodhouse Street and the other in Meanwood Road. I doubted whether I fancied venturing out in the present weather conditions anyway.

"That brings me to another thing," she went on. "We were supposed to be visiting your grandad tomorrow afternoon, but I don't think that's likely to happen now either."

Grandad Miller was undergoing a period of convalescence on Ilkley Moor after having been in hospital following an asthma attack just before Christmas from which he had almost died. Fortunately he did seem to be on the mend and I had been looking forward to seeing him again.

"He should be coming home soon, shouldn't he, mam?"

"I reckon so, but I can't see it being before Easter, so maybe we can go to see him then,"

I loved Grandad Miller's stories about when he was a young lad around the turn of the century and how he and his best mate were always getting into mischief. On my previous visit to the convalescent home I had discovered that both of them, by a strange coincidence just happened to be resident there at the same time, though unbeknown to either of them, and when I imparted this knowledge to my grandfather I felt sure that it must help him on the road to recovery. Having not visited him since that day I was unable to test the validity of my surmise.

My thoughts on this matter were interrupted as Nell gave a sudden bark, stared at my mother, then at the fire and finally at the cellar door.

"The fire's getting low," indicated my mother by pointing at the dull glow emanating from the fireplace, "You'd better bring a shovelful of coal up. I want it to be warm when your dad comes home. He'll be freezing in this weather."

Nell, satisfied that her demands were about to be met, settled down again on the clip rug.

I switched on the light and made my way down the stone steps. At the bottom I entered what was really the first of two cellars as the original room had been divided several years previously by a wall having been erected with an opening on the right-hand side just wide enough, in the absence of a door, to gain entrance without the necessity of having to walk sideways. It was this second room to which we used to retreat during the war whenever the siren announced an air raid in the middle of the night, thus prompting us to leave the comfort of our beds and hurry down the stairs to sanctuary. Being very young at the time and failing to understand the dangers of air raids I used to look forward to this change in routine as being awakened in the middle of the night and taken to a new location always seemed to me like a great adventure. The bunks that my brother and I used to lie on were still there. Along one side of the room was my father's work bench along with a cupboard in which he used to store his tools. The first room, which I entered after leaving the stairs, was the one where the pile of coal was stored. This was delivered through a grate, sacks being emptied haphazardly so that an untidy pile was formed on the floor. As I took hold of the shovel propped up against the cellar wall the light bulb suddenly flickered and went out, the consequence of which was that I tripped over something and fell headlong, face forward, onto the pile of coal. Within seconds the light was back on again. I was relieved to only have some slight grazing on my left knee. I completed my task and set off again up the cellar steps holding a full shovel when the light flickered again and went out. I tripped on one of the steps and dropped the shovel which clattered all the way down to the bottom. The light immediately came back on. This time my mother decided to make an appearance and demanded to know what all the noise was about. She was accompanied by Nell, who peered down at what remained of my shovelful of coal dispersed along the stairway and gave me a look of disgust as if wondering why I was unable to complete what she regarded as a comparatively simple task. My mother, however, was more concerned about the state of my clothes than anything else.

"How on earth did you get in that state?" she asked, completely ignoring my grazed knee and directing all her attention onto the considerable number of black patches that had mysteriously appeared on my shirt and trousers.

"The light went out twice, mam," I told her in an attempt to justify my dishevelled appearance.

"It looks all right to me," she replied with a disbelieving look on her face. "Are you sure you haven't been larking about down there?"

"Yes, mam; and look, I've grazed my knee."

"Well, you'd better sweep all those pieces of coal back down the cellar steps," she said, handing me the sweeping brush. As she did so the light flickered and went out but within seconds came back on again.

After doing as she asked and we had re-entered the living room Nell looked up from the clip rug, stared at me, then at the fire and then at my mother.

"Look, there's a torch in the cupboard. You'd better go back down because we still need a shovelful of coal. I want the house to be nice and warm for when your father gets back from work. If the light goes out again just shine the torch. I'll get him to put a fresh bulb in after he's had his tea."

Nell seemed to think this was quite a reasonable solution to the problem and settled down again, putting her head on her paws.

After the task had been performed I was spared the embarrassment of having to get clean by immersing myself in the tin bath, though I suspect that this was only because of the proximity to tea time. I was, however, made to have a thorough wash in the sink and to change my shirt and trousers. The graze on my knee was again totally ignored. My father arrived at the expected time, my mother greeting him with the news that the light bulb in the cellar was behaving strangely.

"I'll put another one in," he said as he took off his coat and hung it up. "If that one does the same I'll have a look at the wiring."

My mother began to lay the table. "By the way," she said, "Brenda's made some new jam. It's on the top shelf in the cupboard next to that tin of dried milk. "She brought it over yesterday afternoon but I forgot to tell you."

My Auntie Brenda made the best jam that I had ever tasted.

"What flavour is it this time?" asked my father.

"It says plum and orange on the jar."

"Oh, now that's an unusual combination. I don't think she's ever done that one before."

"It's really nice, Tom. I had some with a slice of bread this morning. Unfortunately, some of the jam must have slipped from the knife as I was spreading it and fallen onto the carpet. Nell must have trodden on it and spread it all over the floor."

The perpetrator of the crime chose that moment to raise her paw and lick underneath it.

9

"This jam is so dark," continued my mother, "That if you drop any it's hard to find where it is against the carpet."

"If Auntie Brenda managed to find something to put in it that would make it glow in the dark I bet she would make a lot of money out of it," I suggested, helpfully. "I bet people are always dropping dollops of jam off the edges of their knives. She could call it luminous jam. I don't think anyone will have thought of it before. Yes, I bet she'd make a fortune."

"Now stop being silly," said my mother, totally unimpressed by my idea of how to make my Auntie Brenda a millionaire. My father, however, was laughing at the thought.

"Why don't you think of some way of making me a millionaire so that I don't have to work on five and a half days every week?"

"I'll think about it, dad," was the only response I could give him.

"Well," he said, deciding to change the subject, "It doesn't look like you and Billy will be going to the Electra for a while, does it? All that scaffolding will have to be re-erected before they can even think about continuing to repair the roof, and they certainly can't do that in this weather can they? By the way, you're surely not supposed to be playing rugby tomorrow, are you?"

Woodhouse Junior School Rugby League Team was in its first season and as far as results were concerned it had been a disaster. We were bottom of the local schools league but had only recently won our first game. With only three games remaining we were keen to win at least another one of them which might enable us to climb off the bottom.

"No, dad," I said, "We don't have a game tomorrow."

"Well, I'm very relieved to hear that because there doesn't appear to be much sign of this terrible weather improving, and it's no good you catching your death of cold, is it?"

"Mrs. On-The-Other-Side," said my mother, "Told me that she had an uncle once who died of pneumonia after being out in weather like this."

My mother's difficulty in remembering people's names frequently caused identification problems for the listener, and on this occasion I hadn't the faintest idea to whom she was referring, except for the fact that her unfortunate choice of name in this particular instance referred to the lady's place of residence and not that she had died and passed over.

"There you are then;" said my father, "That just reinforces what I'm trying to say. So I expect you to stay in tonight as well. You can always listen to 'Up The Pole' on the wireless. I know you like Jewell and Warris."

I walked over to the window and peered out at the atrocious conditions that persisted outside and I was very much relieved that I did not have to take part in any kind of sport on the following morning. However, it left me with the unpleasant realisation that the following day would almost certainly prove to be an extremely boring one.

CHAPTER TWO

Saturday, as we had expected, was a horrible day. The wind and rain continued, almost incessantly, until the early evening. When I looked out of my bedroom window on the following morning, however, I could see that Sunday was going to be different; not remarkably different as the sky was still overcast, but the wind had subsided considerably and the rain had ceased altogether. It was what you might expect from the weather in mid March.

"I'm just going to see if Billy's playing out," I told my mother immediately after having devoured my breakfast. I was not expecting any objections now that the rain had ceased and the force of the wind had become much less severe, so I was rather surprised at my mother's next statement.

"I want you to go see how your Grandma Cawson is, and to take her one or two things. She won't have been able to go out during the terrible weather that we've been having over the last few days."

Grandma Cawson lived in the only house that remained standing in Chancellor Place near the nursery at the bottom of Speedwell Street, all the other houses having been demolished just before the outbreak of the war. I suppose she had led rather a lonely existence since my grandfather died three years previously.

"And don't think about taking Billy down there with you. I know what you two are like when you get together. You'd probably get distracted and forget what you're going for. Your grandma needs a bit of company on a Sunday morning and she's always telling me she doesn't see you enough; so make sure you go on your own."

I had long suspected that my mother, in certain situations at least, was able to read my thoughts. She handed me four home-baked buns, a couple of pikelets and a small malt loaf all neatly placed in a paper carrier bag with a string handle.

"Make sure you don't rush straight back," she went on. "Your grandma needs a bit of company on a Sunday at her age. Come back in plenty of time for dinner though. I was hoping the weather might have improved sufficiently for us to go see your Grandad Miller this afternoon, but I don't think that's very likely."

I set off down Speedwell Street, tucking the carrier bag under my arm in as masculine a way as possible instead of holding it by the handle in the way that a girl would. The last thing that I wanted, if I happened to meet any of the lads from school, would be to resemble little red riding hood carrying goodies on her way to her grandma's house.

"Oh, come to visit your old grandmother at last then, have you?" was her greeting after I had knocked on the door. She usually greeted me in a similar fashion whenever I called, though on this occasion I suppose it was justified as I hadn't seen her for several weeks.

"My mam asked me to call with a few things, grandma," I replied.

"So, you're only visiting me because your mother asked you to, are you?"

I could provide no satisfactory answer to this as I handed her the carrier bag.

"Three buns, two pikelets and a malt loaf," I said, expecting her face to beam with delight.

Three buns, eh," she said, eyeing me suspiciously, and I suppose you can explain to me where those crumbs at the corner of your mouth came from."

Again I could not find an answer that would satisfy and just remained silent, looking guilty.

"Well then, it's very thoughtful of your mother anyway. Now, before you take your coat off you can do a little errand for me if you will. I want you to call at the newsagent's shop in Meanwood Road and bring me a copy of the 'News Of The World'.

"Yes, grandma."

"Oh, and you can see if they have a copy of 'Woman's Own' left. You can get yourself a comic as well if you like."

She handed me a two shilling piece and I set off down the remainder of Speedwell Street and turned into Meanwood Road. I spent a couple of minutes gazing into the newsagent's window before stepping inside.

"By heck, Jimmy, I'm fair clemmed," said the elderly gentleman to the proprietor of the establishment as he was handed his Sunday newspaper.

"Well, I'm not surprised George. It's a fair way to walk from your house. I mean, the wind's still blowing a bit as well, isn't it?"

George's face took on a puzzled look as he said goodbye and walked out of the shop.

"What does 'clemmed' mean?" I asked the man behind the counter.

"Well, I've always taken it to mean being out of breath, exhausted, so to speak though I have known people to disagree with me, and he did look a bit puzzled, didn't he? Now, lad, what can I get you?"

I decided to buy a copy of the 'Hotspur' comic after having seen the exciting front cover artwork in the window and as I left the shop I made sure that my grandmother's copy of 'Woman's Own' was placed neatly inside the folded newspaper so that no one would see me carrying it.

"Grandma, what does it mean if anyone says that he's 'fair clemmed'?" I asked her after handing her the newspaper and magazine. I've never heard it before, but the man at the newsagent's said that he thought that it was something you would say if you were exhausted and out of puff."

"Well, I've never heard that explanation before. I always thought it meant that you were hungry, but not many people seem to use the expression these days. Mind you my brother always used to say the opposite. He used to say it when he'd over-filled himself with food and had to loosen his trousers. So you can take your pick of those, if you like."

I stayed with her for what I considered to be a reasonable period of time which passed pleasantly enough and included a glass of Dandelion and Burdock, plus another bun to add to the one that I had shamefully deprived her of earlier.

I began to walk back up Speedwell Street, but decided to hang back for a while and look in Lawson's shop window after I noticed two familiar figures who I suspected must have just got off the tram in Meanwood Road. I waited until they had gone past then began to walk slowly behind them as I had always found their conversations fascinating.

"I'll swing for that ginger-headed tram conductor yet, Phyllis, so help me," said the larger of the two ladies. "I'll give him patting me on the bottom and calling me Tootsie, and I'm not the only one he's tried it on with, oh no, not by a long chalk. Well I'll tell you this, Phyllis, and I don't care who hears me, he'll soon find out that I'm not a woman to be trifled with."

"Oh, you're not, Edna, you're not."

"He struts about that tram as if he's a famous film star seeking attention. I could understand it if he looked like Don Ameche."

"Who's she then, Edna?"

"Who's who?"

"Who's this Donna Meechey? I've never heard of her."

"That's because it isn't a woman, Phyllis. It's a man."

"Well, I don't think that was very nice of his parents calling him Donna. Why did they give him a girl's name? I bet he had a terrible time of it when he went to school. All the other lads would have been pulling his leg all the time."

"Look, I didn't say he was called Donna Meechey. I said he was called Don Ameche."

"Now, you're really confusing me, Edna. You didn't say he was called Donna Meechey, you said he was called Donna Meechey. What kind of sense is that?"

I was struggling not to laugh out loud and betray my presence as Edna was getting more and more exasperated at her companion's failure to understand what, to her, was a simple statement of fact. She let out a long sigh and began to speak again.

"Now listen carefully, Phyllis and play close attention. I'll say this very slowly. He isn't called Donna. His name is Don."

"Well that makes more sense, Edna, but if you'd told me in the first place that his name was Don Meechey instead of calling him Donna Meechey then I'd have understood. So if there's been any misunderstanding I reckon it was your fault and I think you ought to apologise."

It was the first time that I had her stand up to her larger companion and I was quite impressed. Edna hadn't finished though and her voice rose until she was almost shouting.

"He isn't called Don Meechey he's called Don Ameche."

"Now you're doing it again," responded Phyllis.

"Look let's just forget about it and talk about something else," announced Edna, finally admitting defeat.

"Who is your favourite film star then, Edna?"

"I quite like that Hedy Lamarr."

"Now I have heard of Eddie Lamarr but I don't think I've seen any of his films though."

"It's a woman, Phyllis," said Edna, breathing out another long sigh.

As I reached the beginning of my street I didn't mind leaving them to continue up the remainder of Speedwell Street as I felt that the topic of their conversation had just about run its course.

"Hiya, Neil," said Nicky Whitehead, who was standing outside his house which was next to Mrs. Ormond's sweet shop. "I was just talking to Johnny Jackson and he told me that a tree had blown down on the ridge because of the strong winds and that it was stretching right across the beck. He said that he and some other lads had been daring each other to walk across it without touching it with their hands and that three of them had fallen in. I was thinking of going to have a look after I've had my dinner. Do you want to go?"

Nicky wasn't in my class at school, being a year younger, but he was a member of our rugby league team, having already broken his arm during a game a few months earlier causing it to be postponed, though he seemed now to be fully recovered. I suspected though that his mother would be very disapproving if she found out what he might be planning.

"It sounds great," I told him. "About the only thing that would stop me going is if my mother decided to take me to see my grandad in the convalescent home at Ilkley, but she said earlier that we'd only go if the weather got a lot better. Did you tell Billy about it?"

"Not yet, but I was going to."

"I'll tell him if you like then and if we're going we'll call at your house after dinner."

With the bargain sealed I walked the few remaining yards home. I could smell the roast beef as soon as I opened the door. My mother immediately announced that we would not be visiting my grandfather and therefore I could eat my dinner in a leisurely fashion without wolfing it down. She was of course completely unaware of my eagerness to join Billy and Nicky on an adventurous escapade on Woodhouse Ridge. Nevertheless, I did my best to eat in what she considered to be the only suitable fashion that was acceptable. The first course, as always on a Sunday, consisted of a Yorkshire pudding covered in onion gravy which filled the entire plate. This was followed by roast beef with mashed potatoes, cauliflower and carrots. For dessert my mother had made a rice pudding. By the time I had completed everything that was on offer I was full to bursting and my eagerness to rush outside had subsided somewhat. However, as soon as I heard a knock on the door my enthusiasm returned only to subside again when I realised the caller was not Billy or Nicky.

"Are you there, May?" asked the intruder, "Only I didn't want to barge right in, do you see, in case you were still eating your dinner."

It was most unusual for our close neighbour to knock. My mother had by now become accustomed to hearing him push open the door and walk in before calling out his usual greeting.

"Good afternoon, Mr. Senior," she said, "What can I do for you today?"

"Well, what it is, do you see, I've Just broken off the handle of my Toby Jug while I was looking for something else in the cupboard and I wondered if you might have a bit of glue I could borrow. It was a present from our Doreen and I was hoping that I might be able to stick it back on before the next time she came round. I'm sure she'd be upset if she saw the state it's in now. I think it was quite expensive, you know."

"Tom, do you think you might have some glue with all that other stuff you've got in the cellar?" asked my mother.

"Yes, I'm sure I can spare a bit, Mr. Senior," he replied, before opening the cellar door and walking down the steps. I noticed immediately that there was no problem with the light, so it was obvious that he must have either screwed it in tighter or inserted a new bulb.

He returned within a couple of minutes. "There's not very much of it left in this tube," he said, "But I'm sure there'll be enough for your purpose. There's no need to bring it back, I have another tube down there."

"Well, that's very good of you Tom," said our neighbour, his face beaming with the satisfaction that he might not, after all, have to face his daughter's wrath."

"By the way, how are you feeling today?" asked my mother just as he was about to step out of the door.

"Well, I suppose I'm just fair to middling lass, just fair to middling, but we mustn't grumble, must we?"

I still don't know why my mother always asked after his health because she invariably received the same answer. He had no sooner left than there was another knock on the door. When I opened it I was not surprised to be greeted by Billy.

"Do you fancy coming out, Neil?" he asked. "I was dead bored this morning."

"Me and Billy are just popping out, mam," I told her while putting on my jacket. I opened the door and stepped outside before she had the chance to think of a valid reason to prevent me.

"What do you want to do then, Neil?" he asked.

I started walking towards the end of the street. "We're going to see Nicky first," I said and told him about the fallen tree that was straddling the beck and what Johnny Jackson and some other lads had been doing.

"Crikey, that sounds great. I wonder if any of the other trees have blown down. The noise of the wind was so strong on Friday night that it took me ages to get to sleep."

"Well if it has blown any more down I hope the Monkey Tree isn't one of them."

The Monkey Tree was the best tree for climbing on the whole of the ridge and it would be a tragedy if the local lads were no longer able to scramble their way through the maze of branches to hopefully reach the top.

Nicky was ready and the three of us made our way to the ridge. As we walked up the slope towards the entrance I couldn't help looking around in the hope of catching a glimpse of Susan Brown, my favourite girl in the whole school, who I knew lived in the area but had never been sure of the exact address. What I would say if I did see her I had no idea as I was always tongue-tied if anyone else was with me. We walked down the steps leading onto the uppermost path on the ridge and made our way down to the bottom path near the old bandstand via the narrow, twisty path known to all the kids in our area as the Indian Warpath. Nicky had a good idea of the location of what we were looking for.

When we arrived I could see that the tree had been completely uprooted and it was obvious that it would be much more difficult to walk across than I had first thought. Although it stretched completely over the beck it lay diagonally across it so that the other end was about twenty yards downstream. The various branches would also make it more hazardous. The beck itself, after the heavy rain of the previous two days, was in full flood. The three of us gazed at the scene with some trepidation.

"I'm not too sure about this, now that I've seen it," announced Nicky.

"Well, there's no one else here doing it, is there?" said Billy. "I thought there'd be quite a few lads trying it out when we got here."

No sooner had the words been spoken than a small figure emerged from the trees on the other side of the beck. He climbed onto the fallen tree and carefully made his way to our side of the fast flowing water. He looked to be about eight years of age and had a very ragged appearance. He sported a scruffy jersey over his shirt and braces. On his head was a flat cap more in the style of an adult rather than a schoolboy, but what surprised us was that he had no footwear at all. He certainly had a cheery demeanour, however.

"Hiya," he greeted us, "My name's Danny. I've walked across here both ways seven times so far. It was hard at first, but I haven't fallen off once. Now that I've got used to it, it's easy."

"Where did you come from?" asked Billy. "Do you live on the other side of Meanwood Road?"

"Nah, do I heckers like. We've got a caravan parked up on the field behind those trees. We came here last year, but we made the mistake of settling on the rugby ground and the police came and moved us off on the same day. This time though, we're hoping they leave us a bit longer like they usually do because we've got cousins who park their caravans on Woodhouse Moor when the feast comes as they own some of the rides and let me and our Shannon go on for free."

"Is Shannon your sister then?" asked Billy.

"That's right. She's fifteen is our Shannon and she eats lads for breakfast. Sometimes she lets 'em see her tits. Though I don't know what mi da would say if he found out."

I think we all thought it best not to comment on this latest revelation.

"Is it just you two and your parents in the caravan then?" asked Nicky.

"That's right. Well, there's Betsy of course, but we don't let her stay inside the van."

"Why don't you let her in then? It seems a bit unfair to me."

"And what would we be doing with a horse in a caravan? That would be really silly, wouldn't it?"

"Betsy's your horse," declared Billy, immediately sizing up the situation.

"I wish I had a horse," said Nicky.

I couldn't help noticing that the sun, which was shining brightly only half an hour previously, had been replaced by black, menacing clouds, but Billy was the first to suggest what was already in my mind.

"I think we ought to be heading back," he said. "I think it's going to pour down."

"So do I," agreed Nicky. "It wouldn't surprise me if there was thunder and lightning as well. We can always come back during the school holiday."

"Well, I can be inside the caravan in two minutes," indicated our new friend, "But there's one thing I'm going to do first. I'm going to run across the tree trunk this time. I've only walked across it before."

"You'll fall in if you do that," I told him, "Especially with having no shoes on."

"Watch this then."

He climbed onto the tree trunk in his bare feet and promptly began running across He must have got a splinter or something in his foot as he yelled out and lifted his right leg in the air which caused him to lose his balance. There was an almighty splash as he tumbled into the centre of the beck.

"Bugger!" was his only greeting as we got as near as we could while not stepping off the bank. His misfortune only reinforced our decision to head home as soon as we had seen he was all right.

"Are you okay?" shouted Nicky.

"Am I buggary," he said as he sat up in the water and examined his foot. "I've ripped my shirt and my trousers. Mi da will give me a right belting. Just look at the state of me; I'm fair clemmed."

CHAPTER THREE

The last day at school before we broke up for the Easter holiday proved to be an interesting one but not until after the midday break. On the final day of each term the headmaster often introduced a welcome change to routine in order to put his pupils in a happy frame of mind for the forthcoming holiday period, by allowing them to wind down a little, though I think it is fair to say that all my classmates were already eagerly looking forward to laying their burden down as soon as the bell sounded at four o'clock. On the day that we had broken up for Christmas he had organized a quiz, the result of which meant that the four of us who had comprised the winning team were allowed to leave the premises an hour early. This had provided me with the sublime memory of sheltering in the doorway of the Electra Picture House with Susan Brown during an unexpected hailstorm.

As we stood in the assembly hall Mr. Rawcliffe announced that he had arranged for a professor from Leeds University to come to the school during the afternoon period and give a talk to all the pupils of the senior class. He promised us that the subject of the lecture was one that would immediately arouse our interest.

As Billy and I made our way home at twelve o'clock at the end of the morning lessons my companion made an observation.

"I've never met a real professor before," he stated. "I wonder if he'll be very old with a long beard."

"I don't think all professors look like that, Billy, but I bet he's got a foreign name that you can't pronounce properly starting with a 'Z' or an 'X'".

"What if he's called Frankenstein and has a secret laboratory where he builds monsters out of dead bodies and brings them to life."

It was obvious that my closest friend, not for the first time, was getting carried away with a situation.

"I can't see that happening in England. That sort of thing only seems to happen in some spooky, foreign country where it's nearly always dark and there's lots of thunder and lightning."

"Anyway, Neil, you said you wouldn't be surprised if his name began with an 'X'. How can anyone's name start with an 'X'? No one would be able to say it."

"Well I remember hearing in a history lesson about a king of Persia called Xerxes, but he probably lived thousands of years ago. Anyway, I think the first letter of his name was pronounced like the letter 'Z'"

"I don't think you could have a Professor Xerxes," said Billy, laughing, "Because it's almost impossible to say, and if you did manage to say it three or four times in succession you'd probably choke yourself."

When we had all re-entered the classroom at half past one we eagerly awaited the arrival of the lecturer from the university and were keen to hear what the topic of his lecture would be, but the room was remarkably empty.

"I've never known Old Rawcliffe not be here at the start of the afternoon lessons," observed Billy.

"I bet they both walk in together," I suggested.

"It was obvious that the other members of the class were also becoming restive."

Just as the noise was on the verge of reaching unacceptable levels, in strode the headmaster with a companion who in no way resembled our perceived notion of what a university professor should look like. To begin with he had no facial hair of any description and that on the top of his head matched the short back and sides that almost every schoolboy was forced to endure on the instructions of his vigilant parents. He also did not look a day over thirty as he smiled at us, though rather nervously, as if he was unsure as to what he had let himself in for.

"I'd like you all to meet Professor Lee who has kindly agreed to come here from Leeds University to give you a short and rather informal lecture. I will now pass you over to him."

Billy and I looked at each other as his name was announced. It was not what we had expected.

The new arrival, after the headmaster had left the room, began confidently enough. "I don't know what you all expected when you were informed about my visit," he said, "But I can assure you this will not be a stuffy lecture, and it is on a subject that I feel sure you will find as fascinating as I do. I am going to show you how to change the future."

An immediate ripple of interest flowed through the class, especially the boys, most of whom held a fascination with science fiction.

"Now," he went on after a short pause to create the desired effect, "Is there anyone who can tell me what Parallel Time Tracks are?"

No one raised a hand.

"Right then, I'll start with the girls." He pointed at one of them. I immediately realised that he had chosen the one girl in the entire class that he shouldn't have done. "Now then girl," he went on, "What is your name?"

"Lorna Gale, sir," she replied.

"Well then, Lorna, what do you think Parallel Time Tracks might be?"

"Is it something to do with trams, sir, because tram tracks are parallel. They have to be or the wheels wouldn't fit onto them. I wonder though; did they put the wheels on to fit the track or did they build the track to fit the wheels? I suppose they must have made them both at the same time. Well, if they made them at the same time, that's parallel, isn't it? So Parallel Time Tracks must be tram tracks that were made at the same time as the wheels."

"Well, I don't think that's quite-----," Professor Lee attempted to say, but Lorna hadn't finished.

"I remember once when the tram came right off the end of the track at the Meanwood terminus and it was ages before they managed to get it back on again. I can't remember how they did it now but I know it took ages because we were supposed to be going to my Auntie Jean's in Church Lane and we stood watching until we were very late getting there. My Auntie Jean didn't seem to mind though. She didn't tell us off or anything. Anyway it's a good job they did get it back onto the track or we would have had to walk all the way home across Woodhouse Ridge. Mind you, it's quite nice walking on the ridge but I think I'd rather be sitting on the tram."

She continued her verbal assault for several minutes while our visitor stared open-mouthed with a baffled expression on his face no doubt wondering whether he had done the right thing in volunteering for this particular assignment.

Eventually, realising that her vocal chords probably needed a rest, she sat down with a smug expression on her face, no doubt feeling that she had probably answered the professor's question in a competent and satisfactory manner, even though she could no longer remember what it was. My mind went back to the previous autumn when she had attempted to acquire me as a boyfriend and I still regarded it as a most fortunate escape.

"Parallel Time Tracks," said Professor Lee, attempting to rediscover his enthusiasm, "Are created by each decision made by an individual. A good example of this would be to look at the decision I just made to ask Miss Gale a question. We now exist in that world or time track if you like, but another one exists parallel in time to this one in which I did not ask that question and it is obvious to me that in that world this lecture would have progressed more rapidly. Now obviously it is not possible to leap from this world into the one I have just mentioned but can you see that the future in this world is now different to the one in which I did not make the decision to ask the question?"

I was beginning to get interested in this, though not yet getting what he was saying fully clear in my head.

Warming to his theme, the professor continued. "A couple of years ago, I had booked a Wallace Arnold excursion to Scarborough, but was ill on the night before and was unable to make it. That bus collided with a lorry just outside Malton and two passengers were killed. A colleague of mine suggested that I must have felt very relieved that I had been unable to travel but I informed him that for the accident to occur the bus and the lorry would have to be in exactly the same spot at the same time, not ten seconds earlier or ten seconds later. With an extra passenger on board, everyone's thought processes, including those of the driver would have been altered and the odds against the collision still occurring would be astronomical. Imagine looking at two giant screens, the first depicting the bus journey without the extra passenger and the second depicting the journey with the extra passenger and you would see that the two journeys would progress in a totally different manner."

There was deathly silence in the classroom as he continued.

"Now I'm sure there isn't anyone who hasn't heard of the Titanic disaster," he went on. "Well, exactly the same principle holds there. If there was one extra or one fewer passenger on board then the odds against the ship colliding with an iceberg in precisely the same manner would again be astronomical. Quite simply, the Titanic would still be afloat today, unless it met with some other disaster subsequently. In order for it to sink everything that happened on board must happen in exactly the same way and at the same time. Nothing, and I mean nothing, must change."

He paused to allow this concept to sink in. "Now does anyone have a question?" Realising his earlier mistake and not wishing to repeat it, he added, "I'd like to hear from one of the boys this time." I decided to get in first and raised my hand.

"Yes boy," said the professor as he looked in my direction, no doubt pleased that someone had shown an interest. "What's your name?"

"Neil Cawson, sir."

"All right then, Neil, what is your question?"

"Well, sir, if I decided to pick up a pebble on Blackpool beach and move it to Scarborough beach, that wouldn't alter the future would it?"

"It would certainly change your future. Picture the two giant screens again. In the first one you have picked up the pebble and in the second one you haven't. There is already a time gap of several seconds and your thought processes would have been changed by thinking what you would be going to do with the pebble. In the second screen you would already be ahead of yourself and you would be thinking of something entirely different. Even without the human element involved the future would be changed but it would take much longer. I know this is a difficult concept to grasp, but I have a reason for presenting it to you today and I feel it is totally relevant, in an advantageous way, to your prospects when you leave school."

I was carefully mulling this over and I could see that most of the class, though mainly the boys, had thoughtful looks on their faces.

"The whole point of this lecture, if that's what you want to call it, is to let you know that you have the ability to change your own future by making the right decisions in life."

He continued in the same vein for about another half hour and nearly everyone admitted afterwards that it had been well worth listening to, with the science fiction theme that ran through his talk being of most interest to the boys. When he was due to leave the headmaster asked us all on behalf of the school to thank him for taking leave from his university duties to pay us a brief visit, and he was so pleased with our response to his efforts that he allowed us all to break up for Easter almost an hour early.

"I thought that was great, Billy," I said as we walked home together.

"I didn't fully understand it all," he replied. "I don't see how the Titanic would fail to sink just because it had an extra passenger on board."

"I know it's hard to take in, but I think I understand what he meant. If you think about it our future's already changed because of him."

"How do you mean?"

"It's because of what we're talking about right now. Remember the two screens he mentioned. On one we're doing exactly what we're doing now, but on the other we'd have been talking about something entirely different, wouldn't we. We might have been talking about when the Electra's going to open again, or that gypsy caravan near the beck, or when we might be going to Woodhouse Feast."

"Yes, but the professor did come, didn't he? So I don't see how this other world could exist. I mean we can't be in two places at once, can we?"

"I know, Billy, but a lot of what he said makes sense anyway. Look, it can't be later than quarter past three and my mam doesn't know we left school early, does she? So we don't have to go home straight away."

"What do you want to do then?"

"I think I want to try to change the future."

"How?"

"By doing something totally different to what we would have been doing."

"But even I don't know what we would have been doing. I mean we haven't thought of anything yet, have we?"

"Then it's got to be something that we wouldn't normally do, hasn't it?"

"Like seeing if we can catch up with Tucker Lane and call him a sissy."

"That's not the kind of future I was thinking of, Billy. I don't want to end up in hospital."

We were holding this conversation while standing outside the Electra and gazing up at the re-erected scaffolding. "Look, Neil," said my companion, "There's Susan Brown walking on the other side of the road with Sally Cheesedale." I watched as Sally said farewell to Susan and began walking down the ginnel opposite the picture house towards Craven Road. "Now's the time to change your future," he continued.

Before I had time to respond, he called her over. "Neil was just wondering if you would be going to the feast over Easter."

My face turned crimson.

"I never heard him ask me," she replied, "But yes, I expect I'll be going, probably on Saturday afternoon," She looked directly at me, and I could tell that she could sense my discomfort. "Why do you want to know?"

"Oh, I just wondered, that's all."

"Me and Neil might go on Saturday afternoon," said Billy.

"I'll probably see you there then. I think I might be going with Sally Cheesedale, and I think she likes you, Billy."

This time it was Billy's turn to blush and I couldn't help laughing at his embarrassment

She left us and continued walking towards the end of Cross Speedwell Street. I wondered though, because of the close proximity of the Electra doorway whether she was thinking, as I was, of the time just before Christmas when we had sheltered there from the hailstorm.

"It looks like we might have girl friends when we go to the feast, Billy," I said. "You told me you liked Sally Cheesedale, anyway."

"I know, but I'm not sure I want to be seen wandering around the feast with a girl."

"Well, I don't think we've really changed the future anyway because Susan already knows that I like her."

"Let's go home, Neil. I'm getting bored now."

I decided to accept his suggestion and when I went to bed I realised that my experiment had not been as successful as I had hoped, but the professor's words still made a lot of sense to me and I thought about them for a long time. It was quite late before I managed to get to sleep.

CHAPTER FOUR

"I want to go see that gypsy caravan," announced Billy as we sat on the lavatory roof with our legs dangling over the side, but ready to climb down via the midden at the end of the row should any adult enter the yard. It was the first day of the school holiday and I had just asked him what he fancied doing. "Look," he went on, taking a carrot out of his pocket and holding it out for me to scrutinise, "I pinched this. I don't think my mam will notice. There must have been half a dozen on the cellar head. I want to give it to that horse called Betsy."

The top of the cellar stairs was known by everyone in our locality who lived on a similar row of terraced houses as the cellar head and each household would have a solitary shelf there where perishable goods would be stored. No one on our street was able to afford the luxury of a refrigerator as the cellar was the coolest room in the house. This shelf served well enough, though the various items would have to be inspected on a daily basis to make sure they were still fresh.

"Shall we go this morning then, or after dinner?" I asked him.

"Well it was half past ten when we came out, so it must be about eleven o'clock now. I think I'd rather go this afternoon because it will give us more time."

"I think you're right, Billy, and anyway I'll probably have to go for fish and chips at twelve o'clock."

"Right!" said my companion. Let's go tell Nicky."

We climbed back down into the yard and walked along the street to Nicky's house. He must have seen us walk past the window because he opened the door before we had a chance to knock.

"Are we going down to the beck to see that gypsy caravan?" he asked.

"That's what we were thinking of doing, but not until after dinner," said Billy. "There isn't much time left this morning. We'll call round for you at about half past one."

I was right about my mother asking me to go to the fish and chip shop, even though there was only her and me at home, apart from Nell who would certainly be begging for her share. The nearest one was just around the corner opposite Doughty's shop, but for some reason which I had never been able to work out my mother never wanted me to go there, always preferring the one in Jubilee Terrace which was further away. My father would be having his dinner in the canteen at the leather factory in Meanwood Road where he worked.

When I arrived at the premises I was surprised to discover that the queue was a very small one, but I was even more surprised when I saw who was at the back of the queue.

"Hello, Susan, "I managed to squeeze out though my voice must have sounded very croaky. "The fish and chip shop opposite Doughty's is a lot nearer to where you live."

"I know," she admitted. "It's nearer to where you live as well, isn't it? Anyway, why did you want to know if I would be going to Woodhouse Feast?"

"That was just Billy. I never actually said anything to him about wondering if you were going to Woodhouse Feast."

"Why would he say it then?"

"To make me feel embarrassed, I suppose."

I was certainly feeling embarrassed at that precise moment, more embarrassed than I had ever felt before, as she gazed at me with a peculiar expression on her face. It was an expression that I just could not read.

"Do you always feel embarrassed talking to me?"

This was not going very well at all and I silently cursed Billy for instigating the intolerable situation I now found myself in.

"Well, sometimes I do, yes." The words seemed to tumble from my mind involuntarily. It was as if I was listening to them from a distance.

"Well, maybe it would be better if you don't talk to me, then I wouldn't be such an embarrassment to you."

She was now at the front of the queue and was placing her order with the proprietor of the shop.

After receiving her order she just said, "Bye, Neil," and walked out of the shop.

"Bye, Susan," was the only response I could conjure up.

I was furious by the time I got home. It seemed like we had succeeded in changing the future, but not in the way that I had hoped. I wondered if I would still have had an encounter with Susan if Billy hadn't decided to do some mischievous meddling on our way home from school, and if I did whether it might have progressed differently.

When I called round for him after finishing eating I really laid into him once we were safely outdoors.

"Susan Brown won't talk to me now and it's all your fault," I said, rather petulantly."

"How do you make that out? What's it got to do with me?" he said, with a genuine look of puzzlement on his face.

I told him the whole story.

"Well, it was your idea, Neil, to try to change the future."

"I know, but I wouldn't have done it that way. I wanted to change it for the better, not for the worse."

"But according to what you told me she didn't say that she wouldn't be talking to you, she said you shouldn't talk to her if it makes you embarrassed. I should just forget about it, Neil. I bet everything's all right once we get back to school. Anyway, we might see her at Woodhouse Feast first. Let's go get Nicky."

I didn't argue anymore and a few minutes later saw the three of us heading up the hill towards the ridge. Coming towards us, however, was Mary Pearson which caused all three of us to look down to make sure that our flies weren't open, the reason being that she was renowned for following any unsuspecting lad into the lavatory yard and pushing open the cubicle door in order to cause maximum embarrassment, all three of us having, on more than one occasion, become victims. She was two years older than Billy and me and three years older than Nicky. The problem, for me in particular, had become exacerbated recently, as her family and mine were now sharing the same lavatory which made an embarrassing encounter even more likely. We had long assumed that she was the proud owner of a willy-spotting book in which she wrote down the names of all the unsuspecting lads that she'd copped. As she approached us now her eyes were open wide as she stared at the carrot in Billy's pocket, obviously mistaking it for something else.

"Hello, Billy," she said, completely ignoring Nicky and me, "You seem to have grown up a lot since the last time I saw you."

As she walked past us Billy blushed while we laughed. He immediately extracted from his pocket the item which had been the subject of such fascination to his tormentor. "That does it. I'm breaking it in half," he muttered.

This he proceeded to do and placed half in each pocket. "And you two can stop laughing, as well."

"But it was so funny, Billy," I said. "Did you see the look on her face?"

He calmed down and his face broke into a grin. "Do you think she knew it was a carrot?" he asked.

"I'm not sure, Billy," I said, "But I bet she'll want to find out."

I always try to make sure she's not there when I go to the lavvy," said Nicky.

"So do we," I told him, "And I bet Billy will be a lot more careful now."

We walked down the steps that led from the street onto the ridge and continued along the top path passing the area known as Death Valley and Table Top, a very popular play area for any child living in our locality. Death Valley was a large, overgrown area which in the mind of an adventurous schoolboy could be easily transformed into a jungle. Table Top was a plateau that towered twenty to thirty feet above it and could be reached via a steep path around the side. As we began to make our way down the embankment towards the beck close to where it was straddled by the fallen tree the stillness was disturbed by the frantic shouts of a young boy.

"Aargh! Get off me you rotten buggers."

There was little doubt in our minds with regard to the owner of the voice. When we reached the location of the noise it was to find Danny, the gypsy boy we had met earlier held by two lads of about our own age while being suspended upside down, the top of his head just coming into contact with a very muddy puddle. We immediately sized up the odds and decided that three against two, or four against two if you included their victim, were favourable enough to warrant our intervention, especially as neither of the two antagonists looked any more muscular than we did.

"Better leave him alone," said Billy.

"Or else what?" snarled the larger of the two boys.

"There's three of us and only two of you," I said, in the most menacing tone I could manage. I don't think I succeeded very well, but it appeared to have the desired effect as they reluctantly decided to release their captive.

"We were only messing around," said the other boy. "He's a gypsy and my dad doesn't like gypsies. He says they're always thieving."

"Who are you calling a thief?" yelled Danny as his two assailants decided to leave us and started to clamber up the hill. "It's a good job you three showed up when you did," he continued, "I was just starting to get my mad up. I might have hurt one of them really bad if you hadn't arrived. People are always calling me a thief just because I live in a caravan, and I'm getting really sick of it. Here you can have this if you want." He handed

Nicky a pen knife. "I think it must have fallen out of the pocket of one of them."

"Why did they attack you, Danny?" I asked him.

"Because they're rotten buggers, that's why."

It occurred to me that there might have been some other reason, but I decided not to question him further.

"We thought we'd have a go at walking across the tree trunk," I told him. I looked down at the beck and noticed that the water was not running anything like as quickly as on the previous occasion that we had been down there.

"It's dead easy now," said our new friend. "I just run across it."

We walked along the footpath alongside the now gently flowing water until we came to the fallen tree. We all agreed that it did not look as hazardous on this occasion.

"Do you think we could have a look at your horse?" asked Billy.

"Well, if you cross over to the other side of the beck you can't miss her because she's tethered in the field close to the caravan."

"Are you real gypsies?" asked Nicky.

"Well, I'd say we are, but we're not Romanies even if we do spend all our time living in a caravan and moving all over Yorkshire. We're from Ireland originally, though I think I was only two when we came over here. My da was born in Tipperary and my ma in Galway, and that's where our Shannon was born."

There was something I needed to know. "Danny," I began, "After you fell into the beck you said that you was fair clemmed. What does 'fair clemmed', mean?"

"I'm buggered if I know, but I heard a man at Woodhouse Feast say it the last time I was there. It was raining really hard and he was soaking wet. 'Bugger me,' he said, 'I'm fair clemmed'. I thought it sounded real good so I said it after I fell into the water, because I was even wetter than he was, but I haven't a clue if that's what it really means."

"I'm going to run across it," shouted Billy as he surveyed the newest bridge across Meanwood Beck, and interrupted my thoughts in the process.

"Are you sure, Billy? asked Nicky. "Don't forget what happened to Danny when he tried it."

"Just watch this, then," he said.

We watched with some apprehension as he managed to get more than halfway across before his right leg slipped off the edge of the trunk. Attempting to steady himself to avoid falling into the water he only succeeded in almost doing the splits as his other leg slipped from the other side of the fallen tree. I winced when I saw the position he landed in. I could almost feel the pain myself. He crawled the rest of the way before settling on the grass and feeling extremely sorry for himself. Danny showed us how it should be done, but both Nicky and I after witnessing Billy's misfortune decided to walk across in a more sedate fashion.

When we were all safely on the other side of the beck a girl about four or five years older than ourselves appeared from the shelter of the trees. "Oy, what do you think you're doing with our Danny," she yelled in a menacing fashion.

"It's all right, Sha," said our companion, "These lads are my mates. They were having a bit of bother with a couple of other lads and I went to help them out."

"Oh, yes," said the person who we assumed to be his sister, "To be sure, I would think it would be the other way round."

She spoke with a pleasing Irish lilt, yet with a strong, commanding voice. She had fiery red hair but it was something else entirely that attracted our attention.

"This is our Shannon," said Danny, by way of introduction.

The three of us stared in wonderment at the erect nipples as they thrust against the thin material of her blouse in a vain attempt to force a way through. It was obvious that she wore no undergarments whatsoever over that part of her body.

"And why would you three be gawping like that, I wonder?" she said, accurately reading the expressions on our faces. "To be sure, I'd be thinking you'd never set eyes on a lass's tits before, and now that I look at you with your eyes popping out of your head it's fairly certain I am that you haven't. Well my boyos I reckon that's something for you to look forward to in the future then, because I think you've seen enough for today."

She reached into her skirt pocket and produced a knitted scarf which she expertly positioned in such a way as to hide her considerable charms from our view. We were all crimson-faced as we stood there, totally embarrassed and not being able to think of anything to say that would provide a suitable response to the gypsy girl's comments. Danny broke the silence.

"Come on, I'll show you the caravan if you like."

"Could we see your horse?" asked Billy. "I've brought a carrot to give her."

He led us beyond the trees onto the adjacent field. The caravan took my breath away. It was much larger than I had imagined, yet retained the character of the Romany dwellings that we had often seen in films. The outside had been painted with bright colours and it had an oval-shaped roof. The entrance was covered by a brocade curtain, which was again very bright in appearance. We could see the horse tethered just a few yards away.

"You'll have to be careful how you approach her. To be sure, Betsy won't be liking it if you walk up to her face to face," suggested the gypsy girl who had so mesmerised us only a few minutes earlier. "You need to approach her from the side."

We watched as she led Billy towards the horse in the manner she had suggested. As she did so we became aware that the scarf she had carefully placed in order to protect her modesty was no longer performing that function with the same degree of accuracy. Billy, however, was so obsessed with approaching the horse without startling her that he failed to notice.

"Now you need to be holding your hand out flat, like this," remarked Danny's sister while holding out her hand in the manner she suggested, "And be letting Betsy take the carrot from your palm."

He removed the two pieces of carrot from his pockets and offered them to the horse. The animal immediately turned its head sideways towards him and proceeded to lick his nose, causing him to take a sudden step backwards.

"To be sure, I think she's taken a liking to you," said Shannon as Betsy accepted the offering.

Billy appeared to be delighted by the response, but Nicky and I were still transfixed by the sight of his human companion, as her scarf had by now fallen to the floor. Our delight at what we were witnessing was soon to end, however, as a formidable looking woman, gaudily dressed yet with the same fiery red hair as the person we assumed to be her daughter was walking across the field in a determined fashion, a knitted shawl in her hand and an angry look on her face.

"Have I not been telling you Shannon to cover yourself up when you step outside? Will you be wanting every lad in Yorkshire to be gawping at your titties?"

"Aw, ma," she replied, "To be sure I had a scarf for cover, but it seems to have dropped to the floor."

I couldn't help noticing that Danny was finding the whole confrontation hilarious.

"Now put this on," demanded the new arrival as she hurled the shawl at her. "I tremble to think what himself will say about it if I tell him."

I could see that her daughter regarded this prospect with some trepidation.

"Ma, you wouldn't," she said.

"Well now, I'm thinking that I might and I'm thinking that I might not. I've not quite made up my mind yet."

Billy was still obsessed with making friends with the horse while Nicky and I were looking guilty though our eyes were still focussed on the gypsy girl whose expression had changed to one of apprehension as she proceeded to drape the shawl over her shoulders. Danny, meanwhile, was having a fit of uncontrollable laughter.

"And I don't know what you can find to be laughing at Danny O'Shaughnessy," admonished his mother. "It's sure I am that you've been up to some mischief. Who are these three lads anyway?"

"These are my mates," said Danny. "I met them the other day down by the beck. When I saw them again today I could see that they were having a bit of bother with some other lads and I went over to help them."

I think we were too aghast at his version of events to make any comment.

"Is it all right if they come and have a look at the caravan, ma?" he continued.

"I suppose there's no harm in that," she replied, turning towards us, "Seeing as how you've befriended our Danny." She looked down at our boots before continuing. "But I'll not be having you stepping inside unless you take your boots off first. It may not be a house, but it's where we all live and I always have it kept neat and tidy."

Billy reluctantly left the horse and we all walked towards the caravan.

"We're gypsies don't you know?" declared Shannon. "Would you not be thinking that we might kidnap you once you set foot inside? That's what a lot of folk around here would expect."

I had read frightening stories when I was younger about such things happening in gypsy encampments, but I immediately dismissed them as everyone seemed so friendly. It briefly crossed my mind that being kidnapped by Shannon might not be such a bad thing anyway. We discarded our footwear at the foot of the stairs leading from the ground to the caravan entrance. The gypsy lady drew back the brocade curtain covering the entrance and bade us step inside. We were really taken aback as we surveyed the dazzlingly bright colours of almost every object inside the van. It was exactly how I had always imagined a gypsy caravan to look like. It had the paradoxical effect of looking larger on the inside than on the outside.

"Himself won't be back until tomorrow," said Mrs. O'Shaughnessy. "He's away on some business."

"That's where I sleep," said Danny, excitedly as he indicated a bunk against the far wall, "But sometimes if it's a clear night and not too cold I sleep outside with Betsy and look at the stars."

We spent about twenty minutes in the crowded van and were treated to lemonade and biscuits, after which time all three of us could safely concede that our perceived view of gypsy life had been pleasantly enhanced.

"Does any one of you three have a girl friend?" asked Danny's mother

Billy and Nicky both pointed in my direction while I blushed crimson.

"Well then, would I not be having the very thing to pass on to your young lady?" she continued, "And it's certain I am that she'll be delighted to receive it."

She walked over to a dressing table and opened a drawer and took something out. I could not at first detect what the object was except that it was very shiny. "Now this," she said, handing it over for me to examine, "Has been in my family for generations. It was given to my great, great grandfather, Patrick O'Brien, by the little people."

The object she handed to me was a pendant and I had to admit it was a very attractive one, but I was puzzled by her words.

"Who are the little people?" I asked.

"To be sure, you can't be telling me that you've never heard of leprechauns. They are the fairy people that have lived in Ireland for thousands of years, but they are a very shy people and not everybody has met one, though my great, great grandfather certainly did and the little chap was so grateful for the help he gave to him and his family during the great potato famine back in 1849 that he gave him this very pendant that you see here now. It transpired that Patrick O' Brien's farm, for a reason he could not understand, was one of the very few that had not been affected by the potato blight and, as he had always been a good friend of the little people, each week he left a sack full of potatoes under the big oak tree at the edge of his farm for them to collect. The leprechaun told him that the pendant had magical qualities as it was struck by lightning shortly after having been made and that it would bring good luck to any girl who wore it, though it would never work if it was in the possession of a man. This particular pendant has been handed down among the female members of my family for four generations. I would have handed it down to my Shannon if it hadn't been for the proviso.

"What's a proviso?" I asked.

"A proviso is a certain condition attached to something, and the proviso in this instance was that after one hundred years the pendant would cease to have any magical qualities unless it was sold for a certain sum, not a penny more nor a penny less, to a complete stranger. I've kept it in this drawer for nigh on two years waiting for a suitable person to turn up and it's a feeling I'm getting that this young lady of yours would be the ideal candidate to receive it, and whenever she wears it around her neck good fortune will always come her way."

She looked at me and stroked her hand across her chin before she spoke again. "Now, do you suppose you could be telling me how much money you might have on your person?"

I knew exactly how much I had in my pocket. I had one sixpence, one threepenny bit and a penny. I was going to use the sixpence to buy a Captain Marvel comic when I got back home, but I was intrigued by the gypsy's story.

"I've got tenpence," I told her.

"Well, glory be," she said. "Now isn't that an amazing coincidence. The little fellow told my great great grandfather that for the pendant to regain its powers it must be sold to a complete stranger for the princely sum of ten pennies. It must be no more and no less. Indeed, it's lucky you are already and I feel it must be leprechaun magic that has brought you to this very spot today."

I decided immediately that I wanted that pendant for Susan as I desperately wanted her to feel warmer towards me than her words earlier in the day suggested. I took the tenpence from my pocket and handed it over. I suspected that Billy and Nicky were grinning behind my back but I didn't care. She placed the good luck charm into my hand.

"Now don't forget," she reminded. "The magic will only work for a female, so you must make sure you hand it over to your girl friend as soon as possible. Don't keep it yourself for too long."

I felt my face burning again. We left the caravan and Danny accompanied us across to the far side of the beck before saying farewell and informing us that he would be going to Woodhouse Feast on the following Saturday and that he might meet us there.

"I don't believe in all that rubbish about little people," announced Nicky as we began to climb upwards towards the top of the ridge.

"Neither do I," said Billy with a mischievous smile on his face, "But it looks as though Neil does, doesn't it?"

"Don't be daft, Billy. I don't believe in fairies and all that stuff," I told him, rather forcefully, "But Susan might."

I think from the point of view of all three of us it had been an adventurous and very memorable day, but the important thing was that the Easter holiday was only just beginning, with a visit to Woodhouse Feast likely to provide one of the highlights.

CHAPTER FIVE

The day following our encounter with the gypsy family was cold, cloudy and damp and, for me in particular, the contrast with the excitement of the previous day was hard to take. I don't think I was in Billy's company for more than half an hour and both of us were so bored because of the depressing conditions that neither of us could think of anything to do that would lighten our mood, the result of which was that I spent most of the day indoors listening to the wireless and trying unsuccessfully to avoid being on the receiving end of one of my mother's chores, the worst of which involved sitting with my arms outstretched while she used my thumbs to wind some long strands of wool into balls. This procedure would probably last for about fifteen minutes, but to me it always seemed more like an hour, especially when I received a clout for allowing my increasingly aching arms to begin to droop which caused the wool to become twisted making it necessary to begin that batch again. Nevertheless, I survived everything that was thrown at me until bedtime.

The following day was very similar. It was Good Friday and, though it wasn't classed as a public holiday, it was always recognized in our locality as the first day of the Easter festival. It was also the one day of the year when you could virtually be sure that ninety percent of house dwellers would be eating fish for their dinner, it being considered extremely unlucky not to do so at that one time of the year. My mother had acquired some cod from the local fishmonger on the previous day which came encased in ice and which she had kept on the cellar head until the appropriate time for cooking. The remainder of the day, however, was just as boring as the previous one and I eagerly looked forward to Saturday with the promise of a trip to Woodhouse Feast, knowing that whatever the weather an enjoyable time would be virtually guaranteed.

When the following morning finally arrived I drew back the curtains and gazed through my bedroom window. Although the sun had not begun to shine, the sky seemed to hold so much promise. The heavy, damp, depressing atmosphere of the two preceding days was totally lacking and my spirits rose accordingly. There was a lightness to my step as I dressed, hurried down-stairs and entered the front room. My mother, of course, was already there, having released Nell from her night time incarceration at the top of the cellar steps and having already relieved the fire grate of the previous night's cinders. During weekdays this task would always be performed by my father but at weekends my mother always allowed him to stay in bed for a while longer. I had already received permission to visit Woodhouse Feast with Billy during the afternoon and I was looking forward to it immensely.

However, there was still the morning and my exhila-rating mood was suddenly about to change. Shortly after breakfast the postman arrived and Nell rushed to the door barking furiously as a solitary letter was pushed through the aperture. She had long since realized that anything falling to the floor from his hands was never for her and she always showed her disgust in the appropriate manner no doubt wondering why she never seemed to be outside when he paid a visit so that she could show her disapproval in a more aggressive manner. I picked up the handwritten envelope and handed it to my mother.

"It's in your grandad's handwriting," she said. "He knew we were thinking of going to see him over the Easter holidays; so I wonder what's so important that he couldn't wait until then."

She extracted a single sheet of paper from the envelope and began to read it.

"What does the letter say, mam?" I asked her, excitedly.

"Don't be so impatient," she replied. "I'll let you read it as soon as I've finished it."

As soon as she had done so she passed the letter to me. "We were hoping to see your grandad over Easter," she informed me, "But it doesn't look like we will now." I began to read the writing on the sheet of paper.

Dear May,

I know you and Tom were thinking of paying me a visit over Easter, but in view of what's happened and the way I feel right now, I think you would do much better to take the lad to Roundhay Park or somewhere. You may remember on an earlier visit that I discovered that my childhood friend Harry Crabtree happened to be staying in the same convalescent home. Well, it certainly got rid of the boredom that we had both been experiencing and, despite the fact that we hadn't seen each other for over fifty years, it was just as if nothing had changed, apart

from our ages that is. For several days our lives were totally transformed until two days ago when Harry tragically suffered a fatal heart attack. Needless to say I was totally devastated that this could happen just a short time after we had got back together. The result is that I'm not in the best of moods for any sort of company at the moment and, as I fully expect to be home by next weekend, I think it best that I see you all then,
Love dad.

As soon as I had finished reading it I experienced an immediate feeling of sadness, especially as I had been the one who had realized that my grandfather and his friend were residing in the same building.

"It doesn't seem fair, mam," was all I could think of to say.

"Well, that's the way things go sometimes and there's nothing that anyone can do about it except to live your life to the full for as long as you're here, and judging from the tone of his letter that's exactly what his friend did. At least we now know that your grandad will be home soon."

I wasn't particularly cheered by my mother's sentiment. However, by the time the mid-day meal was placed on the table, my spirits had revived sufficiently enough to enable me to get excited again about my intended trip to Woodhouse Feast with Billy. Nicky had already informed us that he would be unable to go in the afternoon as he was visiting relatives with his parents, but he did manage to express his annoyance about it. Billy called round for me half an hour after we had finished eating and we walked up towards Melville Road before turning left and continuing towards Woodhouse Street.

"Do you remember, Neil?" he asked, as we began walking up the hill, "Susan Brown said that she'd be at the feast this afternoon. Are you going to give her that pendant when you see her?"

"You're forgetting that she said that she might not even talk to me and I still blame you for that, Billy. Anyway, she also said that she'd probably be going with Sally Cheesedale who told her that she likes you."

"Well, I don't care if she does, or if she doesn't. I don't want a girl friend. I think that hanging around with girls is all sloppy."

"But you told me that you liked Sally Cheesedale, Billy."

"No I didn't. You said that, if I had to get married to somebody from our school who would I want it to be, and I only picked her because her brother might play cricket for Yorkshire someday and I might get loads of free tickets."

"Anyway, I've decided to hang onto the pendant until the right time and I don't know when that will be."

"That gypsy lad, Danny, said that he'd be going to the feast today, didn't he?"

"I know, but I hope his sister comes with him as well."

When we reached the edge of Woodhouse Moor we could see immediately that the feast was not as large as the one we had visited six months earlier which had overflowed onto the other side of both Rampart Road and Woodhouse Street. It was, however, still a substantial size and the various noises emanating from the rides and sideshows were just as deafening.

"Well, at least we're not likely to get soaked this time," observed Billy, no doubt recalling the discomfort we had experienced on the previous occasion that we had attended the festivities. The sky was clear, though a little chilly. However, I knew that once we had crossed the road to join the excited throng there would be no possibility of feeling cold.

"Do you remember last September, Billy?" I asked him as we reached the other side and began to penetrate the crowd. "We spent ages trying to find out what had happened to Elsie Waterman to make her stop going to the feast anymore." I had heard from my parents while eavesdropping that the young woman had been the victim of some unpleasant incident while she had been enjoying a ride on the chair-o-planes two years earlier. She had lived in the house next to the one currently occupied by Nicky Whitehead but the family had moved to another part of Leeds just before Christmas.

"Of course I remember," he said. "We spent all the time we were there trying to figure out what happened, but we never did, did we? Don't tell me you're going to waste time on it again."

"There's no need to, Billy, because I already know."

He stopped in his tracks at the foot of the Helter Skelter. "What do you mean, you already know?" he gasped. "How can you?"

"Because my mother told me all about it as soon as I'd asked her if I could go to the feast."

I could see that his interest had been aroused. "Well, come on then, what happened?" he asked, eagerly.

I looked around at the hustle and bustle surrounding us. No one seemed to show any interest in two eleven-year old boys in conversation. However, I didn't want to say what I had to say where anyone else might hear. "I can't say it out loud, Billy," I indicated. I leaned over and whispered in his ear everything that I had been told.

He burst out laughing as soon as I had finished my explanation "Crikey!" he said. "So that's what it was all about. It's a pity that it wasn't Mary Pearson who was sitting on the chair-o-planes. It wouldn't have stopped her coming back, would it?"

This time we were both laughing hysterically.

"Where shall we go first, Billy?" I asked him as soon as the mirth had subsided.

"Why don't we just walk around everywhere first and see if we bump into anybody from school?"

"There's no need to, Neil. There's already someone over there that we know." He pointed in the direction of the coconut shy. I couldn't determine who he meant at first as quite a sizeable crowd had gathered, but as a gap appeared in the centre of it I could see the person to whom he was referring standing at the front. It was also obvious that quite a rumpus seemed to be taking place. We walked over to observe what was happening.

"I've hit a coconut at least four times," said the young voice that seemed to be the centre of attraction, "And not one of 'em has dropped from its perch."

"That's right," said an older voice. "I've seen him hit a coconut three times myself."

"Well, you have to hit it in exactly the right spot," shouted the stall owner in an attempt to defend himself from what was rapidly becoming an ugly situation.

"Five balls for a tanner you said," voiced the original complainant. "And I've spent a shilling trying. Ten balls I've thrown and I know four of 'em hit their mark. I'm buggered if Al Capone himself, armed with a machine gun, could shoot any of 'em down."

"Well I think the least you can do is to give the lad his shilling back," said another gruff voice from near the front of the crowd."

"Aye, and a coconut as well for his trouble," said another.

The exasperated stall holder finally decided that it was more prudent to give in on this occasion and he handed the lad his money back as well as a coconut. I couldn't help noticing that he took it from underneath the counter rather than attempt to dislodge one of those that were on display.

Satisfied that his protests had reached a successful conclusion the lad who had been at the centre of the disturbance began to move away from the stall holding his trophy. As the rest of the crowd dispersed Billy and I walked over to him.

"Hello, Danny," I said.

"Hello, you two," he replied. "He was a rotten bugger was that one. I reckon he should have given me four coconuts instead of one."

"Well, it's not worked out too badly for you anyway. At least he gave you your money back."

"No he didn't."

"We both saw him hand you a shilling," said a surprised Billy.

"I know," grinned Danny, holding the coin in his hand for us to see, "But this isn't the same shilling. The one I gave him was a dud. I'll have to get my Uncle Seamus to make me another one now. He kept telling me not to try using it as a real coin or I'd probably get into bother, but I couldn't see much point in having it if I couldn't use it."

"I wish I had an Uncle Seamus," said Billy, pensively. "He sounds quite useful. Is he living in a caravan at the feast?"

"He comes sometimes but he's travelling up in the North Riding at the moment. My Auntie Kathleen's here though. I'll take you to see her if you like. She tells fortunes, my Auntie Kath does, and if you give her sixpence each she'll tell you yours for free."

Despite his rather unusual description of a free fortune-telling session we nevertheless followed him towards one of the caravans close to the edge of the moor.

"What are you going to do if we do bump into Sally Cheesedale and Susan Brown?" I asked Billy.

"Nothing!"

"But what if Sally's brother does end up playing for Yorkshire and gets loads of free tickets?"

"I don't think it's likely to happen and I don't want to be seen by anybody going around with a girl."

Our immediate impression on reaching the caravan belonging to Danny's aunt was that it in no way resembled the one that our companion lived in. It had a distinctly shabby appearance but our attention was drawn to a sign just outside that read KATIE McBRIDE – GENUINE GYPSY FORTUNE-TELLER.

"Just wait here," said Danny, "While I see if it's all right if she sees you."

A couple of minutes later he beckoned us to follow as he climbed the three steps to the entrance. With some reluctance we did as he asked. The inside of the caravan, though it in no way rivaled the previous one into which we had been invited, was much better than our first impressions led us to expect.

"I've brought you another coconut Auntie Kath," announced Danny.

"Thank you son," You're a good lad," said Katie McBride –genuine gypsy fortune-teller, her long, straggly hair making her look much older than she probably was. "Just put it over there with the other one. It isn't often that you get two coconut shies at the same feast, I'll be thinking."

"So who are these two?" she asked, gesturing in our direction.

"These lads are my mates," he replied. "I met them last week on Woodhouse Ridge. They were getting into a bit of bother with about half a dozen other lads so I went to help 'em out."

Billy and I just stared at each other in exasperation.

"So, you're both here, I'll be thinking, to find out what future secrets are lurking in my crystal ball."

I could see that Billy's mind was focused on the sixpence he was expected to hand over. "Not really," he said, though without much conviction.

"Well, that's a great pity it is, because I can already see that everything is becoming less cloudy and that something quite exciting seems to be happening to you." Her eyes briefly rose above the orb and stared at him as if trying to read his expression.

"What can you see?" asked Billy, excitedly.

"Well, first you must cross my palm with silver," she said, "Otherwise my powers will not work."

He took a silver sixpence from his pocket and handed it over. She gazed at it, put it between her teeth and bit on it.

"Now, you wouldn't have been getting this from Danny's Uncle Seamus, would you?" she said, suspiciously.

"No, my dad gave it to me this morning."

Apparently satisfied by his explanation she peered once more into the crystal ball. "Now," she said. What's this I can see? To be sure, it looks like some sort of queue and a very long one at that, and it appears to be outside. Now what could they all be queuing for on what appears to be a warm, sunny day?"

"If it's summer it might be a cricket match," offered Billy.

"I do believe you're right, and to be sure I'm thinking it must be Headingley, for am I not recognizing the street?"

I could see that Billy was getting very excited. "Can I come round and have a look?" he suggested.

"No, I'm afraid that won't do. Would you want to be breaking the spell? The images only make themselves known to me. It was the same with my mother and her mother before her. No, you must stay on that side."

"Can you see me in the queue?"

"I can see a young man that looks like you. Well, just a minute, I do believe it is you, but you're quite a few years older. You're not standing in the queue, mind you. You're strolling past everyone right up to the gate, waving an admission ticket in the air. Now, you're entering the ground through the ticket-holders entrance while everyone in the queue is giving you envious looks."

She paused for a few seconds. "I'm sorry," she continued, "I'm afraid that's all I'll be able to tell you. Everything's getting cloudy and the image has disappeared."

"Wow, said Billy, his face beaming with delight, "I'm going to get my own ticket to see Yorkshire play at Headingley."

"And what about you, young man," said the fortune-teller. To be sure I 'm thinking that you'll want to
know you're own fortune?"

After witnessing Billy's delightful expression I was in
no mood to resist her persuasive words. I handed over
my sixpence and watched her go through the same coin
testing procedure that she had performed earlier.

"Are you going to tell him something about his girlfriend?" asked Billy, mischievously. "She's called Susan
Brown."

I blushed, and flashed him an annoying glance.

"Well, didn't I already know that someone like you
would have to have a girlfriend somewhere? And I
think I can see her now. Yes, she's a very pretty girl and
she appears to be searching for something she has lost.
Her hand goes up to her neck. Perhaps it could be a
necklace or something."

"Could it be a pendant?" I asked, eagerly.

"Well, to be sure, that's exactly what it is, for isn't
the girl at this very moment replacing it around her
neck? Now, just a minute, what do I see here? I can see
you coming into the picture and the girl is giving you a
hug."

"What happens next?" I asked.

"She's taking your hand and you seem to be going
for a walk. Oh, dear, I think that's all I'll be able to tell
you. The crystal ball has gone all cloudy again. I'm
sorry but you'll have to leave me now, I'll be thinking.
These intense sessions often leave me feeling very tired."

The three of us made to leave the van. "Just a minute,
young Danny," she said, "You'd better watch out for
that sister of yours, for didn't I just see her a few minutes
ago walking past the van with a boy's hand wrapped

around her waist? You know what your da will say if he finds out."

"How did she know all that stuff, Billy?" I asked as we stood outside the caravan.

"My Auntie Kath's been telling fortunes for ages," said Danny. "Anyway, you heard what she just said. I'd better go see if I can find my sister."

We didn't need any prompting to decide to accompany him. Uppermost in our minds was the display we were treated to on our first meeting.

"I think I know where she'll be if she's got a boy with he," said our companion.

We soon found ourselves standing outside the Caterpillar, a circular, undulating ride which was very popular with courting couples. The ride was about ten minutes in duration, but about halfway through a canopy would slide over the carriages and the ride would continue in darkness. Some of the occupants would take this opportunity to indulge in the kind of behavior that they would not dream of doing if they were under observation. The unfortunate thing for them, though not those who were watching the ride, was that there was no warning when the canopy was raised again, and there was always someone who found themselves in an embarrassing situation though I am sure, from their point of view, it was worth the risk. The caterpillar always attracted a large crowd of onlookers.

The canopy was down when we arrived, but within seconds it flew open initiating several shrieks from those who had been caught unawares. We recognized the fiery red hair of Danny's sister immediately, despite the fact that she had her back towards us. She was locked in a sensual embrace with some boy and both seemed oblivious to the fact that they were now in full view.

"I can see you, our Sha. You wait till I tell my da," yelled Danny.

The person to whom his words were directed released the boy's grip on her and turned around with a look of horror on her face. "Don't you dare, Danny O'Shaugnessy," she shouted. "Just you wait there until this ride's finished."

I was disappointed that on this occasion her normally hidden charms remained that way.

We left Danny waiting for his sister and set off to explore the remainder of the feast. I wasn't sure whether I was hoping to encounter Susan Brown and Sally Cheesedale or not, but so far we had met none of the pupils from our school.

"What do you want to go on, Billy?" I asked, conscious of the fact that, with the exception of our visit to the fortune-teller, we had spent nothing yet.

"Let's find the dodgem cars," he suggested.

Before we arrived, however, it started to rain and we were forced to shelter under the awning of one of the stalls. As the force of the rain increased we were joined by others and before long the small area was crowded. It must have been about ten minutes before the conditions were such that we felt able to step out. By that time much of the crowd had dispersed and the conditions underfoot were extremely uncomfortable.

"Have you ever been to Woodhouse Feast when it hasn't rained, Neil?" asked my companion.

I gave the matter some thought. "Maybe, a couple of times," I told him, "But I think I was very young at the time."

"Look, there's Sally Cheesedale over there. She isn't with Susan Brown, though. She's with Wanda Aspinall and Norma Clayton."

It was obvious that they were walking in our direction. "Don't tell them we've been to a fortune-teller, Billy or it'll be all over the school and we'll never be able to live it down." I was curious as to why Susan wasn't with them and I just hoped that it wasn't to avoid seeing me. I still remembered her parting words after our encounter at the fish and chip shop, but I knew that I had to ask the question. "Didn't Susan say she was coming with you?"

"We were supposed to meet her at the end of Melville Road but she never turned up," said Norma Clayton.

Billy decided to get a question in. "Is your brother still hoping to play cricket for Yorkshire?" he asked Sally Cheesedale.

"Yes," she replied, and he's already started training with them, but it might be a year or two before he gets to play for the first team."

The three girls left us and started walking towards the carousel.

Within minutes the rain began again and, not wishing to leave without going on a single ride, we continued on our way to the dodgems and spent five or ten minutes speeding around the track before deciding that the rain was unlikely to ease up this time.

"How did that Katie McBride know that I had a pendant for Susan?" I asked Billy as we made our way down Woodhouse Street heading for home.

"And how did she know that I was hoping to get free tickets to go see Yorkshire play?" he replied.

We could think of no satisfactory answer to either question, but after I arrived home my mind was focused on the possible reason for Susan deciding not to attend the feast, and it stayed that way for the remainder of the day.

CHAPTER SIX

As Easter Monday was a bank holiday I was surprised when, just after we had finished eating breakfast, a letter was pushed through the letter box.

"I didn't think that postmen worked on Easter Monday, mam" I said.

"Well now, don't forget that your grandad was a postman before he had to retire and I've known him work on bank holidays on many occasions, but he always used to be paid overtime for doing it." She picked up the letter and scrutinised the envelope. "And it looks to me as if the address is in your grandad's handwriting."

"I wonder what that's all about," said my father, walking across the room to join her. "We only got one from him two days ago. I hope it isn't anything serious."

His comments started me worrying.

"It looks like dad's coming home tomorrow, Tom," she said to my father after finishing reading the letter. She then handed it to him to peruse.

"I thought he might be leaving the convalescent home next weekend, but having read his reasons I can perfectly understand them," he said a few seconds later.

"Can I read what he's written?" I asked, impatiently.

My father handed me the letter and I began to read.

Dear May,

I hope you received the letter that I posted on Friday. I am writing this one only a few hours later after having received permission to be able to leave on Easter Tuesday. I told you in the previous letter about my childhood friend Harry having passed away and for me it has changed the whole feel of the place. I know that being here has done me good because I have noticed a definite improvement in my breathing, but I just think I'd be happier back home now. I was just wondering if I might call on you first and possibly stay the night. If you've already arranged something for the Bank Holiday then please don't change your plans, I don't want to deprive the lad of an outing. I realise it's also possible that this letter might not reach you in time. Anyway, I expect to arrive about the middle of the afternoon. If you happen to be out I'll just leave a message with either Molly, Eileen or Brenda to say that I've gone back home to the flat. Sorry if I've caused you any inconvenience, Love Dad.

I put the letter back in the envelope and handed it to my mother. If I was in the same room Grandad Miller would usually refer to me as 'this lad' rather than by name as if I was some alien entity who had suddenly appeared from nowhere, but when I wasn't in the same room it would be simply 'the lad'.

I realised that this was one occasion when it was useful to have three aunties living in the same street. Surely one of them would be at home even if we weren't, though I suspected that my mother, now that she was aware of the circumstances, would make sure that she wasn't out when my grandfather called.

"What do you think, Tom?" she asked my father. "I know it'll mean that we won't be able to go out anywhere on the last day before you have to go back to work, but I don't see how we can refuse him, do you?"

"No, of course we can't. In fact, I think it would do him good to stay for two or three days. Anyway, we're still going out today, aren't we?"

So it was settled, and I was already looking forward to seeing my grandfather on the following day.

"Where are we going today then, dad?" I asked him.

"Well, I haven't quite decided. I know it's not raining yet but the weather's a bit dull, isn't it?" What do you think love?" His latter remarks were directed to my mother.

"Well, there's Roundhay Park, Temple Newsam or we could just go for a walk in Meanwood Woods, but why don't we wait until after dinner and decide then. The weather might have picked up a bit."

My father was quite happy to agree to her suggestion and it certainly suited me. I decided to call on Billy as he had already told me that his parents hadn't decided on going anywhere special on this particular holiday.

"Are you coming out?" I asked him as soon as he opened the door.

"Hello, Neil," he greeted me, without answering my question. "Have you seen what's happening at the Electra? All the scaffolding's been re-erected and there are workmen trying to repair the roof. If they're working on Easter Monday, it must mean that it'll be opening soon."

"Don't forget, Billy, Easter's early this year and it's still March. We always get a lot of winds in March. It might blow the scaffolding down again." Despite the negativity of my statement I really hoped that Billy's assessment of the situation proved to be the right one.

"My grandad Miller's coming out of the convalescent home tomorrow," I said, as we began to tire of watching the workmen scrambling backwards and forwards along the scaffolding.

"You thought he'd be in a bit longer, didn't you Neil?"

I explained to him about how upset he was about the death of his childhood friend, it happening so soon after they had been reunited. "He'll be staying at our house for a day or two before he goes home," I informed him. "So, what do you want to do this morning, Billy? I might be going out somewhere with my mam and dad this afternoon."

"Where will you be going?" he asked.

"I don't know yet, but it might be Roundhay Park."

"The last time I went there was on Children's Day."

"Yes, it was with me. Billy."

Children's Day was an annual event that took place in the park in July. There were numerous events, many of them involving schools in the Leeds area and always included was the crowning of one delighted schoolgirl who had been designated carnival queen for the day. When evening came there was always a fireworks display on the far side of the lake to look forward to. What my father always enjoyed most, however, was the seven-a-side rugby league match in the afternoon.

"I think they have a feast there as well at Easter," remarked my companion.

"I know, Billy, but it's nowhere near as big as the one that's on Woodhouse Moor."

Nevertheless, it remained an interesting option.

When I returned indoors I was told that Roundhay Park was, indeed, the chosen destination as the weather was showing signs of improvement, though it had been decided to have a quick meal first. I knew how much more I would enjoy the afternoon if I had a companion and begged for Billy to be included in the trip.

"He might be going out with his own mam and dad," suggested my mother, with some reluctance.

"No, they're not going out today. He told me so, and he was hoping that we'd be able to play out together today."

"What do you think, Tom?" asked my mother.

"Well, I can't really see any harm in it I suppose, but he'll have to get permission from his father first."

I was about to suggest that we ask Nicky too, but I didn't want to risk the possibility that they might change their minds.

"You'd better go out and ask him then," added my father. "We'll have to leave at about one o'clock because it will take us nearly an hour to get there."

I immediately rushed out and found my closest friend, as I had expected, delighted by the suggestion. His parents had planned to visit relatives on the following day which was also a public holiday and raised no objections. In fact they seemed quite pleased to have him off their hands for a while. Billy agreed to call round at about ten to one.

When I re-entered the house and informed them that they were quite happy for him to join us, Nell suddenly began running around in circles with her tail wagging furiously, and that was when I was told that our numbers had grown from a party of four to one of five, having made the suggestion while I was outside the house that if Billy was coming they might as well include my canine companion as there would be an extra pair of hands to look after her.

The small expedition set off a little before one thirty with Nell insisting on leading the way by tugging on the lead, that I attempted to retain in my hand, in her desire to leave the boring concrete and cobblestone surroundings that she knew so well, her mind fixed no doubt on the more exciting sights and smells of the greener landscape that she was anticipating.

My father had decided that it would be a total waste of money to board the tram at the Primrose in Meanwood Road and alight at the Golden Cross at the bottom of North Street before taking the number three which would take us to the very gates of Roundhay Park. In his mind, it was well within walking distance to walk to the very end of Buslingthorpe Lane and to board the tram there. Nell, who hadn't the faintest idea of the location of the intended destination, was quite happy to fall in with these plans, secure in the knowledge that she would be able to take command again when the little band reached somewhere more interesting.

When we arrived at the tram stop we did not have long to wait, but it was immediately obvious that it would be standing room only on the lower deck. Nell, however, was all for galloping up the staircase on the platform at the end of the tram.

"No dogs allowed upstairs," announced the overweight conductor. "At least one of you will have to go inside with the dog."

His victim rewarded her antagonist with her fiercest glare of disapproval, the one she only used when registering extreme displeasure.

"You two go upstairs," suggested my father. "We'll stay down here with Nell. I'll get the tickets."

He pointed out what appeared to be the only vacant seat in the lower saloon and my father took hold of the suspended strap as the tram began clanging its way up Roundhay Road. My mother sat down with Nell mounting guard at the side of her taking up as much room in the aisle as she could in order to create as big a problem as she could for the only person on the tram that she had taken an instant dislike to. At the same instant Billy and I began to climb the staircase to the upper deck.

The journey to the park from our vantage point was a very pleasant one, even though the front seats which we always headed for were already occupied. The best part was when the tram reached the Clock cinema opposite the Astoria ballroom and left the heavy traffic to enter its own purpose-built track between two grass verges in the centre of the road. The speed always increased on this part of the journey and it was easy to imagine that you were actually travelling by train rather than by local transport.

Just before the tram was due to halt outside the park gates, Billy and I began to descend the stairs to the lower level. As we reached the platform we could hear an altercation taking place.

"It should be half a crown for bloody dogs rather than tuppence," shouted the red-faced conductor, "What with all the trouble they cause."

I was surprised to hear my father's voice raised in reply.

"Well, if you didn't spend your dinner break drinking so much beer, you wouldn't be so overweight and you wouldn't have tripped over her in the first place. I can smell it on your breath. It reeks of it."

"Now, don't get excited Tom," said my mother, trying to calm down the situation. "She was taking up quite a bit of room."

"Well, it's his own bloody fault. I don't think he even bothered trying to get out of the way."

Nell averted her gaze from her mistress and looked up at her defender with adoring eyes.

As we disembarked from the tram it soon became obvious that most of the other passengers took the same view as my father, some of them declaring that they had become victims of this same conductor's abusive and domineering manner before.

"It's about time he was taken down a peg or two," said one. "He's always drunk on duty."

Nell was quite contented to be declared the hero of the moment and receive several pats from the other travellers. As she led the way through the park gates with her head held high and her tail wagging furiously, Billy whispered in my ear. "I think that's the first time I would rather have been sitting downstairs on a tram." I laughed, and knew exactly what he meant.

"I think I could do with a cup of tea, Tom," declared my mother. "There's a cafe in the Canal Gardens, isn't there?" Whenever she alighted from any form of public transport it always seemed to be the first thing on her mind.

"Why don't we walk down to the Lakeside Cafe and have one there?" responded my father.

Roundhay Park was one of the largest city parks in the United Kingdom and included two lakes of varying size. The one indicated by my father was the larger of the two and various water sports took place on it during the holiday periods. The cafe which overlooked it was extremely popular as it was also quite close to the open-air swimming pool, and most visitors would pay a call there at some point during the afternoon.

My mother was quite happy to fall in with his suggestion and we all made our way past the Mansion House before heading downhill. It soon became obvious that there was a funfair on the site as we heard the sounds emanating from it before it came into view.

I got in first. "Can me and Billy go to the feast, dad?" I asked him.

As we got our first proper sighting of it we realised that it was certainly on the small side, but also very welcoming.

"Wouldn't you like to come to the cafe with us first for a glass of lemonade or something?" asked my father.

"What do you think, Billy?" I said, addressing my companion.

"Well, my dad gave me two shillings to spend, but he told me that I had to pay my way and that I couldn't be expecting your dad to be buying ice creams and things out of his own pocket. So I think we'd better call at the feast later when I know how much I've got left to spend."

So the decision was made and we all continued to the bottom of the hill.

"Look, Neil, there's a maze," he said, excitedly, as we walked past it. "I wonder how much it is to go in there."

"Well, I'll tell you what," suggested my father. "Why don't we have a look at it after we've all had some refreshments?"

"No dogs aloud," said the red-faced man at the door, who was apparently in charge of the seating arrangements. "You'll have to tie it up somewhere or all of you sit outside." He gazed down at our four-legged companion with a look of disgust. "What sort of a dog is it, anyway? It looks like it's got a bit everything in it. Are you sure it is a dog?"

I could sense my father's temper beginning to rise again, but my mother interrupted the proceedings. "Look, there's a dog sitting over there," she said in a calm voice, indicating a table at the far end of the room.

"That's Colonel Melly's dog," was the reply. "He played a very significant role in the war. He never goes anywhere without Skipper and it's a very exclusive breed you know. The colonel doesn't take kindly to other dogs being in the vicinity, especially one as scruffy-looking as the one you've got there."

Nell's hurtful growl was interrupted by my father, his voice rising until he was almost shouting. "Well, you can tell your Colonel Smelly or whatever his name is, that as far as I'm concerned he can stick his bloody bayonet up his arse."

"Tom," said my mother with a look of horror on her face. I knew that her indignation was not with the sentiment he was expressing but with his choice of words.

"Look," she said in a lowered voice in an attempt to calm things down, "There's a kiosk by the lake. We can get a drink there."

Satisfied with his response to the situation my father retraced his steps, but not before Nell peed in the doorway. She then took her place at the side of us with her head held high as we walked over to the kiosk indicated by my mother.

Both Billy and I had remained quiet while the altercation at the cafe was taking place but normal conversation was resumed shortly afterwards.

"I think I fancy going into the maze," he told me as we supped our lemonades by the side of the lake.

"Yes," I said in reply," It looks great, doesn't it? I've never been in there before."

Realising that the only item that the man in the kiosk had to offer that might have been of any interest to her, namely ice cream, was not at that moment on my father's list of priorities, Nell suddenly became distracted. Deciding that the proper habitat for geese was on the surface of the lake and that they had no right to invade the grassy bank which was, in her mind, reserved strictly for the pleasure of dogs with perhaps the occasional human in tow, she suddenly lurched forward, pulling Billy off his feet and forcing him to let go of the lead, to which she had been attached ever since we had approached the Lakeside Cafe with the intention of venturing inside. Sensing her new-found freedom she hurled herself among the birds, scattering them in all directions. Unfortunately, her actions had a similar effect on some of the human visitors, resulting in their landing on their backsides on the slippery bank, several of whom had only a few seconds earlier been enjoying the drinks that they had purchased at the kiosk. It was left to my parents to attempt to make amends and apologise for her behaviour.

Meanwhile Nell, realising that one of her attempted victims had not run off with the others but was moving slowly towards her with a determined and angry look on its face, decided to change tactics and ran back towards us before hiding behind my father who, by now, I think was beginning to regret his decision to bring her.

"Bloody dogs," said one of the unfortunate visitors. "They shouldn't be allowed in the park if they can't be kept under control."

On this occasion it was deemed prudent for no member of our party to make a comment. My mother and father decided to walk around the lake with Nell firmly on the lead while Billy and I visited the funfair. We arranged to meet outside the entrance to the maze half an hour later. The amount of time we had been allocated, considering the smallness of the fair, proved to be just about right and we both had a good time there. When we met up again it was with the news that there had been no more awkward moments caused by our canine companion and my parents did appear to be much more relaxed.

"You two want to go into the maze then, do you?" asked my father, dipping into his pocket to find money for the tickets. "What about you, May? Shall we all go in?"

"I don't think so, Tom. It looks a bit too claustrophobic to me. I don't want to get lost in there. It might give me nightmares."

"Right, just the two of you then and you might as well take Nell in with you. She might help you to find your way out again."

"Is it all right to take a dog in?" asked my father of the ticket attendant, no doubt expecting a refusal bearing in mind what had occurred previously.

"Is it well-behaved?" came the reply.

"Of course she is. She has a very gentle nature and never gives a moment's trouble." I couldn't help noticing that my father refused to make eye-contact with his listener. To add weight to the discourse Nell walked over to the attendant, sat down at the side of him, and offered her paw.

"Very well," he decided, "She seems gentle enough, but make sure that she's kept on the lead."

I knew that this condition would not be exactly in line with Nell's sense of justice, but it seemed totally acceptable to everyone else.

My father paid for the tickets and our canine friend was allowed to accompany us without charge.

"What a nice man, Tom," I heard my mother say as the three of us entered the confines of the maze while they waited outside.

Nell immediately began to pull on the lead, which Billy had handed over to me, not wanting, no doubt, for his previous mishap to be repeated. She ignored a path to the left and a path to the right before coming to a full stop in front of the hedge, which was a very high one. I pulled her back and we retraced our steps before taking the second of the two paths that we had previously ignored. I have to admit that within a few minutes she did seem to realise what was expected of her and began to take charge again.

"Shall we let her lead?" asked Billy, "And see if she manages to get us to the middle of the maze?"

I could already see several people standing on the high platform in the exact centre. We decided to let her assume command and, despite her earlier mistake, we emerged barely five minutes later at our designated destination. We ascended the stairs to join the other hopefuls on the platform.

"Welcome to the castaways," greeted a rather plump, middle-aged man. "How long did it take you to get here, then?"

"Just over five minutes," replied Billy.

"Five minutes," said a younger, bespectacled lady, rather incredulously. "I've been in here for about forty minutes and the gentleman that was just speaking to you has been here for almost an hour."

"Is it that hard then?" I asked.

"I'll say it's bloody hard," uttered a third voice. "Every time we try to find our way out we end up back here. Just before you arrived we'd made a decision to stop trying to find our way back individually but to group together. How did you get here so quickly anyway?"

"It was her really," said Billy, pointing to our canine companion.

"I suppose it was her sense of smell," I added as Nell, sensing her opportunity to be elected as leader of the expedition, began sniffing the ground

"Well," said the original speaker who seemed to be the dominant member of the group, "I reckon that's just what we need then. I can't be stuck in here much longer. The dog will get us out of here,"

I would have preferred to remain in the centre of the maze for a short while longer having just arrived there, but I could see that Nell was anxious to take command and the ones we were hoping to liberate from their unintended incarceration were desperate to escape. I could tell that she sensed that this was her moment as we left the sanctuary with her leading and entered the first pathway. From then on she sniffed at each junction before making a decision and within minutes we had retraced our steps and found ourselves back at the entrance to the maze without having taken one wrong turning. She basked in the adulation she received from each of our companions.

"That dog's bloody marvellous," exclaimed one.

"You can say that again," said another.

"She deserves a medal," said a third.

Billy and I smiled as my parents came over wondering what all the fuss was about.

We could still see from our vantage point the doorman of the Lakeside Cafe, and I felt enormous pride as Nell turned towards him with an expression that seemed to say "What about that then?" before turning her back on him to receive the pats and hugs that she had surely earned.

"Well," said my father, exasperatedly, That's a turn up for the book. I'm fair clemmed."

"What does clemmed mean, dad?" I asked him.

"Well, I'm pleased; dead chuffed in fact, after all the bother she's been getting into today, and I think on that note it's time to be making our way home."

"We've usually had a look at the swimmers in the outdoor pool," said my mother.

"I know, but I think it's best not to tempt providence. I don't want to see Nell running off with someone's bathing trunks."

Billy and I both laughed at the mental image that this remark invited as we turned up the drive towards the Mansion House on the first stage of our journey home. There was no unsavoury incident on the tram and as I said goodbye to Billy and the rest of us had stepped through the welcoming door of number sixteen Cross Speedwell Street my mother's first job was to light a fire in the grate and watch Nell settle down on the clip rug in front of it and bask in the triumph of her first and only visit to Roundhay Park.

CHAPTER SEVEN

The following day, Easter Tuesday, was still a Bank Holiday and I was looking forward to the arrival of Grandad Miller. The letter he had sent us stated that he wouldn't be arriving until mid afternoon. Billy called round immediately after I had finished eating breakfast and asked if I fancied going with him to see if the gypsy caravan was still there. I knew that Woodhouse Feast would be gone by tomorrow and, as that was the main reason why Danny and his family were parked at the bottom of the ridge it might be our last chance to see them. I was as enthusiastic as he was and we called to see if Nicky felt the same way. Eventually, all three of us made our way onto the topmost path before descending towards the beck. As we got nearer it became obvious that the tree trunk was still straddling the water, but our attention was immediately drawn to the fact that Danny, the gypsy boy, was sitting on the far end of it. He answered our greeting but we could see straight away that he looked far from happy.

"What's the matter, Danny?" I asked him, after we had joined him on the opposite bank. "You look really upset about something"

"I was hoping to go back to the feast tonight, but my da says we can't stay any longer and we'll have to leave."

"Why, has something happened? Have the police moved you on?" I asked him.

"No, it's worse than that." he replied. "Our Shannon's gone missing. She didn't come home last night and my da thinks she's run off with that lad that she met at the feast. He told her that he lived in Skipton so we're going up there to see if we can find her."

I could see that the horse had already been harnessed to the caravan which had now moved into view from beyond the trees. We sympathised with our new friend and I was disappointed that he and his family would be leaving as they had provided a most welcome diversion to our usual routine over the past few days. He did inform us, however, that there was a very good chance that they might be returning in the summer especially now that they had found a pitch where they were unlikely to be disturbed. We stayed and chatted for a while before making our way home. I had already told Billy that I might not be coming out again during the afternoon as Grandad Miller was visiting and that I wanted to be there when he arrived.

The clock on the mantelpiece showed twenty past four when he actually made an appearance. Nell looked up from her usual place in front of the fire, realised that it was somebody she knew but not, at least in her mind, anyone to make a fuss over and promptly settled down again.

"Sorry, I'm a bit later than expected, lass," he began, directing his words to my mother. "The people from the convalescent home dropped me off at the bus stop, but it seems that Sammy Ledgard's are running a bank holiday timetable today and I had to wait a long time for a bus, and then when it got to Otley bus station it waited for another twenty minutes before setting off again. Anyway, I'm here now."

I could see that his period of convalescence did seem to have done him some good. He had a lot more colour in his cheeks and he looked considerably younger than when I had last visited him when he looked so bored and depressed.

"Sit yourself down, dad," said my mother. "I'm making a nice salad for tea, if that's all right with you."

"Aye, lass that'll be grand," he replied settling himself into the comfortable armchair close to the fire, which my father had kindly vacated as soon as he had arrived. Nell, however, did not appear to be too happy with this change to routine and moved a little closer to the fire as the person that she considered appreciated her the most had been replaced by someone who was only a fringe member of the family and who only made the occasional appearance.

"How are you feeling now then, Sam?" asked my father. "It certainly looks as if the break has done you good."

"Oh, aye, I feel much better that I did the first week I was in there, and much of that is down to this lad here. I didn't feel that I was getting anywhere," he continued, "Until he told me that my old mate Harry Crabtree was staying on the same premises, though I'm not sure I would have recognized him after all this time. Anyway, as soon as we got talking it was just as if we'd never been separated and we spent hours in each other's company reminiscing about all the things we'd got up to when we were children."

He wiped his eyes and gave a little sniff before continuing. "It came as a great shock to me when he had the heart attack and keeled over. The thing that will always stay in my mind though is the fact that he died laughing. We were both having hysterics while remembering the time we put one over on Old Ma Tubshaw. I'm grateful for one thing though. If I hadn't decided to go convalescing I would never have met up with him again. Anyway, I'll console myself with the thought that it probably won't be all that long before we're back together."

"Dad," exclaimed my mother, "You must not talk like that. It's like tempting providence. You'll probably live for years yet."

"Well, that's as may be, but I'm not frightened of it anymore."

My mother began to lay the table and we all took our places around it. Nell took up her usual position at the side of my father before realising that all that was on offer was salad and not her favourite fish and chips. She decided to settle back down again on the clip rug in front of the fire, though not without giving my mother a look of disgust for not providing more interesting fare and for failing to realise that a dog's need was something more substantial and appetising; this despite the fact that she had already devoured her own doggy meal half an hour previously.

"I see they've got scaffolding all around the Electra," said my grandfather as we were all tucking into the salad. "I thought they'd have finished the repairs by now."

"They would have done," exclaimed my father, "But most of the scaffolding blew down during those strong gales we had a few days ago and they've only just put it back up."

"Oh, I remember them all right," said Grandad Miller. "They kept me awake half the night. I thought the roof was coming in. It's a long time since I've known anything as fierce."

"It all made an awful clatter," I added, for greater effect. "Me and Billy were just walking past on our way home from school when it happened. Those iron bars were rolling around all over the place. It's a wonder they didn't knock us over."

"I reckon a couple of weeks should do it," suggested my father. "At least they've started working on it again."

"When I got off the bus at Hyde Park I walked down Woodhouse Street and passed that picture house halfway down," said my grandfather.

"I think they call it the Astra now, grandad," I told him.

"Do they? Well, I never knew that. I've always called it the Woodhouse Picture House. Anyway the point I was trying to make before I was rudely interrupted was that the film that's on tonight is a film about pirates called 'Treasure Island', and It's supposed to be very good. Most of the picture houses seem to put on a really decent adventure film during the Easter holiday period. I bet there'll be a cartoon or a comedy short on as well. I thought I might pop over to see it after tea if you've no objection."

I waited for the follow-up sentence that I was expecting, such as an invitation for me to join him, but it didn't come.

"Of course we've no objection," declared my mother. You can do whatever you like now that you're here."

"Right then, I noticed it starts at 7 o'clock and it'll probably take me a quarter of an hour to walk up there so I'll leave just after half past six."

I went quiet and picked at the salad on the plate in front of me. Did he really intend to go by himself and leave me at home? It went on like this for perhaps a couple of minutes before he spoke again.

"Yon lad's gone quiet. If he doesn't make quicker progress with that there salad we aren't going to get there in time."

Realising that he had intended to take me with him all the time my appetite miraculously increased and so did my mood. I had read bits of 'Treasure Island' at school and if the picture was as good as the book it would be brilliant. I decided not to tell Billy until the following day as I knew how envious he would be and I did not want to place my grandfather in the position where he would feel obliged to increase the amount he would have to spend out of his meagre pension by taking him along as well. On the previous time that I had been to this particular cinema I had received a thorough soaking due to the appalling weather, but as I looked through the window at the pleasant conditions outside I knew that there was no chance of the same thing happening on this occasion.

We set off shortly after half past six just as it was beginning to get dark, and as we made our way along Melville Road towards Woodhouse Street my grandfather told me about how much his stay in the convalescent home had improved since he became aware of the presence of his childhood friend, Harry Crabtree, residing in the same building and of the joyful hours they had spent together reminiscing. He also went on to say what a shock it had been when he suddenly clutched his heart and died while they were both indulging in hysterical laughter while remembering a particular escapade they had been engaged in when they were children.

"I could have stayed on for another two weeks," he said, "But I knew it just wouldn't be the same without Harry and so I decided that my health had sufficiently improved for me to make the decision to leave early."

"It doesn't seem right," I said, "Him dying just after you'd got back together."

"Well, that's just the way things go son, but he died laughing and what better way to go is there than that?"

As we turned the corner at the end of Melville Road and began to walk up Woodhouse Street we saw a middle-aged man walking towards us and it soon became obvious that he and my grandfather knew each other.

"Hello Phil," greeted Grandad Miller. "Are you out for an evening stroll?"

Hello Sam," said the newcomer. "No, I'm just calling at the chemist to get some medicine for my lass. She's been diagnosed with tonsillitis. Doctor Dunlop reckons she ought to go to the hospital in a few days time and have them taken out. Anyway, I hear you've nearly been at death's door yourself."

"Aye, you can say that again. I had a really bad do just before Christmas, but I've just come out of that convalescent home at Ilkley and I'm pleased to say I'm feeling much better. This is my grandson." He pointed at me. "And we're just on our way to the pictures."

After the brief conversation my grandfather's acquaintance continued to walk down Woodhouse Street while we continued in the opposite direction.

"That's Phil Brown," said Grandad Miller. "He worked at the Post Office in city Square while I was a postman there."

"Wasn't he a postman then, grandad?"

"No, Phil worked in the office there. It's a shame about his daughter though having to go into hospital. Anyway, you might know her because she's about your age and I think she probably goes to your school."

A shiver went through me. "Did you say his last name was Brown?" I asked.

"Aye, lad, that's right. His name is Phil Brown."

"Is his daughter's name, Susan?"

"I don't rightly know. It could be, I suppose. Anyway, we're nearly at the Picture House now, and look, there doesn't seem to be much of a queue, so we'll be able to go straight in."

The film was every bit as good as I had expected it to be, but I couldn't help feeling sorry for Long John Silver at the end of the film and I wondered what it would be like to be cast adrift on the open seas in a boat. As we made our way home my grandfather made a big point of stressing how grateful he was that I had re-introduced him to his childhood friend and he gave me a two shilling piece for my trouble. I was only too pleased to see him looking so much better. I could never forget how ill he had looked when I went to see him in hospital before Christmas. As we turned the corner into Melville Road my thoughts turned towards Susan Brown and the obvious explanation for her non-appearance at Woodhouse Feast. I wondered how long she might have to remain in hospital. It seemed that the gypsy pendant would have to remain in my possession for a while longer.

CHAPTER EIGHT

I know why Susan Brown didn't go to the feast, Billy," I said as we watched the beer lorry pull up outside Doughty's off-licence and waited for them to unload the barrels. "It's because she's got tonsillitis and will have to go into hospital to have them taken out."

"Crikey!" exclaimed my companion, "I bet that hurts."

"My grandad says that tonsils don't really do anything and that there's not much point in them being there anyway, so why not have them taken out? At least it means that she'll never get tonsillitis again. I know that what he says is right because I had mine taken out at the dispensary when I was five years old. My throat was sore for ages afterwards but it hasn't bothered me since."

As two men began moving the barrels from the truck we eagerly awaited for the main event to begin. All in all six barrels were removed. They were unconcerned at being watched as the cellar flap was raised having become used to young spectators being entranced while this particular task was performed. We gazed intently as all the barrels in rapid succession were rolled down a ramp into the proprietor's cellar. I can't really explain what it was about this activity that Billy and I and most of the other kids in the area found so fascinating;

perhaps it was the noise they made as they rolled or maybe the possibility that something might go wrong. However, we were always enthralled.

After the cellar flap had been placed back into position we walked up the hill towards the ridge. I had already explained to my companion that Grandad Miller would be returning home after dinner and that my mother and I would be accompanying him; my mother to do some cleaning and me to go to the shop for some groceries. We decided, therefore, to just lean on the metal barrier at the top of the steps at the entrance to the ridge.

"When are you going to give Susan that pendant, Neil?" asked Billy. Do you remember what that gypsy woman said, that you shouldn't keep it for too long or the magic might wear off?"

"You don't really believe all that stuff, do you? I think she just wanted to sell it to somebody, but I still think Susan might like it anyway."

"So when are you going to give it to her?"

"Well, I can't give it to her when she's in hospital, can I? It'll have to wait until she's back at school."

"She isn't in hospital yet though, is she?"

"What difference does that make? I don't know where she lives, do I? I only know it's not far from the ridge."

"I know what you could do. Why not start knocking on people's doors in the area and when they answer just ask them if they know where Susan Brown lives? I bet you wouldn't have to knock on more than half a dozen before somebody told you."

"That's daft, Billy. Anyway, even if I did find the right house I wouldn't be knocking on her door and explaining to whoever opened it why I'd bought her a present."

"You could just say that you'd heard that she was poorly and that you were wondering how she was."

"That sounds too soppy. You know I couldn't say that." I was beginning to get annoyed with him at that point for making me start to feel embarrassed.

"How about going to see her when she's in hospital then?"

"Shut up, Billy I don't want to talk about it anymore," I said, rather forcefully. "Let's talk about something else."

Realising that he was winding me up a little too much, he decided to change the subject. "Did you know there's a new comic out, Neil? It's called the LION and the front page is an adventure about a space-man called Captain Condor."

"I know. I got the first one. You can borrow it if you like."

"Is it as good as the Eagle because I really like that Dan Dare that's on the front cover?"

"I don't know yet. I've only read the one."

We continued talking about nothing in particular before our stomachs informed us it was time to go.

"You'll have to go to the fish and chip shop," declared my mother after I had arrived home. "I haven't got time to do anything else. We need to get to your grandad's as soon as possible if I'm going to have time to do a bit of cleaning and still get home before your dad arrives from work."

"If we're in a hurry, mam, it'll be quicker if I just walk to the one round the corner opposite Doughty's."

Nell looked up in alarm from her position on the clip rug in front of the fire.

"No, that's not necessary," she replied. "It'll only take you a few minutes longer to go to Jubilee Fisheries and it'll also give me a bit more time to warm the plates and do some bread and butter."

Nell settled down again. I had already known what my mother's answer to my suggestion would be as she never wanted me to go to that particular establishment, though I never knew her reason.

When I arrived at the fish and chip shop there was quite a queue and there was just enough room for me to step inside. The first thing that I realised was that I didn't recognize the lady (or young girl, as she appeared to be about sixteen or seventeen years old) who was doing the serving. The wife of the owner was usually the one behind the counter while her husband Eddie was always, or so she usually informed us, in the back making chips. To my knowledge no one had ever seen him and Billy and I had often doubted his existence. We had no idea, however, who this young server was, but it soon became apparent that her lack of skill in the role she was attempting to fulfil was causing no small measure of discomfort among those who were waiting. The person at the front of the queue was watching her clumsy attempt at arranging the fish and chips in front of her.

"What the Hell are you doing?" said the customer. "What are you counting the chips for?"

"Well my auntie asked me to step in today because she had to go visit my granny at Seacroft because she's very poorly, but the job's a lot harder than I thought it would be."

"So why are you counting the chips?" repeated the irate customer.

"Well, I was told to treat everybody fairly and the person before you had fourteen chips on the paper and you've got seventeen, so that's not really fair, is it? You can't count them when they're on the scoop because they're all bunched up. So you have to wait until they're on the paper and spread them out."

"And have you been doing this with every customer in the shop?"

"Well, I can't think of any other way of doing it."

"Are all the chips the same size then?"

"How do you mean?"

"Well, if some chips are bigger than others how is everybody going the get the same?"

The young girl pondered this for a few seconds before answering. "Fourteen chips is fourteen chips."

A lot of people in the queue, myself included, were beginning to find the whole situation extremely funny and no one attempted to leave the premises because of the poor service. The lady being served, however, could not see the funny side and was getting redder in the face.

"I want to see the owner," she said, raising her voice.

"My Uncle Eddie's in the back making chips."

"Well, you'd better go and get him then, hadn't you?"

"He doesn't like being disturbed when he's making chips."

"Maybe he's trying to make them all the same size," suggested a voice from the queue, causing everyone to laugh even louder.

I couldn't help wondering if my earlier suspicion regarding Eddie might just be true as, with all the commotion, I couldn't understand why he hadn't already made an appearance.

"Well God knows why they put you in charge of serving," shouted the irate customer, going redder still. "It seems to me that you're bloody useless."

The young girl was beginning to cry by now and I half expected her to run into the back of the shop which prompted me to wonder whether we might at last catch sight of the elusive Eddie, but help was at hand from an unexpected quarter.

"I don't make any wonder that yon lass is struggling, "declared Mrs. I-Make-No-Wonder rather forcefully. "Nothing would satisfy you, Mabel Penderghast. You were just the same when we were at school together. I couldn't make any wonder at it then and I don't make any wonder at it now. Leave the poor girl alone. She's doing her best."

The real name of the young girl's champion was Annie Chapman, but because of her unique manner of speaking she was known by most of the local kids as Mrs. I-Make-No-Wonder.

"Well she's not making a very good job at it. She must have been a bloody dunce at school if she thinks she has to count out the chips. Just look at her. She doesn't seem to have a bloody clue."

"Do you make any wonder with the way you're shouting at the poor lass, because I don't make any wonder at it, and I'll tell you this Mabel Penderghast, when you were at school you were the thickest one in our class. You must have been about twelve before you could even say your times tables. Mind you I don't think anybody would make any wonder at that after what they've heard coming out of your mouth today."

Realising that she had met her match and not wishing to be berated any further the young girl's assailant muttered several expletives and stormed out of the shop. The lady who now found herself at the front of the queue had a much kinder expression. "Don't worry about counting all the chips, love," she said, in as soft a voice as she could muster. "Just scoop up what you think is the right amount and put them onto the paper. No one's going to complain."

"That's right," said several voices from the queue, almost simultaneously.

With that re-assurance the girl dried her eyes and willingly did what had been suggested.

"What's your name, love?" asked another lady in the queue.

"It's Wendy."

"Well then, Wendy, the next time I see your auntie I'll make sure I tell her what a good job you made of it and I'm sure that goes for a lot of other people in this shop."

This seemed to satisfy everyone, not least the girl herself, and the queue progressed more rapidly. When I got home I found myself having to explain the reason for my delay which seemed, despite my protestations, to be received with disbelief. It was the idea that someone would actually take the time to count out chips that they found the hardest to take in. Anyway, my mother was too busy placing everything onto the dining table to make any more of the issue. Nell took up her usual place at the side of my father's chair in anticipation of the occasional offering coming her way.

After dinner my mother and I accompanied Grandad Miller down Speedwell Street to the tram stop in

Meanwood Road. After taking the tram to the Corn Exchange we walked across the street to board a number ten to Compton Road. From there it was a five minute walk up the hill to my grandfather's house. When we arrived the first thing my mother did was to check his pantry to see if there was anything left in there. Anything perishable she threw out; anything in tins she kept after ascertaining what the contents were. It soon became clear that my job was to hurry down to the shop with a list of all the items that my mother thought he needed while she tidied up around the house.

"It's freezing in here, dad," she said. "It's a good job you've got plenty of coal available." She laid out a fire in the grate and by the time I arrived back after about twenty minutes it was blazing fiercely.

My mother moved into the bedroom and began making the bed which enabled me to sit in front of the fire with Grandad Miller and ask him a question that had been on my mind for several days.

"Grandad, do you believe in leprechauns?" I asked him.

"Leprechauns, is it? Now where on earth did that question come from?"

I had already decided not to tell him anything about the pendant to save me from embarrassment. Instead I just told him about the gypsy lady at the bottom of the ridge and her story about how one of her ancestors had helped out the little people during the potato famine. He thought for a minute and stroked his chin.

"Now then, do I believe in leprechauns? Well happen I do and happen I don't."

I hated it when he gave that sort of answer. He'd said something very similar when I had asked him if he believed in ghosts.

97

"Well I'll tell you one thing," he went on, "I know for a fact that my old granny believed that they existed. She came from Donegal in Ireland you know, and she used to tell me lots of stories when I was a nipper, some of which would include leprechauns. I remember that she told me that they were mischievous little beggars and not entirely trustworthy. 'Never put your trust in the little people' she used to say. Anyway, as far as I know there are none over here, so you've nothing to worry about, have you?"

I decided to try to get a little more information from him, again without mentioning the pendant.

"This gypsy lady told me that they can be very lucky and that if they took a fancy to you they would sometimes give you something that had magical qualities and would bring you good luck."

"Aye, that's as maybe, but don't forget what my old granny used to tell me; that they're mischievous little beggars and that they'd probably attach some condition to it so that if you didn't obey that condition then you'd probably wind up getting a run of bad luck instead."

Grandad Miller's last statement wasn't really what I had wanted to hear. I think he must have noticed the despondent look on my face and begun to suspect that there was a little more to my interest in the subject than I had revealed to him.

"Now look," he said, "If this gypsy woman that you speak of gave you something claiming it was from a leprechaun I wouldn't worry about it. You've got to think about it sensibly you see. Do you really think it's possible for a race of little people to be running about all over Ireland without anyone being able to prove that they exist? Oh, my old granny believed in them all right, but she never knew anyone that had actually seen one. So, in answer to your earlier question, no I don't believe in leprechauns."

I was relieved at my grandfather's answer, because over the past few days I had begun to wonder if there could have been an element of truth in the gypsy's words.

A few minutes later my mother decided that there was little more that could be done to make Grandad Miller more comfortable and as we put on our coats and prepared to leave he thanked us for our efforts on his behalf, and as we walked out of the door his parting words were addressed to me.

"Mind you," he called as we opened the gate, "I could be totally wrong about leprechauns. I mean I suppose you can never be absolutely sure, can you?"

CHAPTER NINE

As far as my father and most other wage-earners were concerned the day that Grandad Miller returned to his own house was the last day of the Easter holiday. Despite both of my parents having suggested that it would have done him good to have remained with us for a few more days, he had said that he was most grateful for having been allowed to stay the night, but was keen to return to the familiar surroundings of his own flat in Harehills. For Billy and me, however, the Easter holiday continued for a while longer. On the following day, therefore, I awoke early and the first thing that I did was to eagerly look out of the window to see if I could determine what the weather might be like for the remainder of the day. This was never an easy thing to do in the north of England especially during the latter days of March for it was sometimes possible to experience all the seasons in the one day. On this particular Wednesday morning, however, the sky was clear and the probability that it might rain did not seem very high. I dressed hurriedly and made my way downstairs. Billy and I did not have anything in particular planned, but sometimes that was just the way we liked it. Any adventure that had not been anticipated always proved to be a more rewarding experience, like the time a few weeks previously when Mrs. Wormley managed to get herself stuck while cleaning her bedroom window and the part that we, with the additional help of Nicky, played in her rescue; or the time that we struggled to find our way home through the thick fog of Woodhouse Ridge, although it was only the surprising but satisfactory conclusion of that particular adventure that caused us to have fond memories of it.

Immediately after breakfast I informed my mother that I was hoping to call round to see Billy. She was usually keen to get me from under her feet. The only occasions when she might object were if the weather was very bad or if she wanted me to perform some errand or household chore. On this morning, fortunately, she seemed quite happy for me to enjoy the outdoors and with the signature tune to 'Housewife's Choice', my mother's favourite radio programme, ringing in my ears I stepped outside.

It was Nicky who decided how we would spend the morning. "Let's go up to Ganton Steps," he suggested. This area was really a wide passageway between two parallel streets but the hilly nature of the locality, being not far away from Quarry Mount School necessitated the construction of steps down each side with a wide sloping area in the centre. Separating this from the steps were metal barriers which, in the mind of a child, were constructed purely for the enjoyment of swinging on, performing somersaults, hanging suspended or simply sliding down. There was also an added attraction and that was the knowledge that any girls attempting gymnastics on the bars would do so in complete disregard to the fact that their underwear would inevitably be on display. We always pretended not to notice of course in case they stopped doing it.

"Have you given Susan Brown that pendant yet?" asked Nicky as we made our way up the hill at the side of the Electra.

I gave him the same answer that I had given Billy. "I asked my grandad if he believed in leprechauns, yesterday. He said that he didn't but that his old granny did when he was a boy."

"I don't believe in all that stuff," said Nicky.

"I don't either," said my other companion.

I told them what he had told me about them being very mischievous and how I kept remembering what the gypsy woman had said about not hanging on to it for too long.

When we arrived at our destination it was not the hive of activity that we had expected. The only other children there were a couple of young lads about seven years old. Nevertheless we entertained ourselves swinging on or sliding down the metal bars for about half an hour, before I became bored.

"I think I'll go to that newsagent's shop in Johnston Street," I said. "I want to get the second issue of the LION comic. I think that it's due out this morning. Are you coming?"

Both of my companions seemed reluctant to leave, though I couldn't understand why, as there were no girls doing somersaults to add a bit of flavour to our activities.

"I'll see you back here then," I said and set off towards the shop. Before I reached it, however, my school friend Ken Stacey, who lived in Marian Road, hailed me from across the street. We chatted about various things, including a discussion about the three remaining games of the school rugby team. We hoped that we could win at least one of the remaining games that might lift us from the foot of the table. After about ten minutes I left him and entered the newsagent's. I could not see what I was looking for on display.

"Have you got the latest edition of the LION?" I asked him. "I think it's due out today."

"I'm sorry lad," was the reply. "I sold the last one not more than two minutes ago. In fact the lad had only just left the shop before you walked in. It's proving to be very popular is that comic. I think I'll have to increase the size of my order for next week."

I made my way back, rather disappointed, realising that if I hadn't stood chatting to Ken Stacey I would have been in time to buy the last copy. When I arrived back at Ganton Steps both Billy and Nicky greeted me with excited looks on their faces.

"Just after you left," said Billy, eagerly, three girls turned up. Two of them looked to be about our age, and one of them tucked her dress right inside her knickers."

"The third girl, added Nicky, "Had right long hair halfway down her back and we dared her to see if she could hang upside down from one of the bars. She said it was easy and did it three times. She had pale blue knickers on and on the third go we could even see her belly button."

"We just stood there watching them," interrupted Billy, "Until they left about two minutes before you came back."

I silently cursed Ken Stacey. "Well, it's nearly dinner time now," I said, "So we might as well go back home."

"Where's your comic?" asked Billy. "Didn't they have one?"

103

I told them how I had just missed out on buying the last copy after being delayed.

"Wow, that's rotten luck," said Nicky. "You'd have done better staying with us and watching the girls doing somersaults."

I really didn't need him to tell me that.

"Anyway, you can use that sixpence you said you had to buy a copy somewhere else and still have three-pence left over."

I put my hand in my pocket. It was empty.

"I've lost it somewhere. I know I had it when I left the shop. I must have dropped it somewhere"

"Maybe you put it in your other pocket," said Nicky. I tried his suggestion, but the only thing I managed to pull out was the pendant that the gypsy woman had given me.

"I must have dropped it in the shop," I said. "Will you come back with me to help me look?"

They readily agreed, but the search proved to be a fruitless one. I resigned myself to my loss and we headed towards home. As we re-entered Ganton Steps we found that the area was now deserted, which wasn't surprising considering that it was almost dinner time.

"I didn't know you had that pendant in your pocket," said Billy. Do you always carry it about with you just in case you happen to bump into Susan?"

"No, I've been keeping it in the bedroom drawer, but I took it out to look at when I went to bed last night. I was trying to work out when to give it to her. I must have fallen asleep because when I woke up it was lying on the top of my trousers so I just shoved it in my pocket."

As we walked along Johnston Street in the direction of home my mood was a gloomy one which soon became obvious to my companions.

"What's the matter, Neil?" asked Nicky. "I've never seen you looking so miserable."

"I'll tell you why. It was a waste of time me coming out this morning, wasn't it? I mean I missed seeing those girls doing somersaults; someone just beat me to the last LION comic in the shop and on top of all that I lost sixpence out of my pocket, which means I can't go anywhere else to buy another one."

"Well, it could have been worse," suggested Billy. "At least you've still got Susan Brown's pendant in your pocket, haven't you? I mean you haven't lost that."

A sudden thought struck me. "Of course," I said. That's it; it's the pendant. That's why I've been having all this bad luck. Danny's mother warned me that I should hand it over as quickly as possible. Yes, I'm sure that's what it is."

"Don't be daft," said Billy. "If you believe all that then it must mean that you believe in leprechauns."

I thought over what he said. "You're right, Billy, it must be just coincidence that's all." I paused for a moment before adding: "But Grandad Miller's old granny believed in them."

"Well that's the sort of thing that old grannies do believe in," he went on. "I bet old grannies all over the world believe in fairies and all that sort of stuff."

Satisfied by his assurances we began to descend the steps that led into the street below. As I was about to negotiate the final step I stumbled and landed head first onto the pavement.

"Are you all right, Neil?" asked Billy as he and Nicky helped me to my feet. As far as I could tell I only seemed to have grazed my chin a bit.

"I think so," I replied, but something didn't sound right. "I just seem to have grazed my chin, that's all. What are you both laughing at?"

"Every time you say the letter 'S' you whistle."

"I knew something didn't sound right," I said, conscious of the whistling sound I made with each 'S' that I attempted to pronounce.

"Try saying 'Sister Susie's sowing socks for sailors,'" suggested Nicky, laughing.

"That's not funny, Nicky," I said, a little irritated. "I can't be talking like this when I go back to school, can I? I'll never hear the end of it; and how can I talk to Susan when she comes back? Her name's got two 'S's in it. She'll just laugh at me."

"I bet you got a hole in your tooth when you fell," suggested Billy.

We began walking down the hill towards Cross Speedwell Street.

"I bet you'll have to go to the dentist to have your tooth out," added Billy.

I hadn't thought about that possibility. Visiting the school dentist in Great George Street at the back of the Central Library in the centre of Leeds was something I always dreaded.

"It's that pendant," I said. "I know it is. It's cursed. I should never have put it in my pocket."

"Don't be daft," mocked Billy. "How can having something in your pocket account for all the bad luck you've been having this morning?"

"I'll tell you what then, Billy. I bet you're too afraid to keep it in your pocket until after dinner."

He seemed to be mulling over this suggestion.

"All right then, pass it over," he said coming to a decision.

I handed it to him and he put it in his pocket. As we reached the bottom of the hill we each went to our respective houses.

"Don't expect to stop whistling just because you haven't got the pendant in your pocket," was Billy's parting shot. "Like I said, I bet you've got a hole in your tooth and the air going in and out is making you whistle."

My mother did not seem overly concerned about my unfortunate speech problem or the grazing on my chin, but it was obvious that Nell assumed I was making those annoying whistling noises on purpose and gave me a look of disgust before settling down again on the clip rug in front of the fire. There was no suggestion of my having to visit the dentist and I decided to play the whole thing down in the hope that everything would soon be back to normal.

As soon as dinner was over I went straight round to see Billy. He needed no persuading to come back outside.

"Say Susie's sister Cicily sells seashells," he said, as we walked along Cross Speedwell Street in the direction of Nicky's house. "It took me ages to think of that one."

"Stop it Billy," I responded, somewhat aggrieved, but not without noticing that the annoying whistling sound was again prevalent with the first word I uttered.

"Anyway, has anything happened to you since I handed over the pendant?"

"Of course it hasn't. I told you all that business about leprechauns making it unlucky unless it was given to a female was a load of rubbish."

"Well you might as well give me it back then."

"Don't you think it would be best if I kept it a bit longer, just to see?"

"I bet you haven't put it in your pocket yet, have you?"

"Not likely, I don't want to start whistling every time I say an 'S'"

"I knew it Billy, you're scared aren't you? You told me you didn't believe all that stuff."

"Well I just wanted to play it safe. It's because of what your grandad told you about his old granny believing in leprechauns. I'll go back and get it if you like."

"No, it's all right. It'll do later." I felt relieved that he did not have it with him.

Nicky came out of the house as soon as he saw us walk past his window. Deciding to get in first I hurriedly informed him that no, my newly-acquired affliction had not disappeared and that, fortunately, no visit to the dentist had been suggested. I also explained to him how Billy had chickened out and was afraid to put the pendant in his pocket.

"Well it wouldn't scare me," he asserted. "You did say you haven't got it with you, didn't you?"

Despite his assertions he seemed relieved when I pointed out that it was in Billy's house.

"I hope I'm not still whistling while I'm talking when we're back at school though. Everybody would be laughing at me. I'd hardly dare open my mouth."

"Look there's Johnny Jackson," said Billy, "He's just coming out of Doughty's."

I sincerely hoped that he didn't walk in our direction.

"Hiya, Johnny," shouted Billy before I had the presence of mind to stop him.

Much to my discomfort he began to walk towards us. I was determined to say as little as possible. If he found out about my speech impediment it would probably be all round the school from the moment I arrived there. Billy, however, I was soon to discover, was intent on mischief.

"We've been trying to say tongue twisters," he said to our new companion. "Tell him, Neil, how you managed to say 'Susie's sister Cicily sells seashells'. You were the only one that could do it at first."

"That one's easy. I can say that," responded Nicky, and proceeded to display his prowess.

Billy glared at him.

Johnny then made a rather unsuccessful attempt and tried another four times before getting it right.

"None of you can say it as good as Neil," said the person who was supposed to be my closest friend. "Come on, Neil, let's hear you say it."

His persistence was beginning to annoy me. Nicky, however, saved me from having to make a response.

"I can say 'Billy blows a big blue bugle'" he said, triumphantly. "It took me ages at first because I kept saying 'blugle' instead of 'bugle', but I can say it first time now."

"What about 'Cook cooked a cup of creamy custard'", suggested Johnny, deciding to join in.

I could see that Billy was getting more and more exasperated in what was increasingly becoming a desperate attempt to cause me maximum embarrassment. After a further few minutes he gave up on the attempt and I kept as silent as possible rather than spend time trying to think of something to say that did not include the letter 'S'.

Not long after Johnny Jackson departed it began to rain quite heavily which saved us the trouble of trying to decide how to spend the remainder of the afternoon. I don't know what Billy and Nicky planned to do for entertainment once they went back indoors but I was quite content to listen to the wireless and read comics and hopefully forget all about my speech problem. First of all though, I made sure that I retrieved the pendant and chided Billy for being too scared to put it in his pocket. I then placed it in my bedroom drawer. What I was no longer sure of, however, was what to do with it afterwards.

CHAPTER TEN

By the time Saturday morning arrived I was much relieved to find that my speech had returned to normal and any prospect of a visit to the dentist was now non-existent. This did not entirely suit the wishes of my closest friend for I know that he had hoped to get a little more mileage out of my discomfort. Grandad Miller was due to arrive in time for dinner and he had agreed to accept my mother's suggestion that he spend the weekend with us by staying the night.

"When do you think it'll all be finished, Billy?" I said, as the two of us watched the workmen scrambling along the scaffolding and working on the roof of the Electra Picture House.

"Well, they haven't always been working on a Saturday, so they must be getting keen to finish it," responded Billy. "My dad thinks that they must have a deadline to meet and are probably being paid overtime. Don't forget there was quite a long time when they couldn't work at all because of the strong winds."

"There doesn't seem to be much more to do. I bet it could be open by next weekend."

"I hope so, Neil. I can't wait to see what the first film will be. I hope it's not one of those sloppy love stories."

"Sometimes my grandad takes me to the pictures. We went to the Astra to see 'Treasure Island' on Tuesday."

"I wish I'd have seen it, Neil. It's about pirates, isn't it?"

"Yes, it was a great film, but I felt really sorry for that Long John Silver at the end. He was the main pirate, you know. Anyway, I don't think it's been to the Electra yet and I wouldn't mind seeing it again, so I'll go with you if it does."

One of the workmen had just descended from the scaffolding and walked towards us. "Nowthen lads," he said. "Can either of you tell us where the nearest fish and chip shop is?"

"Well, there are three close by," volunteered Billy. "If you walk down the ginnel opposite and turn right into Craven Road, there's one there. There's Jubilee Fisheries opposite the far end of the school and if you go to the end of Cross Speedwell Street and go round the corner there's another one."

"Do you know what time they all open?" asked the man in overalls.

Billy looked at me.

"I think they all open at half past eleven," I said.

"Is the one round the corner at the end of Cross Speedwell Street the same one that's opposite Doughty's?"

"Yes."

Our inquisitor was joined by one of the other workmen. "Did you find out, Alf?" he asked.

Alf repeated everything he had been told.

"Is the one round the corner at the end of Cross Speedwell Street the same one that's opposite Doughty's?" he asked.

"Yes it is. I've already asked that question," said Alf.

"Which is the best, Jubilee or the one in Craven Road?" asked his companion, limiting the choice to two.

"Well, we usually go to Jubilee Fisheries," I informed him, but it's nearly always the one with the biggest queue."

"I'll tell you what, lads," said Alf, "Me and Ted here will give you each a shilling if you go and get some for us, and if you go as soon as they open there shouldn't be much of a queue should there?"

I looked at Billy. "What do you think?" I asked him, knowing in advance that my mother wouldn't be asking me to go for fish and chips as she was already planning something totally different for dinner with my grandfather arriving.

"What time is it now, mister?" asked Billy

Ted looked at his watch. "It's just ten past eleven, lads," he announced.

"Tell them to get them from Craven Road." This latter statement came from above.

"What was that, Gerry?" shouted Alf.

"Tell them to get them from Craven Road," he repeated, "And there's another tanner each for them if they deliver a message for me."

I looked at my companion again. "That'll be one and six each, Billy, and our mams won't even know about it, will they? Just think what we can do with it."

"Well, lads, what do you reckon then?" asked Ted.

"We'll go," I said, safe in the knowledge that Billy would already have arrived at the same decision.

Gerry had by now stepped off the scaffolding. He walked over to us and handed Billy an envelope.

"One of the two young ladies who serve behind the counter is called Andrea," he explained. "Now I want you to make sure that you hand the envelope to her and not to the other one. They are both about the same age but you should be able to tell the difference because Andrea's hair is lighter. If you hand it to the wrong one then I could be in serious bother and if that happens I'll see that you know about it the next time I set eyes on you; and make sure that you don't open the envelope before you give it to her, because Andrea is certain to know if you have, and it will get back to me. Now that's not too much to remember for sixpence each, is it? And to show that I trust you I'm going to hand over the money to you now." After concluding his instructions he placed a sixpenny piece into the hand of each of us.

"Are you at it again, Gerry?" admonished Alf. "You're bound to get caught one of these days."

"Bugger off, Alf," he replied. "It's my life not yours."

"Forget it Alf," said Ted. "You're just wasting your time with that one. We're never going to get him to see sense. God knows we've been trying long enough."

"Right lads, it's time for you to set off I reckon," said Alf, deciding to accept Ted's advice. He told us what the order was, gave us the money to pay for it and promised to give us our reward when he returned. "Make sure that they're all individually wrapped," he added, "Or it'll take us ages to separate them all."

With Billy clutching the envelope and me holding a cardboard box we walked down the ginnel and turned into Craven Road. When we arrived at our destination we found that three people had already formed a queue as they waited for the premises to open. Now, it was a well-known fact in our locality that there was nothing more likely to strike panic in a fish and chip show queue than the sight of a cardboard box.

"I'm glad I got here in front of you," said the lady standing immediately in front of us. Which factory are you collecting for?"

"It's for the workmen repairing the roof on the Electra," I explained.

"Well, it's about time that got finished," she said. "Me and my Albert haven't been to the pictures for ages. I can't get him to go to any of the other ones, but it doesn't stop him going to the football match every Saturday."

"It's the same with my Jack," said the lady in front of her. "These men have no idea. They expect us to cook and slave for 'em every day and then begrudge us the little pleasure that a trip to the pictures might bring."

She turned towards Billy and me. "So you two," she added, "Had better watch your step when you grow up because, mark my words, there's a revolution coming and by the time you choose your bride, you'd better choose very carefully because I'll tell you now, life won't be so cushy for you in the future."

"I don't know what she's telling me for," whispered Billy. "I'm not getting married. I want to join the army or the navy and see the world."

"What about your free tickets to see Yorkshire at Headingley," I reminded him.

"I don't think that's worth getting married for," he replied.

"How much are you hoping to get in that cardboard box?" asked an elderly man who had just joined the end of the queue?"

"Fish and chips, eleven times," I told him.

"They're for the men repairing the roof at the Electra," explained Billy.

"I didn't know they had that many working on it," said the newcomer. "Mind you, I did hear that they were hoping to finish it all by next week. Maybe they've put a lot of overtime on. I don't suppose if I gave you threepence each that you'd let me move in front of you, would you?" He took two threepenny bits from his pocket."

Billy looked at me. "All right mister," he said, correctly reading the satisfied expression on my face. It was rapidly becoming a profitable morning. We stepped behind him just as the shop door opened and we were all beckoned inside, but not before an awkward thought struck me.

"What was that girl's name, Billy, who we were supposed to hand the envelope to. I've forgotten it."

Billy thought for a few seconds. "It was Angela, wasn't it?"

"Yes, Billy. That sounds right. I'm sure that's what he said."

The first thing we noticed was that there was only one lady behind the counter.

"Do you think that's her, Neil," whispered Billy. "Her hair's fairly light."

"I know, but how can we find out if it's lighter than the other lady if she's not here?"

"We could just ask her if her name's Angela and if it isn't when will she be back?"

Before we had a chance to speak to her, she spoke to us. "Hand me that cardboard box," she said. "I'll keep it behind the counter until it's your turn. Customers don't like to see a cardboard box when they come in and I don't want them walking out again."

"I decided to take a chance. "Is your name Angela?"
I asked.

"No love," she replied.

"What do we do now, Billy?" I whispered.

"I don't know yet."

The shop was beginning to fill up and all the new-comers looked reasonably happy now that the one item that could darken their mood was no longer in view. When we reached the front of the queue and were asked what we wanted we both realised that the smiles on the faces behind us were about to disappear."

"Fish and chips eleven times, please" announced Billy.

Groans of protest could immediately be heard. The serving lady, I realised, had been very astute by insisting on hiding the cardboard box as customers would now think twice about leaving the premises because of the length of time that they had already queued.

"You'll have to wait a while for them to be cooked," declared the lady who wasn't Angela, "But Frank's in the back making chips so they shouldn't be too long. I'll go to collect them in a few minutes."

Billy and I looked at each other. I couldn't help wondering if Eddie from Jubilee Fisheries and Frank were part of the same fish and chip fryers union, dedicated to preserving the secret of the correct and proper way of making perfect chips by never appearing in front of the customer in case they were asked prying questions that might be unwittingly passed on to other fryers in the locality.

"I've got one fish ready and a couple of scoopfuls of chips if that is enough for anybody," she suddenly shouted. There were no takers.

I decided to take a chance with a question. "What time does the other lady come in?" I asked.

"Jackie, do you mean? She won't be in today, love, but she'll be back in on Wednesday. Why, was there something you wanted her for?"

"No, it's all right," I replied, rather confused and not knowing what to say.

"That Gerry must have got it wrong," whispered Billy. "There isn't anybody working here called Angela. Do you think he's getting mixed up with Jubilee Fisheries?"

"I don't think so. He particularly asked us to go to this fish and chip shop, didn't he?"

After a further few minutes she went into the back room and emerged with a tray full of uncooked chips which she emptied into the boiling pan to accompany the pieces of fish that were already in there. Frank, however, declined to make an appearance.

"There," said the serving lady, "I told you they wouldn't be long."

Over the next few minutes the queue grew longer and Billy and I became the most unpopular customers in the shop.

"Nowthen lads," she said eventually, "Eleven times wasn't it?"

"That's right," agreed Billy, and our popularity decreased even further with his following remark. "Could you wrap each one separately, please or they might all stick together?" As this meant eleven separate pieces of newspaper I could tell that she wasn't very pleased either. Nevertheless, she decided not to comment and eventually handed over the cardboard box which was now full and quite heavy.

As we left the premises I was concerned that we had been unable to hand over Gerry's letter. The queue was by now stretching outside and the reason for the holdup was obvious to everyone who was standing there as soon as they saw us. However, I was determined to find out one thing.

"Does anybody work there called Angela?" I asked a man at the end of the queue.

"No lad there's just Jackie and Andrea, and that's the lady that should be serving today."

"Okay, thanks mister," I replied.

"That's it, Neil," said Billy, forcefully. "He didn't tell us to give the letter to Angela, he said Andrea."

The validity of his reply hit me immediately. "You're right Billy," I said, "So what do we do now?"

"We'll have to go back or he'll make us give him his money back."

I knew Billy was right and we made our way back to the shop. It was immediately clear, however, as we ignored the queue and stepped inside, that Andrea wasn't particularly pleased to see us again.

"What is it now, love?" she exclaimed, though the disapproving look never left her face.

"Is your name Andrea, then?" I asked her, though my voice was quiet and hesitant as I wasn't sure whether she was going to tell me off. I could see that most of the other customers, who had been extremely pleased to witness our departure just a few moments earlier were not too happy to see us return, no doubt thinking that we had got the order wrong and were hoping to jump the queue on this occasion.

"Well, Gerry, who's working on the repairs to the Electra roof asked me to hand you this." I handed over the envelope. "We thought he said your name was Angela at first, but then we remembered he must have said Andrea."

With this statement the expression on her face immediately changed to one of delight. She put the envelope to one side, took her purse from her overall pocket and gave us each a sixpence. "Thank you very much lads," she said, "But I reckon you'd better be going now so that I can serve the rest of these patient customers."

We left the premises for the second time, though this time in a much better frame of mind.

"That's one and threepence each we've got so far, plus another shilling to come from Ted and Alf," said Billy.

"Let's hope they keep their promise then," I replied.

We had little to fear, the workmen's only concern being the length of time we had taken, and Ted and Alf handed over our reward without any thought.

"When do you think the Electra will be open again, mister? asked Billy.

"Well, if we've anything to do with it, lads, I can't think of any reason why it shouldn't reopen by next weekend. We should be all finished by Tuesday."

"I'm glad we didn't go anywhere else," said Billy as we walked back along Cross Speedwell Street. I can't believe we got two and threepence each just for going to the fish and chip shop. Are you going to tell your mam about it?"

"Don't be daft, Billy. I'm going to keep it at the bottom of my drawer in the bedroom."

"Me too, I don't know what I'm going to spend it on yet."

"You know, we might be able to make a lot of money doing this sort of thing."

"You could be right, Neil. Why don't we have a think about it?"

I suddenly realised that it was quarter past twelve, and that Grandad Miller must surely have arrived by now. "I might not be coming out again this afternoon, Billy. I want to talk to my grandad."

When I entered the house my mother was already laying the table, but my father hadn't arrived yet. My grandfather was already occupying the armchair near the fire.

"You've certainly taken your time, lad," was his greeting." I thought you'd be keen to see your old grandad."

I decided not to explain what we had been doing as my mother would surely realise that we probably wouldn't have agreed without some financial reward. I was glad that the coins I had received were small ones so that they didn't make a jingling noise in my pocket when I walked. At the first opportunity I would take them upstairs and place them at the bottom of my drawer.

"Well get your hands washed," said my mother. "We'll be eating as soon as your dad gets home."

My father duly arrived and we sat down to a dinner of stew and dumplings. After we had finished eating, my grandfather announced that if my mother had no objection he would retreat into the other downstairs room for an afternoon nap.

"Of course, dad, it'll do you good," she replied. "You need your rest."

"Right then, lass, I'll just have an hour then," he decided, and rose from the chair.

I waited a few minutes until my mother wasn't paying particular attention and followed him. I knew it would save me a lecture about tiring him out by asking questions. I could see that he was just sitting on the settee and had not yet closed his eyes.

"Can I ask you something, grandad, before you go to sleep?"

"Aye lad," he replied, turning towards me, "As long as you're quick about it"

"When you were a boy," I said, "Did you and your mate Harry ever play April Fool jokes on people?"

"Now what prompted that question?"

"Well it's April Fool Day on Monday and I thought you might be able to tell me a good one to play on somebody."

"Well, happen I might and happen I might not, but I'll still be here tomorrow morning. So why don't we leave it until then. I'll tell you what, I'll have a think about it as I'm drifting off to sleep, so how's that? I'd rather not go into it in detail at the moment because to be perfectly honest, I'm fair clemmed."

This latter statement prompted a new question, but I daren't ask it and decided to leave him to his repose. One thing that I couldn't understand was the fact that an expression that I had never heard used until a couple of weeks ago was now being used by so many.

CHAPTER ELEVEN

"I've been thinking about what you were saying yesterday," declared Grandad Miller immediately after breakfast.

My father was visiting Grandma Cawson, which he often did on a Sunday morning while my mother had popped next door to have a chat with my Auntie Molly.

"Do you mean about April Fool Day?" I asked him.

"That's right. You were wondering what sort of things me and my best friend Harry used to get up to. Well, to tell you the truth, by the time we got to your age we'd started to find the whole thing rather boring. We'd done the same things so many times that none of them seemed to work anymore. Harry would tell me my shoe lace was undone and I'd tell him that someone had pinned a note onto his back. Neither of us had much imagination. Sometimes we'd tell someone that they had an extra-special bargain at the local shop, but eventually everyone just got wise to what we were doing and we just stopped bothering with it anymore."

"That's what it's like with Billy and me. Neither of us can come up with anything different."

"Anyway," continued Grandad Miller, "Harry came up with a different way to celebrate April Fool Day. We would conjure up some mystifying puzzle and bet all the other lads at school that they couldn't solve it.

I remember one year it was about a farmer trying to get a fox, a chicken and a sack full of grain onto an island by boat in such a way that the fox didn't eat the chicken and the chicken didn't eat the grain. I could tell you how to work that one out if you like, but by far the best one that we came up with is the one that I'm going to tell you about now."

My interest was immediately aroused as I waited for him to continue. "On one April Fool day we gathered all the lads together in the school yard and bet them that we could show them something that no one in the whole world had ever seen before and that after showing it to them that no one would ever see it again."

"I don't see how that can be possible grandad. I mean somebody somewhere must have seen it before," I told him, with a disbelieving expression on my face.

"I'm afraid you're wrong there lad with the object that I'm going to show you now. In fact I've never even seen it myself."

"How can you never have seen it before grandad, if you're going to show it to me?"

"Like I said, this object has never been seen before by anyone in the whole world."

I was totally baffled by his statement and waited eagerly to see what it was that he was going to show me.

"Now this," he said, extracting something from a bag that had been residing in his trouser pocket, "Is called a monkey nut." He held it in the palm of his hand for me to scrutinise.

"Well that can't be it," I said. "Someone must have seen that before, like the man at the shop who emptied them into a bag, for instance."

"You're right there, lad, but just watch this." He broke open the shell with his fingers and took out the kernel. "Now then," he continued, "You can't tell me that anyone has seen this before, can you?"

"Well, no, because it's been inside the shell all the time." I had to admit to being impressed and I was already contemplating the looks of astonishment on the faces of my school friends as I won the bet.

"Anyway, lad, that's only the first part. If you remember I said that after a few seconds no one would ever see it again," and he proceeded to place the object into his mouth and, after chewing for a while, he swallowed it. "And very tasty it was too," he added.

"Like I said earlier," he went on, "Me and Harry, by the time we got to your age, found April Fool Day incredibly boring. We had been repeating the same pranks for so long that no one was ever taken in by them and we could never think of anything new. So one day Harry came up with the puzzle about the fox, the chicken and the grain which seemed to baffle everyone and on the first of April every year it became a sort of a challenge for us to find a new puzzle and I'm pleased to admit that we were nearly always successful."

"How can I get hold of some monkey nuts then, grandad?"

"Well, you only really need one, don't you, and I can supply that. The reason we always used monkey nuts was because you can break the shell with just a little pressure from the fingers. Try it with any other sort and you'd need a pair of nutcrackers to break it."

"I can't wait to tell Billy," I told him. I'd already decided to let him in on it so that we could both have a laugh about it afterwards.

"Like I told you," said Grandad Miller doing silly April Fool pranks that you've tried before are a waste of time. You'll get a lot more fun out of this escapade when you see the looks of wonder on the faces of your schoolmates. I want you to promise me one thing though. Under no circumstances must you take money from anyone by way of a bet."

I knew it would be a waste of time trying to attempt that anyway, as none of my fellow pupils ever seemed to have any money on them, so the promise was an easy one to make. After begging my grandfather for a monkey nut I couldn't wait to run outside and tell Billy what I was planning and, after I'd shown him how the trick worked, I wasn't surprised that he accepted Grandad Miller's view that once you got to ten or eleven years old April Fool Day seemed to have lost its attraction as it was almost impossible to think of something that hadn't been tried before. This way we would be doing something that was completely new.

"I can't wait to see their faces when we show them," said my companion.

"Anyway, Billy, it's the last day of the Easter holiday so what do you want to do?"

"Why don't we go down to Meanwood Road and see what's on at the Royal Picture House at the weekend?"

That seemed a reasonable suggestion to me, as it was by no means certain when the Electra would be re-opening. "Let's go now then, because it must be nearly eleven o'clock and we'll both have to be back for dinner time," I said.

We walked to the end of our street and turned left down the ginnel before turning right onto Craven Road.

Before reaching Woodhouse Street we were met by two of the girls from our school.

"Hello, Billy," said Sally Cheesedale, while ignoring me. I couldn't help grinning, however, at Billy's embarrassment, while Wanda Aspinall just giggled.

My friend seemed tongue-tied.

"Aren't you going to talk to me?" persisted Sally.

"I can't think of anything to say," mumbled Billy.

"Well you were talking plenty at Woodhouse Feast. I thought you were going to ask me to be your girlfriend."

Wanda Aspinall giggled again and I was beginning to find Billy's attempts to get out of his embarrassing predicament hilarious.

Sally Cheesedale decided to turn her attention to me. "I don't know why you're laughing either, Neil, because we all know who you like."

Now it was my turn to be embarrassed, and I made no reply to her statement.

"I bet he likes Sophie Morton," said Wanda.

I knew I had to make a remark this time. "Don't be daft," I said, "Nobody likes Sophie Morton."

Billy seemed relieved that it was now my turn to be the object of their mischievous probing. "We heard that Susan Brown might be going into hospital to have her tonsils out," he said.

"She's already in there," said Sally. "She's in the dispensary in North Street, but she'll only be in for a few days. I saw her brother Peter in the fish and chip shop, and he told me."

"Why don't you call in to see her?" suggested Wanda, grinning.

I was getting really uncomfortable again and I desperately wanted to change the subject. It was obvious that Billy was in a similar frame of mind. "When we go back to school tomorrow, me and Neil are going to show everybody something that's never been seen before by anyone in the whole world."

"That's not possible," declared Sally.

"Somebody must have seen it somewhere," voiced her companion, in agreement.

"Not only that," I added, "But after we show it to you it will never be seen by anyone again."

"No, it's not possible," repeated Sally.

"I'll bet you anything you like," offered Billy. "If I'm right, will you ask your brother to see if he can get me a free ticket for the Roses Match at Headingley?"

"All right, "She replied, "But I can't promise that he'll be able to do it; but it doesn't matter because what you say you're going to do is impossible. Anyway, if you lose the bet will you agree to kiss me on the lips in the schoolyard in front of everybody?"

I could see that Billy was hesitating. "Don't worry," I whispered in his ear. "How can we possibly lose?"

Realising the validity of my words his enthusiasm returned. "All right," he said, "And I'll even give you a hug at the same time." The expression on his face, however, gave clear indication that he would not enjoy the experience. Whether or not his would-be girl friend had noticed, I had no idea.

"Me and Billy are just going down to the Royal to see what's on at the weekend," I said.

"I heard the Electra might be re-opening a week tomorrow," explained Wanda.

"I know they've nearly finished working on it," Said Billy, "Because one of the men on the scaffolding told us; but even if they do re-open then we still need to find a good film to go see on Friday."

"After you lose your bet tomorrow, Billy, you'll be able to take me with you, because everybody will expect you to," suggested Sally, her face beaming with delight.

Billy's face turned crimson and I couldn't help smiling as I recalled my own embarrassment a few months earlier when Lorna Gale had set her sights on me as a suitable boyfriend.

"That wasn't part of the bet," spluttered my closest friend. "Anyway, I won't lose the bet, will I?" He turned towards me for confirmation.

"Don't worry, Billy," I told him. "There's no way we can lose, is there?"

With Billy satisfied with my words of reassurance, we left the girls and made our way down Woodhouse Street and Cambridge Road, and before long were standing outside the Royal Picture House in Meanwood Road. With it only being a Sunday I wasn't too sure that they would be displaying the title of the film that would be showing at the weekend, but we were in luck.

"Look'" said Billy, delightedly, "It's a cowboy picture." JAMES STEWART in 'WINCHESTER 73', the poster proudly displayed.

"That's it then, Billy," I said. "We've got our film for Friday, and if there's a cartoon or a comedy film on with it, it'll be even better."

As we made our way back home we were entirely satisfied with the result of our expedition and we were both looking forward to Friday night, neither of us being able to think of any parental objection as to why we would not be able to visit the cinema.

I noticed that my companion was looking thought-ful. "I really like your grandad," he said, suddenly.

"I know, Billy. You've told me before."

"Well, he's not really like a grown-up, is he? He's more like one of us, and he's always coming up with these great ideas from when he was our age. Take this idea for April Fool Day. I mean, I've been getting fed up with the same old stunts being pulled every year that don't seem to work anymore because everyone knows what to expect. This idea about the monkey nut is fantastic. I wish I had a grandad like yours, anyway. I just can't wait to see Sally Cheesedale's face when she loses the bet."

As soon as I arrived home my nose informed me, as soon as I opened the door, that the Sunday joint of roast beef was already cooking. In fact I had noticed the same aroma as I had passed Billy's house. On this one particular day of the week it is fair to state that at least seventy-five percent of all the houses in the street would be cooking a joint of meat, though in some cases it would be roast lamb or roast pork rather than the more popular roast beef. This would always be after a first course consisting of a Yorkshire pudding which filled the entire plate and which was smothered in onion gravy. The fat from the joint, if it was beef or pork, would be gathered in a pot container and allowed to cool down, after which process it became known as dripping and was used to spread on bread. Every house in the street would have a pot of dripping in the house somewhere. The best tasting bit was always located at the bottom of the pot. I would always, much to my mother's annoyance, attempt to reach the bottom part before anyone else, which meant creating a large hole in the centre.

I knew that my grandfather would be going home during the afternoon and that he usually took a nap after finishing his dinner, so immediately after my mother had cleared the table I went to have a word with him. He had, already anticipated, however, what I wanted to talk to him about.

"I can see that you want to show this trick with the monkey nut to your friends at school," he said, "But remember what I told you. I think it would be very unfair of you to make bets with them in a situation where you can't lose."

I told him about the bet that Billy had made.

"Well, don't let him make any more, "he said. "Anyway, it's very unlikely that this girl would be able to get him tickets for the Roses Match. They're in very high demand, you know.

Now, to make it look more interesting and mystifying you don't want to just present the nut out of your pocket. You need to place it in a sealed envelope and explain that inside of it is something that has never been seen before. This will make them believe that someone must have seen it when it was placed in the envelope and that therefore what you are telling them has to be impossible."

I was visibly warming to his idea of the best way to present the illusion. He took from his pocket what to me, from the shape of it, resembled a small packet rather than an envelope, but yet it had a flap that sealed. He took a monkey nut from his pocket and dropped it in. "Now, before I seal it, are you sure you know what to do, and how to break into the shell with your finger nail?"

"Yes, grandad," I said, impatiently.

"Right then, now I suggest you put it on the table where you'll be having your breakfast in the morning, then there'll be no chance that you might forget to take it to school with you, will there?"

Billy called round shortly afterwards and we spent most of the afternoon playing outdoors. I went back inside just in time to say goodbye to Grandad Miller before he went to catch the tram in Meanwood Road to take him home. I gazed at the envelope containing the monkey nut and found myself looking forward to returning to school on the following day.

CHAPTER TWELVE

"Are you sure you've got it?" asked Billy as we walked the two hundred yards to school.

I reached into my trouser pocket and extracted the small envelope just as I had done on three previous occasions since placing it there immediately after getting dressed. I gave the nut, which nestled at the bottom, a reassuring pat.

"I don't know what you're worried about, Billy. Here, examine it for yourself if you like." I handed the envelope over to him and he performed the same routine that I had just undertaken.

"I just want to make sure that nothing goes wrong," he said. "I wish I hadn't made that bet with Sally Cheesedale."

"I don't see how anything can go wrong. Anyway, what about your chance of getting a free ticket for the Roses Match?"

This statement seemed to cheer him up, even though I was in agreement with my grandfather's expectation that a free ticket would be very difficult to obtain.

As we vaulted over the low wall into the school playground the bell calling the pupils to assembly was just being rung and we formed two lines, girls to the left and boys to the right. This meant that we had no opportunity at that particular time to tell anyone about the prank we were going to play.

"Your shoe lace is undone," said Ernie Peyton.

"Get lost," snarled Billy without bothering to check.

"What if it actually is undone this time Billy?" I said. "You might trip up and fall down."

"Stop it," he persisted. "I'm not even going to bother looking."

Miss Hazlehurst began marching the two neatly formed lines into the assembly hall, where the headmaster, Mr. Rawcliffe and his deputy, Mr. Barnes, would be waiting. As we reached the bottom of the four steps leading to the school entrance Billy glanced down at his shoes.

"April Fool," said Ernie Peyton, laughing.

"Get lost, Ernie," said Billy, more forcefully this time.

Once inside we all attempted a woeful rendition of 'He Who Would Valiant Be' accompanied on the piano by Miss Greenop, the senior teacher of the infants section of the school. She had been there for so long that many of the adults in our locality recall being taught by her when they were children.

There was no long lecture from the headmaster, which was most unusual considering that it was the beginning of a new term, and we soon found ourselves seated in the classroom. I took the envelope out of my pocket again for reassurance and felt the comforting shape of the monkey nut inside it. I was thinking about how I was going to astound everyone during the morning break when I heard a familiar name being mentioned.

"I'm sorry to have to inform you," announced Mr. Rawcliffe, "That Susan Brown will not be with us for a while as she has had to go into hospital to have her tonsils removed. While this is by no means a serious operation in this day and age, the after-effects can be quite painful. Now, as this is supposed to be an English lesson I think it would be a good idea for you all to compose your thoughts and express them in the form of a short letter which we can then send to her in the hospital with our good wishes for a speedy recovery."

I thought hard about what he was saying. I could actually write a letter to Susan without any embarrassment as everyone else in the class would be doing the same thing. Would I be able to write what I really wanted to say? I knew that this prospect would be very unlikely. If I couldn't say what I wanted to her face then it would also be unlikely that I would be able to do so in a letter. I realised that the headmaster had continued speaking.

"Each letter, of course," he went on, "Will be personally vetted by me as I have no wish for anyone to bring shame onto this school by poor spelling and grammar. The content of what you have written will also be keenly observed in order to ensure that no inappropriate comments have been made. You can all write these letters this afternoon when you have had time to think about what to write."

I knew that if my letter was going to be scrutinised I could only talk about general things and not let my feelings be known. I decided to concentrate on the remainder of the lesson.

As soon as the class was dismissed Billy came over to me immediately.

"Sally Cheesedale and Wanda Aspinall have been telling everybody about the bet," he said, looking rather worried.

I had heard the sound of mumbling accompanied by a fair amount of girly giggles and was surprised that the headmaster, who was usually so vigilant in such circumstances, had either failed to notice or had simply ignored it. The concern on the face of my closest friend suggested that he had not accepted the undeniable fact that there was very little that could go wrong. There was no need to mention to anyone what we were about to do as virtually everybody in the class was by that stage aware of it. Nevertheless, I wanted to get my presentation right and with Billy by my side and about twenty of our fellow pupils facing us I reached into my pocket and began to speak.

"Now, in this envelope," I said while patting the nut reassuringly, "Is something that no one in the world has ever seen before and, after showing it to you, no one will ever see it again."

Tucker Lane made the first challenge. "That's impossible," he said. "You must have seen it if it was you who put it in the envelope."

"I've never seen it either," I told him. I was reluctant to make a bet with him even though I knew there was no way that I could lose, and I was relieved when he didn't make one either. All he said was "This had better be good."

"Billy's promised to hug and kiss Sally Cheesedale if they're wrong," said a female voice in the crowd.

Knowing that I had their full attention I emptied the content of the envelope onto the palm of my hand and waited for the gasps of astonishment from my captive audience.

I gazed stupidly at the rough-looking stone about the size of a monkey nut. Placing my hand back inside

I retrieved the only remaining item that was there and held it up. There were two words written in large letters on the piece of paper. They read 'APRIL FOOL'. I looked at my companion in desperation.

"I hate your grandad," said Billy, his face a picture of abject dismay.

As we made our way home from school at midday Billy's utter humiliation and, to a lesser extent my own, dominated our thoughts.

"That was the worst morning ever," he declared. "How did your grandad manage to swap what was in the envelope?"

"I've no idea, Billy. I wish I did, but it has to be him, hasn't it? He must have steamed it open."

Billy's ordeal had certainly been worse than mine. Almost everyone in the class knew about the bet so there was no way he could have avoided his romantic interlude with Sally Cheesedale. In fact, his face was still burning for the remainder of the morning as the headmaster's attempts to teach geography were frequently interrupted by the sound of laughter. I suppose in comparison I got off fairly lightly. I was a little concerned of what Tucker Lane's reaction might be, but he tended to find the whole episode to be a source of amusement.

Billy's frame of mind had in no way improved by the time we had returned to school. However, though I was initially furious about Grandad Miller's deception I was by now beginning to see the funny side. Was it not, after all, the sort of escapade that we would have enjoyed initiating? I found it difficult trying to compose what amounted merely to a 'Get Well Soon' type of letter to send to Susan, especially as it would be scrutinised by the headmaster before being bundled with all the others from her fellow pupils and when, after having re-started it on three separate occasions, I read the final result, it seemed very bland and impersonal and did not include anything that I really wanted to say. Nevertheless, there did not seem to be much I could do about the situation. I thought about the pendant, which still lay in the bottom of the drawer in my bedroom. I had no desire to take it out of there until I could hand it over to its intended recipient, though I did not know how long it would be before that day arrived. Despite knowing that it was illogical to think so, I still harboured suspicions in the depths of my mind that it might have been in some way responsible for the unfortunate events that had happened to me when it was housed temporarily in my pocket. When the bell rang to signal the end of lessons for the day both of us were immensely relieved.

"That was the worst day at school that I've ever had," said Billy as we were leaving the classroom.

"You're not going straight home, are you, Billy?" asked Phillip Thatcher. "Aren't you going to kiss a few of the girls first? Sophie Morton hasn't left the classroom yet."

"Back off," he said, visibly annoyed. "I've had more than enough for this afternoon and I'm not taking any more."

His antagonist, realising that he meant it, wisely decided to say no more on the subject.

"Don't ever tell me about any of your grandad's ideas again," said my companion as we walked home. "She thinks I'm her boyfriend now."

By the time I reached home I had been unable to change his mood and I was just glad that I had not made any foolish bets myself. My face fell when I saw my mother's knitting basket on the floor. I knew that my most hated chore was about to manifest itself.

"As soon as you've taken your coat off you can help me wind some wool," confirmed my mother.

"Aw, mam, do I have to?" I complained. "My arms always feel as though they're going to drop off."

"Now, stop being silly. "Hold your arms out and make sure that you don't get the wool twisted around your thumb this time. Otherwise it'll take me ages to get it right again."

"Mam, what does it mean if you say that you're 'fair clemmed?'" I asked after taking up the dreaded position for the ordeal to begin.

"Nothing, as far as I know. I don't think I've ever heard that expression before."

"Yes, you have. My dad said it when we were at Roundhay Park."

"Well I didn't hear him. Why don't you ask him then?"

"I have. He said it means that you're pleased about something, but everybody else seems to say something different."

"Well I don't know what it means, so you'll have to find out from somebody else. Now, stop moving your arms about, otherwise it'll take twice as long to wind this wool up."

That threat was sufficient to make me agree to her demands, but suddenly there was a knock on the door and it was opened simultaneously.

"Are you there, May?" asked the voice.

"Come on in Mr. Senior," responded my mother. "What can I do for you today?"

Her next words were addressed to me. "Now, don't you dare move your arms until I get back to you"

As there was never any way of ascertaining how long one of my neighbour's frequent visits would be I viewed this demand with some trepidation. To make matters worse, Nell rose from the clip rug in front of the fireplace, sat in front of me and stared as if to make sure that my mother's demands were strictly adhered to. With my arms beginning to feel like lead weights I attempted to listen to the conversation.

"Well, what it is, do you see?" he began, "I was wondering if your lad might go on an errand for me. I need to get in touch with our Connie."

"Is that your sister, Mr. Senior?"

"Aye, that's right lass. She lives up on Johnston Street, but I find these hills a bit too much for me these days."

"Of course he will," she proclaimed, "As soon as he's finished helping me to wind this wool. I hope she's not ill."

"Nay, lass, It's nothing like that. It's just that she usually visits me on a Thursday, do you see? Now I've just remembered that I've got this appointment at the Infirmary on that day, so I'm trying to save her a wasted journey."

"I'll send him round to see you in just a few minutes," decided my mother on my behalf. "Now let's get the rest of this wool sorted, shall we? You haven't let your hands droop, I hope."

Nell, satisfied that her mistress had now resumed command, ceased her observation and settled down again on the clip rug. Our close neighbour departed, for once without the obligatory question regarding his health, and my ordeal continued for a further five minutes.

"It's a good job he doesn't want me to bring anything from the shop, mam," I said, as I allowed my arms to relax, and with as much of a complaining tone to my voice as I dare muster, because I don't think I'd be able to carry anything heavier than an empty paper bag."

"Now stop it," she said with some force. "You're always exaggerating. You can go see him now, because your tea won't be ready for an hour yet."

I called at Mr. Senior's house and he gave me the address in Johnston Street, stating that if there was no answer to my knock I was to push the note that he'd written through the letter box. I decided to see if Billy was willing to go with me, though I knew he was still smarting over his humiliating experience at school. Nevertheless, the two of us were soon on our way up the hill towards our destination.

"What am I going to do about Sally Cheesedale?" he asked as we walked past Burrell's shop on Melville Road and began climbing again. "I helped you, didn't I when Lorna Gale was pestering you to be her boyfriend?"

My mind went back to my ordeal of the previous October and he had, indeed, got me out of a very difficult and embarrassing situation.

"I don't think it's quite the same, Billy. I don't think Sally's really looking for a boyfriend. I think she just wants to make you feel embarrassed. Girls are like that sometimes." Did my words come from experience? I wasn't really sure.

"I hope you're right, Neil, but I'm still going to get a lot of stick from everyone else at school, aren't I?"

We arrived at the designated address and I knocked on the door. A lady with a cheerful, smiley face opened the door. She looked about five years younger than the instigator of the message. "What can I do for you two lads?" she asked, pleasantly.

"Are you Mr. Senior's sister," I asked, "The one who lives in Cross Speedwell Street?"

"Yes, I am," she replied. "I'm Mrs. Lancaster. What's the daft beggar been doing now?"

"He sent me to tell you that he's got an appointment at the Infirmary on Thursday, the day that you usually go to see him and he wants to save you the trouble of trailing down there"

"Do you know, I'll swear he gets dafter by the week. I know he means well, but he's already told me all about it. What it is, do you see, he's been having this nasty cough for quite some time now and Dr. Dunlop decided that he ought to get it investigated at the Infirmary, so I'm afraid you've had a wasted journey, lads. Still, the least I can do for your trouble is to offer you a glass of lemonade. So get inside and make yourselves comfortable."

We did as she asked while she disappeared into the kitchen, before returning shortly afterwards with two glasses of dark liquid.

"There you are lads," she said, smiling. Get that down you. It's Dandelion and Burdock. I did have a bottle of Tizer, do you see, but I finished that yesterday."

"I'd know she was Mr. Senior's sister," whispered my companion, as she popped back into the kitchen, "Even if I'd accidentally met her in the street."

"So would I, Billy. So would I."

After she had rejoined us and we had finished our drinks I knew that there was just one question I had to ask before we departed. "Thank you very much Mrs. Lancaster. Anyway, how are you feeling today?"

"Well, thank you for asking love. I suppose you could say that I'm just fair to middling, but we mustn't grumble, must we?"

CHAPTER THIRTEEN

With the arrival of April the weather became perceptibly brighter and the days noticeably longer. Daylight Saving Time had been operating since the end of the previous month and very welcome it was to all the children in our locality. Over those first few days Sally Cheesedale's romantic designs on my closest friend had virtually fizzled out as indeed I had expected them to and references to his humiliating experience on the first day of the month had become virtually non-existent. Billy and I had enjoyed our visit to the Royal Picture House on the Friday night, especially as the threat of his having to have a girl friend in tow had disappeared, and the suggestion that the Electra would be re-opening on the following Monday had been officially confirmed. On the Saturday morning Woodhouse Junior School Rugby League team had resumed its activities and we went down to a narrow defeat as the opposing side scored a try followed by a conversion in the very last minutes of play. Only two games now remained to enable us to climb off the bottom of the league table. The pendant that I had bought for Susan remained in my bedroom drawer as I was still reluctant to carry it about with me, not having fully accepted as illogical the idea that it had in some way been responsible for the misfortunes that had befallen me when it had resided in my trouser pocket.

As I gazed out of my bedroom window on the morning following I reflected on all these events of the previous week. Outside the sun was shining but everything was peaceful and quiet as it always was at 8 o'clock on a Sunday morning. I got dressed quickly and hurried downstairs, not wanting to miss out on the fine weather. My mother, of course, was already up, having released Nell from her night time incarceration behind the cellar door and having brought up a shovel full of coal to place on the fire which was already smouldering on the wooden chips that we always used to get it going properly. My father would perform this task on any other day of the week before going to work, but this was the one day when my mother insisted that he have a morning free from the chore.

"What are we doing today, mam?" I asked, realising that the pleasant weather might indicate a leisurely day out somewhere.

"I don't know," she replied. "Let's wait until your dad gets up, shall we? Then we'll see what he thinks."

My mind was torn between the benefit of having a day's outing somewhere and spending the day with Billy.

"Before you have your breakfast I think you'd better remind yourself of what you need to do first," added my mother.

Realising what it was that she wanted me to do, I walked over to the kitchen sink and turned on the solitary tap. The water that came out of it was extremely cold. In winter my mother would add to it by boiling some in a kettle, but as we were now into the month of April I knew that this luxury would not be forthcoming.

Once I had finished eating the first meal of the day I ventured outside. My immediate thought had been to call on Billy to see how he wanted to spend the morning, but something prompted me to turn in the opposite direction and knock on my Auntie Molly's door, which was the one next to us. I knew that if I had something on my mind or some puzzle that needed resolving then my Cousin Raymond would invariably find the answer I was looking for. Despite his being six years older he always seemed to have a lot of time for me and I think I probably learnt more from him in my earlier years than I did from any other acquaintance.

"Is Raymond in?" I asked as my Auntie Molly opened the door.

"Come on in," she responded. "He's in the other room. You can go straight in if you like."

I did as she suggested and found him like I often did, reclining on the sofa while reading a magazine. Hesitating to disturb him, I gave a little cough. He put down the copy of Picturegoer, a very popular film publication dedicated to reviews of the latest films, and looked up. Even though I knew exactly what I wanted to say to him I was still reluctant and a little embarrassed to put it into words.

"I want to ask your advice about something," I eventually managed to get out.

"Don't tell me you've got yourself into trouble with the school bully again," he said, no doubt remembering the time when I had unwittingly placed myself in a situation where I was expected to fight Krusher Kershaw with all the school watching. I had sought his advice on that occasion too, but the return to school of Tucker Lane after illness had rendered the meeting unnecessary, and I considered myself very fortunate at the way things had turned out.

"No, it's nothing like that, Raymond. It's this girl at school." I found myself blushing as I forced the words out.

"So, you've got a girl friend, have you? Well, what's wrong with that?"

"Well, no, she's not really my girl friend."

"But you'd like her to be, is that it?"

I was starting to feel really uncomfortable and beginning to regret my snap decision to call round. What I really wanted from him were his feelings about the pendant and whether he believed it could possess any special powers. I decided that now that I was in his presence I ought to go through with it.

"I've got this present for her," I told him, "And I'm a bit worried about it."

"What is there to worry about? I've never met any girl yet who didn't like to receive presents. Why, what is it?"

"It's a pendant that I got from a gypsy woman who was camping at the bottom of Woodhouse Ridge. She told me that her great, great grandfather received it from a leprechaun that he had helped out during that potato famine that they had in Ireland a hundred years ago and that it had been struck by lightning and possessed magical powers."

"Now, don't tell me that you believe in all that stuff," he said. I could see that he was doing his utmost not to laugh. "Of course I've heard all that nonsense about the little people in Ireland, but that doesn't mean that any of it is true."

I explained to him that I was supposed to hand it over to a female as quickly as possible for the recipient to begin receiving good fortune and how it wasn't supposed to work if in the possession of a male. Though the gypsy woman hadn't actually said that the reverse would happen I explained about the misfortune that I had experienced when I had carried it around in my pocket, while omitting the part about missing out on the chance to catch a glimpse of some girl displaying colourful knickers while swinging on the bars on Ganton Steps.

"I'm sure all that was just coincidence," said Raymond. "I'm sure that when you give her this pendant she'll be begging you to be her boyfriend."

"Do you really think so?"

"I'm sure of it. All girls love to receive presents."

Before I had a chance to reply the room door opened and a lad of about Raymond's age walked in. There was something about him that made me feel that I had seen him before somewhere.

"Hello Pete," was my cousin's greeting to the new-comer. "I'm just helping Neil out here with a personal problem."

"Oh, dear," said the visitor, "Not girl trouble, I hope."

I felt my face beginning to turn crimson again.

"Pete's very observant," declared Raymond. I hoped that he would say nothing at all about the pendant. "Well, I reckon we can be discreet, can't we Pete?"

"Sure thing, but at least I think we ought to know the girl's name. My sister's probably in your class because she's about the same age. Unfortunately, she's off school at the moment as she's just come out of hospital after having had her tonsils removed."

That was the when I realised where I had seen him before. It was at the finish line of The Long Sledge that Billy and I had successfully completed just before Christmas. Why had he arrived just at that precise moment? If it had been in my pocket, I would probably have blamed the pendant.

"Yes, come on, Neil. At least you can tell us her first name. What harm can that do?" agreed Raymond.

I knew it could do a great deal of harm, but I had to say something.

"Just a minute," said Peter Brown. "It's not my sister, is it?"

"No," I managed to splutter, "Her name's Dorothy." I was desperately trying to hide the fact that it actually was his sister that I was interested in as the increase in my feelings of embarrassment had I told him the truth would have been unbearable.

"I might have a word with our Susan then," suggested Peter Brown. "If she is in your class she'll probably know her and she might be able to put in a good word for you."

"No, please don't do that," I begged. The only girl in our class named Dorothy was Dorothy Steedman. Why I had chosen her in particular I had no idea. It was the first name that came into my head, though I had at least picked on one of the more attractive ones.

"Well, I'll tell you what then, I'll have a long, hard think about it when I get home," said my cousin's friend.

"I think we'd better talk about something else, Pete," suggested my cousin because I think Neil is becoming a bit embarrassed. "How is your sister now, anyway?"

I was more than a bit embarrassed and was wishing that I had never called round, but now that the topic of Susan had cropped up I listened intently.

"Well, she's over the worst of it and she's starting to eat better, but she's still croaking a lot. However, the doctor said that her voice should get back to normal in a day or two, so she should be able to get back to school soon."

I stayed for a few minutes longer while the topic of conversation turned to football and the fortunes of Leeds United, but as I said goodbye and left I could hear the sound of laughing coming from the room.

'What have I done?' I thought. The possible consequences of my naming someone else as the object of my affection were just beginning to dominate my mind. 'What if he tells Susan? What do I do then?' With these thoughts uppermost I re-entered my house. My father had completed his Sunday morning lie-in and had finished his breakfast.

"What are we doing today, dad?" I asked him.

"Don't be so impatient, Neil," admonished my mother. I haven't had time to ask him yet".

Nell chose this moment to look towards the cellar door, behind which hung the dog lead. She much preferred to roam freely, but she had long since learned that a glance in that direction often had the desired effect. The second part of this well-practiced manoeuvre involved her walking towards him and sitting by his side, while gazing longingly into his eyes.

"I suppose we could take Nell for a walk on the ridge," suggested my father, as if the idea had originated in his own brain rather than a canine one. "We could go this morning and come back in time for dinner."

"I don't think so, Tom," said my mother. Look it's started raining."

He walked over to the window and looked at the sky overhead. "It looks like it's settled in for a while, love. We'll see what it's like this afternoon."

Nell walked over to the front door and grabbed hold of the hem of my father's raincoat, which was hanging from a hook there, in a desperate attempt to get him to reverse the decision he had just made.

"Come here, Nell," he shouted. "A damn raincoat isn't going to make much difference in this weather."

The rainfall had increased considerably and I was resigning myself to spending a miserable day indoors.

Deciding that if it was going to rain all morning, the next best thing for her would be to sleep through it on the clip rug in front of the warm fire, Nell walked away from the door with her tail between her legs, while casting accusing looks at everyone in her vicinity as if we were in some way responsible for the change in the weather.

It was three o'clock in the afternoon when it stopped raining and a further half hour before the sun made an appearance, by which time both my parents had abandoned any idea of venturing outside. Even Nell seemed reluctant to move away from her favourite spot. For my own part, however, I was anxious to be in the open air away from the confinement of the room in which I had spent the last five or six hours. I also wanted to inform Billy about what had occurred at my cousin's and see what he thought about my predicament. I informed my mother that I was going out and that I would be back in plenty of time for tea.

I could tell he was pleased to see me as soon as he opened the door. "I've been bored stiff all day," he informed me. "Let's do something interesting."

"I think It's too wet to go onto the ridge, Billy," I said. "We'll have to stay around here."

"What about the schoolyard then?"

"Okay, but why don't we see what's on at the Electra on Friday first?"

"Great, it's a western," remarked Billy, as we stood in front of the doorway that held such memories for me.

I looked at the poster. It read 'Showing on Thursday, Friday and Saturday, BROKEN ARROW, starring James Stewart and Jeff Chandler'.

"I don't think we need to find out what film is showing at the Royal or the Astra, do you?"

"No, I fancy seeing this one, and I think we might have to go early, Billy, because I bet it'll be packed on the first Friday after opening."

With the decision agreed upon we made our way to the schoolyard. Often there'd be a few other kids hanging about, but it was eerily silent. Instead of vaulting over the low wall like we usually did we decided to sit on it for a while, despite it still being wet from the rain. I thought it was a good time to explain what had taken place when I went round to see Raymond.

"Crikey, Neil, why did you tell him that you wanted Dorothy Steedman to be your girlfriend?"

"I didn't, Billy. When they asked me her name, I couldn't tell Susan's brother that it was her that I liked and Dorothy was the first name that came into my mind. What am I going to do if he tells her?"

"Well, she's going to think you don't like her any more isn't she? She'll think that you've found someone that you like better."

"I don't know what to do now," I said despairingly, "And it's all because of this stupid pendant. I wish I'd never bought it."

"Why don't you get rid of it then?"

"What, just throw it away, do you mean?"

"Well, I certainly don't want it. Maybe you could sell it to somebody. You could give it Tucker Lane and see if he has a run of bad luck like you did."

"Don't be daft, Billy. Can you really imagine Tucker with a pendant on him?"

I realised I was still no wiser with regard to what to do with it, but uppermost in my mind was the explanation I had to give to Susan if her brother decided to reveal the contents of our discussion. It was obvious that I had a lot to think about.

CHAPTER FOURTEEN

"A collective noun always takes a singular verb," declared Mr. Rawcliffe on the first day of the school week. He peered over the top of his glasses while moving his head to scrutinise everyone in the room in a determined attempt to ensure that the words he had projected had successfully reached their targets. He held up an exercise book with a look of displeasure on his face and continued his lecture. "This book belongs to one of the boys in this class, isn't that correct Master Rogers?"

Peter Rogers looked decidedly unhappy. "Yes, sir, I think it's mine," he managed to say. "Why sir, what's wrong with it?"

The headmaster glared at him. "I'll tell you what's wrong with it. I asked you all to write a composition about the sort of things you might observe from a helicopter if you were looking down onto a peaceful countryside scene, and I asked you to pay particular attention to using correct grammar. Is that right, boy?"

Yes, sir," said his victim, uncomfortably.

"Now, to be fair, I was reasonably pleased with the first half of your composition until I came to one particular sentence." He began to quote from the book. "A FLOCK OF SHEEP ARE MAKING THEIR WAY ALONG THE LANE, CLOSELEY FOLLOWED BY A SHEEPDOG."

He paused and looked around the room before continuing. "Now, can you see what is wrong with that sentence?"

"No, sir."

"Well, perhaps you can tell me how many flocks of sheep there were. Was there only one flock of sheep, or were there two?"

"Just one flock, sir."

"Then you should have written that 'A FLOCK OF SHEEP IS MAKING ITS WAY ALONG THE LANE.' You should have used a singular verb, do you see?"

"But there was more than one sheep, sir."

"Yes, but the subject of the sentence is the word 'FLOCK' which is a collective noun. A similar example would be 'A GROUP OF PEOPLE IS IN THE DOCTOR'S WAITING ROOM', the subject of the sentence in this case being the word 'GROUP'."

I knew what he was getting at but for many of the pupils in the room it was a difficult concept to take in. He continued to cite other examples before bringing the final lesson of the afternoon to a close. Before he dismissed the class, however, I was determined to get in one further question. He was always telling us how he was a fervent supporter of Leeds United Football Club and he always expressed disappointment if his favoured side lost. I already knew the result of the game that had been played at the weekend but I was keen to see his reaction.

"How did Leeds United do on Saturday, sir?" I asked. I could sense that everyone in the class was wondering why I was delaying the length of time that they had to remain in the classroom.

The headmaster's face beamed in delight. "I'm pleased to say, boy, that they beat Leicester City 3-2."

With a bravado that surprised even me I sprung the trap. "Is Leeds United a collective noun, sir, because we're only talking about one team, aren't we?"

I could see him mulling this over and wondering to where it was all leading.

"It is indeed boy. I'm pleased to see that you have been paying attention. Now, if you'd all like to put your books inside your desks you may all leave the room."

I wasn't, however, prepared to let him off the hook so easily. "Well, sir, if a collective noun takes a singular verb, shouldn't we say 'IT beat Leicester City 3-2, instead of THEY beat Leicester City 3-2'."

I could see that the looks on the faces of the other pupils suggested that they were beginning to side with me on this issue, being keen to discover how he was going to squirm his way out of the awkward situation that he now found himself in, whereas just a few moments earlier they had been wondering why I was delaying the time that they could all escape the confines of the school.

"Well done, boy," He said. "Leeds United is indeed a collective noun, being the name of a football club, "But what I was really saying was that the players of that club won the game, so I used the word 'THEY'."

He obviously thought he had successfully answered my question, but I hadn't quite finished with him. "So there are some instances," I said, "Where a collective noun doesn't take a singular verb. Is that right, sir?"

The other pupils seemed to have lost all interest in making a dash for freedom, being curious to see how things played out. There were smiling faces all around the class, as there always was if the headmaster appeared to struggle while attempting to prove a point.

"Sometimes," he managed to splutter," A collective noun might take a plural verb by implication or by local usage, but only in certain circumstances."

"What circumstances would they be, sir?" I persisted.

"I think we had better continue this discussion another time, boy" he replied. "I don't want to be accused of keeping pupils after school for no reason."

I realised I was pushing him a little too far and decided to let go. As we left the school premises Ken Stacey came over and whispered in my ear. "That was great," he said. "I didn't know how he was going to talk himself out of it. It was worth waiting an extra five minutes just to see him squirm."

We stepped out into brilliant sunshine and I was immediately joined by Billy, who expressed his own satisfaction to the way things had turned out.

"It's very warm, Neil," he said as we began to make our way along the street, "I don't really want to go straight home, do you?"

"No," I told him, "I'd much rather stay outside. What do you want to do?"

My mother was quite used to my not going home immediately that school finished, but she always expected me to be within shouting distance.

"I fancy going onto the ridge," decided my companion.

"I don't know about that, Billy. We'll end up forgetting what time it is and be late for tea."

"Okay, I'll go on my own then if you're scared of your mam."

"I'm not scared, Billy, but I don't want to miss my tea. If we're up on the ridge I won't hear her shouting, will I? You know we always forget what time it is when we're doing something interesting. I think we should find something to do round here."

I could see that my companion was giving this suggestion careful thought.

"Let's climb onto the nursery roof, then," he suggested, excitedly.

The nursery school was close to the bottom of Speedwell Street , and the flat roof was very easy to climb onto as the wall on the nearer side was much lower than the one on the playground side and I had to admit that we had spent some enjoyable times larking about up there. Nevertheless, I greeted his suggestion with some trepidation as in the previous year Nicky Whitehead had had the misfortune to sprain his ankle after bragging that he could jump from the roof onto to the grassy area adjacent to the playground. Unfortunately, he missed his intended target and landed on the concrete, therefore causing the aforementioned injury. My mother, after she had heard about it, made me promise that I would never climb up there again. As Nicky was later to break his arm playing for the school rugby team, it had not been a good year for him. In addition to this, the nursery was very close to the house where my Grandma Cawson lived and I knew I would get a severe ticking off if I was spotted.

"I'm not sure about that, Billy," I told him, giving him my reasons for being apprehensive.

"Well, I wasn't thinking of jumping off the roof like Nicky did, anyway," he said.

We had already begun walking down Speedwell Street, but my thoughts about what we were going to do were interrupted when I spotted Susan Brown and her brother walking towards us. I could think of absolutely nothing to say as they approached, but I sensed that Billy was becoming intrigued and rather amused as he considered all the possible outcomes of the encounter. I knew that there was no possibility of my avoiding the pair and I mentally prepared myself for an embarrassing encounter.

"This is the very lad I was telling you about, our Susan," declared Peter Brown. "The one who says he's taken a fancy to one of the girls in your class."

"Yes, I know her," she said, but her voice was cold, almost without emotion.

I was grateful that Billy remained quiet. It was as if he knew that he would be intruding in the conversation.

"I'll leave you to carry on chatting," said Susan's brother. "I want to call at Doughty's, so I'll see you back home," and he began walking up the street.

"I didn't know you liked Dorothy Steedman," she whispered, so low that I could hardly hear her.

"I don't like her," I attempted to say, though it seemed to lack conviction. "Well, that's not entirely true. I do like her, but I like you better." I knew that what I said was an inadequate response and was not what I really wanted to say. I wanted to put my arms round her and tell her it was all a terrible mistake, but I just couldn't do it.

"Well, I'll be going back to school soon and I'm not really bothered who you like. I might have a word with Dorothy anyway and see what she thinks."

Billy decided it was time for him to join the conversation. "Neil's bought you a present, Susan," he said.

"Why would he do that?"

"Because he likes you, that's why."

I didn't know whether to be pleased or annoyed that he had mentioned the pendant as I was still undecided as to what to do with it.

"Why hasn't he given it to me then?"

"Because you haven't been at school for ages and I don't have it with me now," I said.

"Are you sure you don't want to give it to Dorothy Steedman?"

"No, Susan, I want to give it to you."

There followed an embarrassing silence which only ended when Johnny Jackson, one of the boys in our class, made an appearance. "Hiya, I bet you didn't know I've joined the scouts. Why don't you two join?" he suggested, cheerfully, indicating Billy and me. "It's great and we're all going camping in the summer. So long as you're eleven or over anyone can join."

"Where do you have to go to join?" asked Billy.

"Just go to the Old Carr Sunday School near Meanwood Road. "Anyway, I'm in a bit of a hurry, so I'll tell you all about it when I get back to school."

"I thought he must have been poorly," I said, as we watched him leave, "Because he wasn't at school today, was he?"

"He looked all right to me," said Billy. "What do you think, Neil? I wouldn't mind joining the scouts, especially if they go camping. I think it would be great."

"Well we know where to go to join, but he didn't tell us when, did he?"

"I know when the scouts are there," announced Susan, "Because my cousin goes. They meet every Thursday at six o'clock."

I didn't get the impression that I might have eliminated any differences between us, because she still looked rather angry as she left us and began to walk up Speedwell Street. However, we were both enthusiastic about the possibility of joining the scouts. "It's a pity Nicky's only ten," decided Billy, "Otherwise he'd have been able to come as well."

"Let's go have a look at the Old Carr Sunday School building," I said. "There might be some notices on the wall telling us about the scout troop."

Despite my unsure feelings regarding Susan's reaction to my attempts to reassure her of my regard for her above anyone else, I found myself in an enthusiastic mood as we walked towards our destination. Neither of us had ever been on a camping trip, but it seemed to be just the sort of adventure that we would both enjoy to the full.

"I like scout uniforms, Billy," I told him, "Especially the hat and the neckerchief. It would be almost like being a cowboy."

"Yes," he replied, "I like the hat as well. I can't imagine my mam having any objections to me joining. What about you?"

"I don't know about my mam, but I'm sure my dad will be all right about it."

We continued down Speedwell Street, passed the nursery, and cut across the road to the building behind Buslingthorpe School, which had always been known in the locality as The Old Carr and which, as well as apparently hosting a scout troop, was also used as a

Sunday school. Billy and I used to go, but it was only recently that both his parents and mine had become less forceful in insisting that we attend. This suited us both as there always seemed to be much more enjoyable things to do on a Sunday afternoon.

"I can't see any notices about the scouts," suggested Billy, as we gazed at the notice board near the entrance.

"Just a minute," I said. "There's one over here on the door. It just says HOME OF THE 25TH NORTH WEST LEEDS SCOUT TROOP. It doesn't give any other information though."

"Well, at least we know we've come to the right place," acknowledged my companion.

With our minds now firmly set on seeking permission from our parents for us to return on Thursday and become fully fledged members of Baden Powell's Boy Scout Movement we abandoned our earlier plan to lark about on the nursery roof and made our way back up Speedwell Street. Before we had walked more than a few strides, however, we spied a familiar figure outside Lawson's grocery shop.

"What's the matter with Tony, Billy?" I asked. "He doesn't look very well, does he?"

"Let's go see if he's all right," he suggested.

Tony was a very recognisable figure among the streets of Woodhouse especially among the younger element. He had pushed his ice cream barrow up and down the hills for as long as I could remember, though on this occasion he was slumped across it and looking thoroughly miserable. His achievements were truly remarkable as his eyesight had deteriorated to such an extent that he was now virtually blind and there couldn't have been that many blind ice cream sellers in the country.

"Are you all right, Tony?" I asked as we approached him.

"I suppose so, lad, but I reckon I'm getting a bit too old for this lark. I've been selling my ice cream round here for years but I suppose it's got to take its toll sometime."

"You must get exhausted pushing that barrow all day," suggested Billy.

"Well that's certainly the case today. I'm fair clemmed, and that's a fact, but I've finished for the day now. Do you think you might be able to give me a hand with it back to my yard, seeing as how there are two of you? I won't be able to give you an ice cream I'm afraid. I've been that busy, I've completely sold out."

We jumped at the opportunity. Letting it be known that we had pushed Tony's barrow back to his yard would undoubtedly give us bragging rights at school. It always amazed us how, with virtually no eyesight, he managed to run his business at all. He could tell the value of each coin that was placed into his hand and it was almost impossible to cheat him, not that we would ever dare to attempt it and now, as Billy and I each took a shaft of his barrow while he walked alongside, he never put a foot wrong. Within a few minutes we walked through an open gate in Meanwood Road, above which was a sign that read 'BRIZOLARA ICE CREAM'.

He thanked us for helping him and promised us a free ice cream each when he was next in our street.

"How does he manage to get all round Woodhouse like that when he can't really see anything?" asked Billy as we made our way back up Speedwell Street.

Tony had for many years been one of the most common and popular characters in our locality, and his famous long drawn-out yell, consisting of only one syllable, to announce his arrival in your street could have put Johnny Weissmuller's Tarzan to shame.

"I'll tell you what," I said. "Let's close our eyes and see how far we can walk without bumping into anything."

My companion looked ahead and observed all the various hazards that would confront him if he did as I had suggested. "Not likely," he replied. "I wouldn't get more than a few yards."

As we made our way home I couldn't help but marvel at the sheer resilience of someone who could well be the only blind ice cream man in the country.

CHAPTER FIFTEEN

At precisely eleven minutes past eight on Thursday morning disaster struck the Cawson household and I was the unfortunate individual who discovered it.

"Mam," I shouted, being unable to disguise the despair in my voice, "There's none of Auntie Brenda's jam left."

Nell rushed over to peruse the contents of the bottom shelf in the cupboard close to the cellar door and immediately cast accusing looks in the direction of my mother.

"It's all right," she said. "I bought a jar from Doughty's yesterday. It should be in there."

I knew that there was no way that any jam bought in a shop could compare favourably with my Auntie Brenda's.

"That's no good," I told her. "It just doesn't taste the same. Can't you get her to make some more?"

"Look, I know how nice your auntie's jam tastes, but you can't expect her to be giving us a jar every day now, can you?"

"If she made a lot more she could sell some to Doughty's, then we could buy it there if we ran out."

"I don't know how she finds the time to make the amount she does do, what with all her housework and everything."

I knew it was not an argument I was going to win, and as I reluctantly took the jar of jam that we did have and spread some thinly onto a slice of bread I found myself looking forward to Billy and me joining the scout troop later in the day. My mother, as I had expected, had raised no objection and my father had even been very keen on the idea. "It'll help to make a man of you," he had said.

As we walked along the street towards school it became obvious that my companion was also looking forward to what the early evening might bring.

"If we join, how soon do you think it would be before we'd go camping?" he asked.

"I've no idea, Billy, but it's not going to happen every weekend, is it?"

"I can't wait to be sitting round a real camp fire singing camp songs. It'll be like playing cowboys and Indians, only more life-like."

I could see that his enthusiasm was beginning to let his imagination run wild.

"Don't forget," I said, attempting to add a little realism to his wild thoughts, "There won't be a yard with lavatories in it like there is in our street. I think they just dig a hole somewhere and you have to go there."

The expression on his face changed to one of disgust. "I couldn't do that. Everyone would be watching."

"You'd have to Billy. There wouldn't be anywhere else. Anyway, they might put a tent over it, or something like that. I think it'd stink a bit though. I mean we're lucky at home. All we have to do is walk down the street and go into a cubicle."

"Well, at least Mary Pearson won't be there," he said, attempting to take some brief consolation out of the situation.

"I wouldn't be too sure. She seems to have a habit of turning up in the most unlikely places, doesn't she?"

As we passed the Electra Picture House and were reminded of the fact that it would be re-opening on the following Monday, he suddenly stopped.

"What is it, Billy. What have you stopped for?"

"I was just thinking, Neil. Why do cowboys never have to go for a pee?"

"How do you mean?"

"Well, let's say I'm a cowboy and I'm in this saloon and I've been drinking beer or whisky all day, like they seem to, and then this gunslinger comes in and tells me that I've to go out into the street to have a gunfight with him to see who's the fastest, I mean I'm not going to go straight out there, am I? I'll be thinking 'Crikey, I'll have to have a pee first', but they never do that do they? They just walk straight out and get on with it."

"Well, you can't expect them to show you John Wayne going for a pee, can you? They wouldn't be allowed to do that."

"I know, Neil, but that's what makes it all seem so phoney. He should say something like 'As soon as I've been to the lavvy I'll see you outside,' then it would seem more realistic."

"Don't be daft, Billy. Can you imagine John Wayne saying something like that? It doesn't sound very tough, does it?"

"Well, that's what I think, anyway."

We left the Electra and continued walking. "I've just thought of something else," said my companion. "Why do horses never get shot?"

"What do you mean this time?"

"Well, do you remember that picture we saw on the night the Electra got flooded?"

"Of course I do. It was called RED RIVER and we never saw the end of it, did we?"

"Well, do you remember that bit where they had the wagons in a circle and were trying to fight off all those Indians?"

"Yes, Billy, that's when the picture broke down and everything seemed to go into slow motion, and all the yells that the Indians were making sounded like deep groans."

"That's right, and it might have been funny if the picture hadn't been so exciting. Anyway, why didn't they just shoot the horses, because they would have been much easier to hit and then, if the Indians didn't have a horse, they would have had to run away, wouldn't they?"

"I hadn't thought of that. Anyway, you'd think that at least one horse would have been hit by accident, but that never seems to happen, does it?"

We had to leave the discussion there as we realised that neither of us had heard the school bell and that the last ones in the two lines of pupils were entering the school premises followed by the formidable Miss Hazlehurst. She glared at us as we hurriedly entered the Assembly Hall to join those who were already in position.

"Look over there," whispered Billy, I looked in the direction he was pointing and my heart missed a beat. "I didn't think she'd be back today, Neil, did you?" he added.

I gazed longingly at the back of Susan Brown as she stood at the front of the group with her hair gently brushing her shoulders. She wore, as she usually did, a ribbon similar to the one that resided under my pillow while I slept, which always seemed to enhance her features.

"She said she'd be coming back soon, Billy, but I didn't think it would be before next week."

"Do you think she's still fallen out with you?"

"I don't know. I hope not. I still haven't given her the pendant yet. In fact I'm still not sure if I should."

Mr. Rawcliffe publicly acknowledged her rapid recovery from her operation and welcomed her back into the fold. I didn't get the opportunity to speak to her before we were all seated in the classroom and on this occasion she was on the opposite side of the room. What did strike my attention, however, was that she was seated next to Dorothy Steedman and while the headmaster's attention was on writing on the blackboard the two of them were engaged in earnest conversation accompanied by the occasional giggle which he didn't seem to notice. I couldn't help thinking that I was probably the main topic.

Susan and I didn't converse together for the whole of the day, partly because I had no idea what to say to her and she never made any attempt to approach me. When the bell sounded for the end of lessons Billy was just as enthusiastic to get home as I was, and as we hurried along the street the topic was the same as it was when we set off in the morning.

"I wonder how long we'll have to wait before we go camping," he said. "I suppose it won't be until the summer."

"It might be at Whitsuntide," I suggested, because we get two extra days off school."

"Have you been for your Whitsy clothes yet, Neil?"

"No, my mam hasn't said anything about it yet and I want to keep it that way."

It was customary throughout Yorkshire, and in particular in those towns where mills and factories dominated, for each child to be presented with a brand new set of clothes to wear on Whit Sunday. While most of the girls found it to be a quite acceptable arrangement, the boys on the other hand were never as enthusiastic as they were expected to visit just about every known relative where they would be told how smart they looked.

"I always hate it," said Billy. "I know we sometimes get money from aunts and uncles when we go round to show them our new clothes, but my mam's always telling me not to play out or I'll get them dirty."

"I know, Billy. I feel the same, but there's one good thing about it. It's the one day of the year when you don't have a problem getting the girls to show you their knickers."

I learnt very early in life that girls love to be dressed in new clothes and show them off. On Whit Sunday in particular some of them would insist on including those that would not normally be on view.

Before we parted Billy agreed to call round at a quarter to six and as I entered the house my excitement at what the evening might bring dominated my thoughts.

"Don't take your coat off yet," said my mother. "I want you to call round to see Mr. Senior. He's got an errand for you."

"Shall I go see Auntie Brenda as well, mam, and tell her that we've run out of jam?"

"You'll do no such thing. It's very nice of her to give us the occasional jar but I'm sure that there's an awful lot of work goes into making it and I dare say it costs a bit too. So I'm sure she'll make some more in her own good time without anyone pestering her."

"Come on in, lad. Come on in," invited Mr. Senior after I had knocked on his door. I assumed that he'd run out of tobacco again, which he seemed to do with regularity. However, he had something different in mind on this occasion.

"I was wondering, do you see," he went on after I was safely inside, "Whether you might get rid of some of these empty bottles for me. The trouble is I'm not entirely sure which shops they all came from. I've had about a dozen of them resting on the cellar head for weeks now and it's getting to the point where I'm frightened of knocking them down the steps whenever I go into the cellar. Best thing to do, do you see, is to take them to Doughty's first. I'm fairly sure that's where most of them came from. Whatever you've got left, just bring them back here and I'll chuck them in the midden later. Nowthen, whatever you get for them, we'll split it fifty-fifty. Now, how does that sound?"

It sounded reasonable to me. You got either threepence or tuppence on each bottle depending on its size, but no shopkeeper would ever accept one that had not been sold in his shop. What I hadn't anticipated, however, was just how heavy twelve empty bottles would be. As things turned out, they accepted eight bottles as having been sold on the premises leaving only four to be discarded. Three of them were worth tuppence each and five of them threepence each, making a total of One shilling and ninepence for me to take back to Mr. Senior. I took the four remaining bottles straight to the midden at the end of our row, after having dispensed with an earlier thought that I might take them round to some of the other shops to see if they belonged to them. It just didn't seem worth the effort.

"Nowthen, lad," remarked my neighbour on my return. "Let's see how you did then."

"Eight of them were theirs and I got one and ninepence." I showed him the money.

"So, if we go fifty-fifty then like I promised, can you work out how much I owe you?"

I'd already done that as soon as I had left the shop. "Tenpence-halfpenny, Mr. Senior," I replied with confidence.

"Well done, lad. You worked that out a bit sharpish like. I reckon you deserve a whole shilling for that." He took two sixpences from his pocket and handed them to me. He must have seen the look of delight on my face. "You've done me a great favour, do you see?" he went on. If you hadn't have taken them back to the shop I'd have just thrown them into the midden when there got to be so many that I kept falling over them."

When I left his house I happened to glance towards the end of the street and my heart seemed to miss a beat when I noticed Susan Brown staring hard into Mrs. Ormond's sweet shop window. Despite her coolness towards me lately, my feelings towards her remained the same and I was still unsure what to do with the pendant. I decided to chance my luck.

"What are you thinking of buying, Susan?" I asked. She obviously hadn't seen me approach and I think I must have startled her, but I was desperate to know whether her reaction would be a friendly or a hostile one.

"I can't really buy anything because I haven't any sweet coupons left," she said in a not unpleasant voice, "But I like Liquorice Torpedoes best. Anyway, are you still thinking of joining the scouts tonight, Neil?"

She didn't seem to be particularly annoyed with me.

"Yes, Susan, me and Billy will be going down there as soon as we've finished our tea. You said it would be starting at six o'clock, didn't you?"

"That's right. My cousin's in the scouts."

After we parted I found it difficult to contain my delight at the way the encounter had gone.

There could be little doubt that Billy's enthusiasm for the evening's prospects matched my own. He must have rushed his tea, as he knocked on the door at half past five while I was still eating. My mother insisted that he call back in twenty minutes as she always, though usually unsuccessfully, encouraged me to eat mine in a leisurely fashion.

"What time does this scout meeting finish?" she asked.

"I'm not sure, mam, but I think it's about eight o'clock."

"Well, make sure you come straight home, and don't be bothering your grandma Cawson. She sometimes likes to go to bed early." She knew that I would have to walk past my grandmother's house on the way home.

When Billy and I arrived at the Woodhouse Carr building, which was also the local Sunday school, we were already a few minutes late.

"What if they won't let us join, Billy, because we've arrived late?" I said, anxiously.

"Well, it would be your fault, Neil. Why couldn't you eat your tea as quickly as I did?"

"Because my mam won't let me, that's why."

"It sounds very quiet, but the light's on, isn't it? Let's just walk in."

We did as he had suggested and found ourselves in the lobby, where we were greeted by a rather rough-looking middle-aged man.

"We've come to join," said Billy. "We're not too late are we?"

"Come to join have you?" he said, his craggy face breaking into an almost toothless grin. "Are you sure?"

"Yes, if we're not too late," suggested Billy.

"Well, I'll tell you what I'll do son. I'll just pop into the main hall and see if it's all right. They always insist on a quiet five minutes before the main activities start. Reckon it's good for discipline."

He shunted us to one side and stepped through the large double doors. A couple of minutes later he rejoined us. "It's all right, lads," he indicated, "You can go straight in."

What greeted us as we entered the hall was nothing like what we had expected.

"These two boys want to join our little group," said the lady who was standing in the centre of the room. "Shall we let them?"

The cry from the girls who formed a semi-circle as they squatted on the floor was unanimous. "Yes," they shouted, before the giggles started.

"They're Brownies," said Billy, his face betraying an expression of horror, while I was struggling to find any words at all.

"Would you like to start today?" asked the leader of the Brownie pack.

"No miss, I think there's been a mistake," I finally managed to stutter, my face going as red as a beetroot.

"Come on, Neil." Let's go, urged my companion.

I needed no more prompting and the two of us rushed for the door.

"By Heck, I did enjoy that little moment," laughed the caretaker as we rushed past him. "If you wanted the scouts, you should have come on Tuesday. That's the best laugh I've had in ages. I'm fair clemmed."

"That was awful," declared Billy as we stepped outside. Just think what it would be like if everybody at school found out that we tried to join the Brownies."

"Well thank god there was nobody in the room that we knew."

"Are you sure? There must have been about twenty girls in the group and surely some of them must have gone to our school."

"Yes, I'm sure, Billy. It was the first thing I thought about. I had a good look at all their faces before we left. I didn't recognise anybody."

I had to admit that it was probably the most humiliating situation I had ever experienced and I'm sure that view was also shared by my companion. I couldn't imagine how things could get any worse, but a few seconds later they did just that.

"Oh, no," said Billy, as we stood outside the building before starting for home, "Look who's over there standing outside the pub."

I stared across at the Fox Public House and my heart sank as I spied Susan Brown standing next to Dorothy Steedman both of whom were staring in our direction. Both of them were having a fit of the giggles.

"Do you remember, Billy," I said, "It was Susan who told us that the scout troop met on Thursdays. She must have known all along that it was the wrong day."

"That's right, Neil. What a rotten trick. It'll be all over the school. How will we ever live it down?"

"Well, I'm sure Tucker Lane will make the most out of it, won't he?"

"Are you still going to give her that pendant?"

"I just don't know, Billy."

The two girls did not give us the opportunity to approach them as they both turned and run off up the hill, their laughter taunting us as they went.

Earlier in the day I had been delighted that Susan had returned to school following her illness, but as the two of us made our way home I was just not sure what my feelings were anymore.

CHAPTER SIXTEEN

"I'm not talking to Susan anymore, Billy," I declared as we walked the short distance to school on the morning after the humiliating experience resulting from our attempt to join the scouts.

"It's all right saying that, Neil, but I don't think you'll be able to do it," replied my companion. "She's only to look at you and your knees turn to jelly."

"But this is different, Billy. As soon as we get to school I bet everybody will know about what happened yesterday. We'll be known as the Brownie Boys for ages."

"She might not tell them," he offered, rather hopefully.

"I can't believe that, and even if she doesn't, Dorothy Steedman will. You saw them both laughing."

"What about the pendant?"

"It can stay where it is. I'm not bothered anymore."

We heard the bell sound before we had entered the playground and the two neatly formed lines of pupils had already made their way into the building before we arrived. Apprehensively, we made our way into the assembly hall, wondering whether either Susan or Dorothy had had time to inform anyone of the events of the previous evening. Talking during the assembly period was strictly forbidden and by the time we entered our classroom we still had no idea whether we were already becoming the focus of ridicule.

"Let's just take our places and see what happens, Neil?" suggested Billy.

In the circumstances I did not see what else we could have done, but I remained very apprehensive. Surprisingly, the first lesson of the morning went by without any of the sniggering or girly giggles that might have suggested that what we were dreading was taking place and I deliberately refused to make eye contact with either of the two girls who had witnessed our humiliation.

"They'll tell everybody as soon as we get into the playground," I said, as we made our way out of the classroom for the morning break.

"Did you two join the scouts last night?" asked Alan Bartle. He did not give the impression that he was getting any sense of amusement from the question, so I assumed he was unaware at that moment of what had transpired.

"No," said Billy. We got the wrong day."

I was glad that he didn't elaborate on that statement.

"When you do join, let me know what it's like, will you? I might join myself," said our fellow pupil.

I couldn't see Susan or Dorothy in our part of the playground, nor very many of the other girls, and it occurred to me that they might be gathering in the area behind the school and having a good laugh at our expense before excitedly emerging to cause us even more humiliation.

"Nobody seems to know yet, Billy," I said as we made our way back to the classroom. All the girls seemed to have been reunited in our part of the playground without any obvious signs that we were about to become targets of laughter.

"Nobody seems to know what?" asked Ernie Peyton, who had walked up behind us.

"Oh, nothing much, Ernie," I said, thinking quickly, "We were just wondering what the picture that's on at the Electra was like, but we don't know anybody who's seen it."

"It's a cowboy picture," he acknowledged. "That's all I know about it. I don't know if it's any good or not."

"Well, we're thinking of going anyway," said Billy.

The remainder of the morning progressed without anyone making any remarks to us of an embarrassing nature, which left me rather puzzled. I had imagined that the happenings of the previous night would have been all round the school by this time, and as we made our way home Billy sounded as perplexed as I was.

"I can't believe that neither of them has mentioned it, can you? I mean, if I knew that one of the lads in our class had tried to join the Brownies instead of the Scouts there's no way that I'd be able to keep it quiet."

"I know what you mean, Billy. I can't understand it either. Even if Susan decided to keep quiet I can't believe that Dorothy would."

Nevertheless, we returned for the afternoon session fully expecting that we would be on the receiving end of all the sarcastic comments that our fellow pupils could muster together. The fact that we weren't left me even more perplexed than I had been earlier. I decided to forget my earlier resolution not to speak to Susan, and confront her as soon as I could. Unfortunately, that opportunity did not occur during the remainder of the day and as Billy and I walked home from school very much relieved, though a little puzzled, that the humiliation that we had anticipated had not taken place our thoughts focussed on our intended visit to the Electra in the evening.

"Are you still all right for the pictures tonight, Billy?" I asked him.

"Well, my mam told me this morning that I could go and I don't think I've done anything to make her change her mind."

"It sounds like a good film. I like westerns."

"Yes, so do I, Neil and if The Three Stooges are on as well, it'll be better still. Anyway, I'll call round for you at ten to seven."

I had barely finished my tea when there was a knock on the door. I looked at the clock on the shelf over the fireplace and found that it was only six forty. Nevertheless, when I opened the door there stood Billy with a look on his face that could only be described as panic.

"You'd better come and have a look, Neil," he said.

I stepped outside to see what was startling him. My heart sank as I perceived the queue which had begun outside the cinema and already stretched around the corner almost up to Burrell's shop on Melville Road.

"Crikey," I said. "Why has that happened?"

"I've no idea," replied Billy, "But we'd better get a move on because the doors opened at half past six, so it could be nearly full already."

"You know why that is, don't you?" asked my father after walking to the door to investigate and satisfying himself of the solidarity of Billy's statement.

"Why, dad?" I asked him.

"Well," he replied, "It's obviously because Friday is their busiest night of the week and this is the first one since the picture house re-opened. What's on, anyway?"

"It's a cowboy picture," volunteered Billy.

"Well, there you are then. They're always popular, aren't they? Mind you, the biggest queue I ever saw was when they were showing GONE WITH THE WIND a few years ago. That picture had received so much publicity that just about everyone in Woodhouse turned up to watch it on the night it opened, and that wasn't even a Friday, if I remember correctly."

"Do you think we'll still be able to get in, dad?"

"I don't know son. It depends on how many they've let in already, but you'll certainly have more chance if you join the queue, won't you? Anyway, here's one and sixpence so you should have enough for an ice cream as well."

I needed no more encouragement and eagerly put on my coat. Billy was already suitably attired. We made our way towards the end of the queue which, although constantly moving, now stretched around the corner into Melville Road. We tagged onto the end just as two familiar-looking ladies arrived and stood immediately behind us.

"I told you we should have left earlier, Phyllis," said the larger of the two ladies. "I knew there'd be a big queue today but I didn't expect it to be this big. Why did it take you so long to get ready anyway?"

"It didn't, Edna," responded her companion, indignantly. "I don't think I was more than five minutes."

"More like twenty you mean."

Before the victim of the verbal onslaught was able to protest she felt her companion's hand on her shoulder.

"Keep quiet, Phyllis. Can you see who's coming up the road? It's her."

"It's who, Edna?

"You know, the one I keep telling you about."

"Oh, you mean ------"

"No, not her Phyllis, the other one."

"You mean----"

"No, not her either."

"I don't know who you're talking about, Edna."

"Of course you do, Phyllis."

"Oh, you mean her that lives next door to the off-licence in Craven Road."

"That's exactly who I mean."

"Is he still going round there then, Edna?"

"He tells me he isn't, but I know differently. I reckon she's been his fancy-piece for over a year now."

"Well, isn't it about time you confronted her then?"

"Oh, there's going to be a reckoning there before long, Phyllis. You mark my words."

Before either of the two ladies was able to say anything more, the object of their animosity stood facing the dominant one of the pair. "Is your name Edna?" she scowled, with a thunderous expression on her face.

"That's right," came the rather startled reply.

"Well, you can just tell that useless, good for nothing, husband of yours to go and get stuffed." With that, she turned and walked hurriedly back down the street.

The two ladies stared at each other with their mouths wide open before Edna broke the silence. "Did you hear that, Phyllis?" she shrieked. "How dare she talk about my husband like that? What right has she got to call him useless and good for nothing?"

"No right at all, Edna."

"He's the perfect gentleman is my Arthur. It's her that's led him astray, the little trollop."

"Do you know what I think, Edna?"

"What's that, Phyllis?"

"I think it's her that's led him astray."

"You're right there, Phyllis. That's exactly what I think. Just a minute, I just said that."

"You just said what?"

"I just said what you said, that it was her that led him astray."

"Funny you should say that, Edna. That's exactly what I think."

At that point we totally lost interest in what had been for both of us an entertaining conversation as our senses were drawn to the fact that the queue appeared to be breaking up.

"What's happening, Neil?" asked Billy.

I did not need to ask anyone the cause of the disruption as cries of ''They're full up. They won't let anyone else in'' came from several voices.

Billy and I stepped out of the line. "What shall we do now?" he asked.

"I'm not sure, but if we go back home I'll have to give my mam the picture money back."

"What's on at the Astra in Woodhouse Street, Neil?"

"I've no idea, but I think it's better to go find out than to go home, don't you?"

Being both in agreement we left what had once been an orderly queue full of eager faces looking forward to an evening of relaxing entertainment but which in one brief moment had changed into a disorganised, grumbling rabble with everyone heading off in different directions. A lot of them, however, were heading the same way as Billy and me along Melville Road in the direction of Woodhouse Street.

"I think they've got the same idea as us, Neil, suggested Billy. I think we'd better hurry or we might not be able to get in there either."

I didn't argue with him and we turned right into Marian Road and began running up the hill. As we neared the top Billy stumbled and grazed his knee on the pavement. I helped him to his feet.

"It must be turned seven o'clock by now, Billy," I said, as if I was blaming him for delaying our hurried dash to the picture house, "And I know that the Astra always starts at the same time as the Electra on a Friday night."

I hurriedly looked behind me half expecting to see a hoard of angry cinemagoers charging up the hill in hot pursuit, but of course I didn't see any such thing as most of the disappointed people from the queue had simply dispersed towards their own homes. Nevertheless, I was eager for us to reach the Astra as quickly as possible.

I helped Billy to his feet and examined the graze on his knee which didn't seem too bad. We hastened to the top of the hill and turned left onto Johnston Street and then right onto Woodhouse Street. When we arrived at the picture house there was, of course, no queue as the performance must have started fifteen minutes earlier. Unfortunately, we hadn't the faintest idea of what film was on offer. We decided to gaze at the poster on the wall before committing ourselves. Our mood of excited anticipation changed to one of extreme disappointment by what we saw. 'FATHER OF THE BRIDE' screamed the poster in an attempt to encourage us to step inside, the illustration on it depicting a bride and groom emerging from a church.

"Oh no!" exclaimed Billy. "We're not going to see that are we, Neil? We're already late, so even if there's a comedy or a cartoon on it'll probably have finished by the time we got to our seats."

I knew exactly what he meant and my feelings were exactly the same.

"No, there's no way I'm going in there, Billy. It'll be dead boring. Why couldn't it have been a Tarzan picture or something like that?"

I couldn't answer that. "I can't see any point going to Meanwood Road to see what's on at the Royal, Billy, can you? I mean by the time we got there it would be turned half past seven and the picture that's on might not be any better than this one."

"What do you want to do then, Neil?"

I didn't really want to admit defeat and have to return the cinema money I had been given yet I was beginning to feel quite cold and listening to the wireless in front of a warm fire was beginning to seem an attractive proposition.

"Let's go home, Billy. I don't even think I want to play out. I'm too cold."

"I've just started shivering as well. I thought we'd have been getting warm at the Electra by now. Why did they all have to turn up on the same night?"

We began to make our way down Woodhouse Street knowing that there wouldn't be much daylight left.

"Are we still going to join the scouts?" asked my companion.

"I don't see why not. We'll call round next week, but let's make sure that we've got the right day first."

As we turned into Woodhouse Street there were far more people walking towards us than we would have expected at half past seven at night, and none of them looked particularly happy.

"What's the matter, mister?" asked Billy to a tall, elegantly dressed man arm in arm with someone who we assumed to be his wife. Why are there so many people? Has something happened?"

"I'll say it has," he replied. "We were all sitting comfortably in the Electra waiting for the big picture to start and the cinema was full to bursting, you know, when all of a sudden the screen went black and we were told that the projector had broken and that they would not be able to show the film. I'm not really surprised when you consider how long it's just been sitting there gathering dust, and I bet it was ancient to begin with. I thought there was going to be a riot at first."

"Didn't they give everybody their money back?" I asked.

"They said they didn't have enough time to be able to do that, but they handed out free passes for next Friday. They won't be any use to us though. We live in Headingley and we usually go to the Cottage Road Picture House or the Lounge in North Lane. I don't think we'll be trailing all the way back down here again. As it is we have to walk all the way back up Woodhouse Street just to get on the tram at Hyde Park. Here you are lads. You two might as well have them."

With that comment he handed me two pieces of card on which were stamped the words 'FREE PASS'. As well as the name of the cinema and the date for which they would be valid.

We stared at them with unconcealed delight. "Thanks mister," was the only response we could muster.

"No thanks necessary, lads," said our benefactor. "I hope you enjoy it, that's if they ever get that bloody museum piece of a projector working again."

As the couple left we looked at the tickets again. "They're both for next Friday," I said. "I don't think things have worked out too badly after all." I handed Billy his and we headed for home in a much better frame of mind than the one that existed just a few minutes earlier.

CHAPTER SEVENTEEN

He was certainly a big lad and he'd been causing us all sorts of problems ever since the game began. With only about ten minutes remaining we were losing by twelve points to eight. It wasn't that we were playing particularly badly against the school from Meanwood but our afore-mentioned adversary had been resorting to tactics which could not in any way be considered to be in the true spirit of the way a game of rugby should be played. The things he had been getting away with in the scrums should have resulted in several free kicks for our side if only the referee had been aware of them. I had never seen Tucker Lane looking more incensed. "I'll do him before this game's finished," he whispered in my ear. "You just watch me."

His opportunity to do what he had promised did not arise until a few minutes before the end of the game. We were only a few yards from the opposing try line when Phillip Thatcher was tackled into touch and the referee indicated a scrum down. As soon as the ball was thrown in Tucker sprang into action and as the whole thing collapsed and the referee blew his whistle the boy who had been causing all the trouble emerged from the mass of sprawling bodies with his nose bleeding profusely. As far as Tucker was concerned it was simply a case of the heads of two opposing hookers colliding as each leaned forward in an attempt to play the ball to the rear end of the scrum but from my vantage point it was the neatest demonstration of a head butt that I had ever seen. The lad with the nose bleed immediately began harassing the referee while pointing furiously at his assailant. Tucker's face, of course, was a picture of innocence. How he managed to display such an image of surprise and indignation in such a convincing manner was a complete mystery to me. If the moment had been filmed his performance would have been worthy of an Oscar. Because of the strong element of doubt no free kick was awarded and the injured party was escorted off the field of play to have his injury attended to. A second scrum was formed and on this occasion we had no problem playing the ball through to the back where it was safely gathered by Alan Bartle who quickly passed it along the line. It was eventually caught by Johnny Jackson who dived over the line right underneath the goal posts. With the score now poised at twelve points to eleven the goal kick was crucial and Tucker had no problem at all sending the ball through the posts to collect a further two points. With only a couple of minutes remaining there was barely time for the game to be restarted before the referee blew the final whistle.

Had we won the game by cheating? If that was the case, what about all the incidents where we should have been awarded a free kick. I found myself having no sympathy whatsoever for the boy who was the victim of Tucker's wrath and Mr. Barnes had no words of recrimination to us after we had entered the changing room.

"Do you think that win's lifted us off the bottom of the league table?" asked Billy.

"It depends what the team above us did," I replied, "But if it hasn't we've only got one more game to go."

It was a very warm and sunny day for early April as Mr. Barnes said farewell to his rugby team and crossed to the far side of Meanwood Park towards his home at Headingley. He had said nothing regarding the incident in the scrum though I suspect he had his suspicions regarding what went on in there. I think he was just pleased about the outcome of the game and was content to leave the matter there. This left the rest of us to make our way towards the tram terminus near the Capital Picture House.

"I told you I'd do him," said Tucker several times to anyone who was prepared to listen. "Did you see his nose? I bet it's still bleeding when he gets home, but it bloody well served him right."

No one dared to challenge him on the rights and wrongs of the situation and I don't think anyone wanted to. We were all elated to have got another win under our belts whatever the circumstances that might have influenced the result.

I suddenly noticed that Billy, who had been walking just behind me was no longer in sight. Leaving the rest of the group to continue their walk along Green Lane I retraced my steps. As I approached a passageway that lead to the old tannery my friend suddenly emerged from it.

"I've just seen a fox, Neil," he exclaimed, excitedly.

"Where is it?" I asked him, my excitement beginning to match his own.

"it just ran into somebody's back garden," he said.

"Crikey, Billy, I've never seen a real fox before. Are you sure that's what it was?"

"Of course, I'm sure. I've seen them at the pictures, haven't I?"

I followed him down the passageway and when he turned left by the side of the beck he pointed to a garden with a privet hedge acting as a boundary. "It crawled through there," he said.

Well we can't see over the hedge, can we? How do we know if it's still in there? I wonder if it lives in Meanwood Woods."

"Either there or on Woodhouse Ridge, I bet"

All thoughts of rejoining our fellow team-mates disappeared as we waited to see if it re-emerged from the garden. After about ten minutes of this we were starting to get bored when Billy shouted excitedly.

"Look, Neil, there it is."

It had apparently emerged from a garden further along and we charged after it as it crossed the bridge over the beck. There was of course no way that we could catch it. If it was successful in evading hounds and riders on horseback what chance did we have? By the time we arrived at the tannery it had completely disappeared.

"Why does this place always stink so much?" asked my companion while holding his nose with a look of disgust on his face.

"I've no idea, Billy, but my Uncle Frank worked here before he died three years ago. He lived next door with my Auntie Molly, and you could always smell it on his clothes when he came home."

We both realised that our quarry was by now out of our reach and further pursuit would be pointless. However, neither of us wanted to retrace our steps and walk up the hill to the tram terminus. We made the decision, therefore, to walk home which wouldn't take much longer than travelling by our previously intended route. We walked along another passageway, crossed over Grove Lane and entered the familiar and welcoming site of Woodhouse Ridge.

It was by now warm and sunny and we saw no reason to hurry. We knew we could be home within half an hour but we were in high spirits and both of us were prepared to risk a telling-off at the prospect of being late for dinner. After all, we had plenty of time to think up a reasonable excuse. We were standing at the top of a grassy bank and I immediately recollected how Billy and I had often slid down it on pieces of cardboard and I suggested that we do the same on this occasion.

"We haven't got anything to slide down on though, Neil," he said, though I could tell he was just as enthusiastic as I was.

At the bottom of the banking was a small copse close to the beck. We made our way down there knowing that we weren't the only lads who had used the smooth, grassy slope for the same purpose as ourselves, our thoughts being that there might be some large, discarded pieces of cardboard under the trees. After arriving at our destination we underwent a methodical search for anything that we could use to sit on while sliding down the banking. Our surmise that there might be something lying about proved to be correct and armed with two sizeable pieces of cardboard we made our way back to the path at the top of the rise. Leaving our duffle bags which contained our rugby kits on a bench on the path we eagerly climbed aboard our make-shift vehicles and enthusiastically slid down to the bottom of the hill. Walking back up, of course, did not provide the same thrill, but at least we had the prospect of repeating the experience. The situation was about to change, however. As we approached the top we caught sight of a rather plump, middle-aged woman with straggly hair approaching the bench.

"I'm Peggy Wiggins," she announced in a rather forceful manner, "And I was born on a Thursday but my friend Helen was only born on a Tuesday." She began to laugh. "So what do you think of that then, eh?"

We both stared at her not knowing what to say.

"The moon's falling down you know," she went on. "Bet you didn't know that, did you? Bet you didn't know that, but I've known for some time. Peggy Wiggins knows everything. She was born on a Thursday you know. My friend Helen doesn't believe that the moon's falling, but she was only born on a Tuesday. I'm going to catch it though when it does fall and put it back in the sky where it belongs."

I was beginning to wish that it was her friend Helen that was standing there instead of this strange creature.

"What have you got in here then?" she asked, seizing Billy's duffle bag from the bench. He tried to snatch it back from her but only succeeded in falling to the floor.

"Give me that back," he said. "It's mine."

"Show me your willy then," she suggested. "Then you can have it back."

Billy made no reply to this, but I couldn't help laughing out loud at his embarrassment.

"Ergh, smelly clothes," said his tormentor, as she looked in the bag. She held her nose in disgust as she threw the offending items to the ground. "Peggy doesn't like smelly clothes."

My companion raced down the path to retrieve his things, but she seemed to have found something more interesting. "Now this is more like it," she said, smiling, "A Mars Bar. Now Peggy does like them," and after taking off the rapper she took an enormous bite.

The expression on Billy's face was amazing. I'd never seen him look so despondent. The problem was that there was nothing he could do about the situation short of attacking the woman, which I knew was never an option. Our attention suddenly focussed on a young nurse and an older man in a white coat heading towards us, both of whom were shouting.

"Peggy, Peggy, you must come back home. Helen's worried about you and she says you mustn't be naughty again."

The effect on their quarry was immediate as she began to start crying. "Peggy didn't mean any harm," she bawled. "Peggy didn't mean any harm."

The man took her by the arm and began walking her towards Grove Lane while attempting to sooth her by telling her that she would be riding home in a big, shiny car, while the young lady in nurse's uniform spoke to us.

"I'm very sorry if she caused you any trouble," she said. "She a resident of Meanwood Hospital which is for patients with mental illnesses and every week we take several of them for a ride and a walk outdoors to save them from being cooped up inside all the time. Unfortunately, she ran off and we couldn't give chase until we'd got all the other patients back inside the van. I'm afraid this lady suffers from what is called a split personality.

"She ate my Mars Bar," said Billy.

"Well, I'm sorry, son. Obviously there's no way that I can bring it back for you, but I can give you sixpence to buy another one." She handed him a coin before continuing. "Her real name is Helen Bradshaw and usually she's very calm and friendly, but occasionally she does the sort of things that you've just witnessed and, unfortunately, these incidents are becoming more frequent."

"She said she was called Peggy and that her friend was called Helen," I informed her.

"Well, they're really the same person. You see Helen, in her placid state, can't face the fact that she has done these things herself so whenever she does something bad she blames it on this character she's created called Peggy Wiggins, but in her mind they are entirely separate individuals and I suspect that as soon as we get her back to the hospital she'll simply be warm and friendly Helen again. Well, I must get back now, lads. They'll all be waiting for me. Once again, I'm really sorry for any trouble that she's caused."

She waved goodbye and left us staring after her as we attempted to digest everything she'd said.

"How can one person split into two?" asked my companion as he took charge of his duffle bag again. "I don't understand that."

"It's something to do with her mind, Billy. She said she's a patient in Meanwood Hospital and I know that's for people with mental illnesses because my dad had an uncle who had to go in there after he came home from the First World War. My Grandma Cawson said that he suffered from shell shock because of all the canon fire. She said there were a lot of people came home like that."

"I didn't know that, but I heard that they used to shoot you for being a coward if you ran away. It must be awful being shot by your own side. I wonder if we'd have run away, Neil."

"That's something we'll never find out, Billy, but I hope not."

"I bet there must be a lot of people like Peggy Wiggins, or Helen Bradshaw or whatever her name is."

"Would you have shown her your willy if that was the only way you could get your things back?"

"Not likely, Neil, not after she'd eaten my Mars Bar anyway. I was going to eat that on my way home. I think I might save the sixpence she gave me for a Captain Marvel comic though."

We decided to abandon any further thoughts of sliding down the slope and make our way home as quickly as possible. Both of us were now feeling hungry and my mother hadn't considered providing me with a Mars bar or anything similar. I was pleased though that I did not have to suffer the discomfort of watching Billy eat one. It only took us a further twenty minutes to leave the ridge and enter the street that led down to Melville Road.

"Let's run, Billy," I suggested. "It's downhill from here."

He needed no prompting and set off ahead with me racing after him. However, something made me slow down and eventually come to a stop. I watched as he disappeared round the corner and focussed my attention on the figure that was emerging from one of the side streets.

"Hello, Susan," I plucked up the courage to say.

"Hello, Neil. Why is your face all covered in mud?" was her response.

"We've been playing rugby this morning."

"Did you win?"

"Yes, we won by thirteen points to twelve." I didn't mention the rather dubious circumstances that brought about the victory as I knew that she would have disapproved. I was surprised to find myself talking to her so easily in view of the difficulties I had always experienced previously, and at least I hadn't knocked her over this time, which was something I had accidently done on two previous occasions.

Billy's head appeared round the corner. He was obviously wondering where I had got to. Noticing who I was speaking to, he gave me a cheerful wave and obligingly resumed his journey. I turned my attention to Susan. There was something I needed to know.

"Why didn't you tell everybody at school that me and Billy tried to join the Brownies?"

"Why would I want to do that?"

"When we came out, both you and Dorothy Steedman were laughing. I thought the first thing you would do was tell the whole school about it."

"I was annoyed when you told my brother that you wanted Dorothy Steedman to be your girl friend when I knew it wasn't true so I decided to teach you a lesson by telling you that the scouts had their meeting on the wrong day, but I never wanted the whole school to be laughing at you. When I told her what you had said she thought it was really funny. She likes Alan Bartle by the way. Anyway, she agreed to come down with me but I told her that if she told anyone else about it then we wouldn't be friends anymore. Why can't you just say that you like me?"

"I don't know." I just do, that's all. Unfortunately, I'll have to go now, Susan. I know I'm already late for dinner and my mam might be expecting me to go to the fish and chip shop."

"There's just one thing," she said, as I reluctantly began to move away. "Make sure you have a good wash when you get home."

My mother wasn't as annoyed as I thought she might have been when I arrived later than expected. I don't think I would have cared anyway after having cleared the air with Susan in a way that had left me feeling warm all over, and I knew now that I had to give her the pendant, a decision that I had been agonizing over for weeks. I wasn't required to go for any fish and chips, as a meal of sausage and mash was already being prepared. The afternoon brought heavy rain which meant that I had to resign myself to remaining indoors, but this was one occasion when I didn't mind at all.

CHAPTER EIGHTEEN

"This jam tastes awful," I complained as I took the first bite of my sandwich at breakfast time.

"Why, what's wrong with it?" asked my mother. It's a brand new jar from Doughty's."

"I don't like the taste of it, that's all. It says Bramble Seedless on the label. I don't even know what brambles are supposed to taste like."

"It's made from blackberries."

"It can't be. I like blackberries but this tastes totally different. Auntie Brenda has made blackberry jam before but this is nothing like it."

"Well, I can't help that. I don't think your Auntie Brenda makes jam anymore."

"Why has she stopped making it then?"

"I've no idea. You'll have to ask her yourself. Maybe she hasn't got time. Now hurry up and finish your breakfast. Your grandad's coming this morning."

This would be the first time I'd seen him since my humiliation on April Fool Day, but I had already forgiven him and looked forward to seeing him again.

"What time is he coming, mam?"

"I just asked him to come in time for his dinner, so I reckon it should be between eleven and twelve o'clock. If you're playing outside you'd better make sure that you're back inside in plenty of time."

I had barely finished eating when Billy called round. The weather was a complete contrast to that of the previous day. The rain had gone and it was warm and sunny.

"What were you saying to Susan, yesterday?" he asked. "Did she say why nobody at school had said anything about us trying to join the Brownies?"

"She said that she hadn't wanted everyone to be laughing at us so she hadn't told anybody. She made Dorothy Steedman do the same. I think if it had been anyone else who saw us it would have been all round the school."

"So are we going down there again on Tuesday to see if we can join the scouts?"

"I think so, Billy. I still want to be a scout, don't you?"

"I want to go camping most of all. That's why I want to join."

"So do I, but I'm sure they don't go every weekend. It could be ages before they do."

"It'll be summer soon though, and that's the best time to go."

Having walked towards the end of the street without particularly planning to do so, we found ourselves standing outside Mrs. Ormond's sweet shop.

"I won't be able to stay outside long, Billy. Grandad Miller's coming soon and my mam wants me to be inside when he arrives. I'll probably be able to come out again after dinner though."

"I used to like your grandad until he played that trick on us on April Fool day. I can still taste that sloppy kiss that I had to let Sally Cheesedale give me. It was really embarrassing."

"Well you shouldn't have made that daft bet, should you?"

"I only made it because you told me that it was impossible for anything to go wrong."

"Well, I didn't know he'd substituted that nut for something else, did I? I still don't know how he did it. Anyway, I've forgiven him."

"Well I haven't."

I decided to change the subject. "My Auntie Brenda's stopped making jam," told him.

"What difference does that make? You can buy jam anywhere."

"Not like my Auntie Brenda's, you can't. No matter where my mam buys it from, it never tastes as good."

"Why has she stopped making it then?"

"I don't know, Billy, but I'd like to find out. I could just ask her, I suppose, but my mam doesn't think I should. She said it must take a lot of time to make jam and that she's probably too busy. I'd still like to know though."

"What do you want to do now then, Neil? We haven't got a lot of time if you have to get back when your grandad arrives."

"We could go down to the Dammy," he suggested.

"I'm not going paddling though. When my feet get wet it takes me ages to get my socks back on." The Dammy was the name given by all the local lads to the beck at the bottom of Sugarwell Hill. "I suppose we could go down there though and find something else to do." Sometimes we would throw a stick into the water and see which one reached the bridge over Buslingthorpe Lane first, but it only really worked when there were several lads there. With only two it quickly became boring.

As things turned out we never actually got there. As we neared Meanwood Road it was obvious from the size of the crowd gathered there that something of immense interest was taking place and as we turned the corner it soon became obvious what it was. A lorry carrying lots of sand had involuntarily tipped its load all over the road immediately in front of the Primrose Public House, resulting in a huge tailback of traffic including two trams in one direction and three in the other, the lines that they were supposed to run on being totally covered.

"I wonder how they're going to clear that lot," I said.

Before I had time to answer two police cars arrived, with sirens blazing. One policeman set up a road block outside the Junction pub opposite Buslingthorpe School while another went to speak to the driver of the offending vehicle.

"This is more interesting than laiking about on the Dammy, Neil," observed Billy.

"When another large vehicle armed with a huge scoop at the front finally arrived to dig up all the sand it got even more interesting. In fact we were so absorbed in what was happening that we became totally oblivious to the time. It was only when a hand grabbed my shoulder and a voice declared "Aren't you going to help your old grandad walk up the hill then," that I realised that I was supposed to be somewhere else.

"How did you get here, grandad?" I asked, rather sheepishly.

"Well, because of what's been happening right in front of you, that you and your pal seem so interested in. I had to get off the tram right outside Buslingthorpe School as did just about everyone else who was on board. I'm afraid you'll have to leave your morning's entertainment because your mother was expecting me between eleven and half past."

"What time is it now, grandad?"

"It's twenty past eleven, lad."

"It can't be that time. I thought it was about half past ten."

He took out his pocket watch and showed it to me. "There look, see for yourself."

The evidence was right in front of me. I couldn't understand how the time had passed so quickly.

"You see, lad, when you're doing something that's interesting or something that you really enjoy time seems to pass very quickly, but if you're doing some-thing extremely boring or something that you really hate, then time seems to slow down."

"I think you're right, grandad. If I was helping my mam to wind wool I bet it wouldn't be even ten o'clock yet."

He laughed. "Yes, that's exactly what I mean."

I was aware that my closest friend had not been paying much attention to the conversation, concentrat-ing fully on the drama that was taking place in Meanwood Road, even though he had seen my grand-father arrive, but I knew that I would now have to be making tracks for home if I didn't want to face my mother's wrath.

"I'll have to go now, Billy," I told him. "If I don't, we'll be late for dinner."

"Well, I'm not going yet. I want to see what happens when they start moving all this sand."

"I'll see you after dinner then."

I was reluctant to end what had proved to be an entertaining morning, but I dreaded the repercussions that would definitely occur if I stayed. So my grandfather and I walked up Speedwell Street together and reached our destination just in time to smell the usual Sunday aroma of roast beef cooking in the oven at the side of the open fire. Nell looked up from her position on the clip rug. She had long ago decided that her main function on this particular day of the week was to guard the dinner. She gleefully wagged her tail at the sight of the new arrivals as it signified to her that the object that was producing the aroma which had so mesmerised her might soon be doing the same to her taste buds. My mother readily accepted my grandfather's explanation for his delay and because of that she felt obliged to accept mine.

"The dinner will be ready in about half an hour," she exclaimed.

"Right," said Grandad Miller to me. "We'll just go into the other room and have a chat then, shall we?"

I followed him down the single step and watched him settle onto the arm chair that I had seen him doze off in on many occasions, although I knew that there was no chance of that happening on this occasion. He enjoyed his Sunday lunch just as much as we all did. I settled myself onto the settee opposite him, wondering if there was anything in particular that he wanted to chat about.

"Now then, lad," he began, "Have you forgiven me yet for that little April Fool stunt I pulled on you?"

"Yes, grandad, but I don't think Billy has. He had made a promise that he would kiss Sally Cheesedale in front of the whole school if we didn't manage to do what we said we would do."

"Oh, dear," he said, though with a smile on his face, "It just shows you that you shouldn't make rash promises. I suppose this Sally Cheesedale isn't very attractive then."

"Well, as a matter of fact grandad, she's one of the best looking girls in the school," (But not the best, I thought).

"So what has he got to complain about? What's wrong with kissing a pretty girl?"

"I know he likes her, really, but he thinks it's all sloppy kissing girls, especially when everyone in the school is watching."

"What about you, then? Haven't you got someone special that you're really keen on?"

There was absolutely nothing I could do to prevent my face from turning crimson.

"Don't bother answering that one," he said, being unable to suppress another smile. "The fact that your face has changed to the colour of beetroot is a dead giveaway. There's nothing wrong in having feelings for someone, but I can see that you find it embarrassing so I suggest that we don't say any more about it."

I was very much relieved by this latter statement. However, he hadn't finished on the subject.

"It reminds me of a situation," he went on, "Involving my old schoolmate Harry Crabtree, God rest his soul. When we were young children, neither of us had any particular interest in girls but when we got to be about your age we started to see them a little differently, or at least Harry did."

I immediately forgot about any embarrassment that my grandfather had made me feel and settled down to listen to what I hoped would be another of his entertaining stories. However, my mother had other ideas.

"The Yorkshire puddings are ready dad," she announced as she poked her head around the door. "I'm just about to put them on the plate so don't let them go cold. I've made some nice onion gravy to put on them as well."

I don't know why she bothered to make this latter statement as Sunday dinners were always the same, and I wouldn't have wanted it any other way. I knew that Nell would already have seated herself at the side of my father's chair waiting for her share, which she always received directly from his hand whenever he thought that my mother wasn't looking.

"It looks like we'll have to continue this conversation after we've finished eating," declared Grandad Miller."

I knew that he always liked to take a nap on the settee afterwards and I would have to get to him quickly if I wanted to hear the story he had been about to relate. Within minutes my mother had placed a giant Yorkshire pudding on everyone's plate, which would be a prelude to the roast beef dinner which was to follow. I'm fairly sure that my canine friend could never understand why she always had to resort to cunning measures of her own devising rather than to be invited to have an equal share along with everyone else who was seated at the table, especially as one of those currently occupying a chair was, in her eyes, only a fringe member of the family who only made the occasional visit.

"By heck, lass, that was grand," said my grandfather with a satisfied look on his face as he devoured the last mouthful

"Thank you for saying that, dad," she said. "It's a pity I don't get the same sort of appreciation from anyone else seated at this table."

My father looked a little sheepish, but Nell, realising that no more tasty morsels would be coming her way, left her comfort zone and sat down at the side of my mother and gazed up at her with adoring eyes.

"You know I don't like you feeding her at the table, Tom," she admonished. "She has her own place for eating, and anyway she's just devoured a dishful of dog food at the top of the cellar steps."

Nell, realising her mistake, slunk off to the clip rug in front of the fire, no doubt hoping that her intrusion would be conveniently forgotten by the next meal time.

When Grandad Miller left his seat at the table and announced that he would be going into the other room for his usual nap, my father retired to his favourite arm chair in front of the fire and opened his copy of the Empire News. My mother, meanwhile, was clearing away the dinner plates and placing them in the sink in the corner of the room. With her back towards me I followed my grandfather. If she had seen me I know she would have insisted that I left him alone to have his relaxing hour, but I was keen to hear the story that he had been about to relate before we had been called into the kitchen. I had no need to worry that he might have forgotten, however, as he invited me to sit down opposite him.

"Now then," he began, "I was about to tell you about my friend Harry's attempt to impress a girl from our school." He paused for a moment before speaking again. "By heck, that was a grand dinner. You're mother certainly knows how to cook, lad. My taste buds are still working now."

"She always makes good dinners, grandad," I felt obliged to admit as I waited for him to re-gather his thoughts."

"Now, where was I?" he asked. "Ah, yes, my mate Harry. Now Harry, you must understand had never seemed particularly interested in girls. In fact he always made fun of any lad his age who did show an interest, so it came as a surprise to me when one day as we were leaving school and walking the short distance home that he suddenly turned to me and told me that he thought he'd fallen in love with Emily Grimshaw. There's no doubt that she was, indeed, a pretty little piece and my closest friend appeared to have fallen head over heels. We were both eleven years old at the time, the same age as Emily, which is also the same age as you are now. Well, I did my best to try to talk him out of it. I didn't want him to be going all soppy on me and going out with a girl when we could be indulging in all sorts of adventures."

Once again his story had me enthralled. I waited for him to continue.

"Anyway it was clear that Harry was having nothing to do with my pleading and said that he couldn't help himself. He was, in my mind, well and truly hooked. His problem was that the girl who was bewitching him did not appear to feel the same way about him as he did about her, and he asked me for my advice on how to resolve the situation to his satisfaction. Now, I was no expert on girls and he knew that, so I suppose he just asked me because he didn't want anyone else to know. I told him that I couldn't think of anything that might help him, but after several days of us doing nothing worthwhile together I realised that I would have to do something. The special companionship that we had always had seemed to have been lost and life for me was becoming incredibly boring. All the mischievous activities that had always delighted us had become virtually non-existent."

"So what did you do, grandad?" I asked him.

"I'm coming to that, lad. I'm coming to that. I remember spending a whole afternoon thinking about it and the only thing I could come up with was for him to buy her something and to explain how he felt. When I told him about it he said that as he hadn't been able to think of anything else then he might as well give my suggestion a try. Harry had never been able to save anything out of his meagre pocket money, but to give him his due, within a few days he'd managed to accumulate one shilling and sixpence. I never asked him how he'd managed it, though I couldn't believe he would have been desperate enough or clever enough to raid his mother's purse without being found out. So I had to concede that he thought it worthwhile to do without some of those things that lads of our age found entertaining."

He paused for a moment and gave a long yawn. I knew how much he was looking forward to lying down on the settee and closing his eyes for a while. However, I desperately wanted to hear the end of his story.

"So what happened, then?" I asked him. "Did he find something to buy?"

"He certainly did, lad. He didn't know what to buy or where to buy it from, so I suggested that he might buy her some sort of trinket that she could wear as I'd heard that girls seemed to like that sort of thing, and that the best place to try with the amount of money he'd got was the bottom of the market in the centre of Leeds. He thought that was probably the best idea and we agreed to go there on the following Saturday morning, which was a time when we were usually left to roam free with the condition that we did not get into mischief; a condition, I might add, that we didn't always adhere to. Now Hunslet, where we both lived at the time is, as you probably know, only a short tram ride into the centre of Leeds and we were both wandering around the market stalls within twenty minute of leaving home, the fare for each of us being one penny."

"Was the market as big then as it is now, grandad?" I asked him.

"If anything, I'd say it was bigger, but there were a lot more stalls outside in those days. Anyway, within a few minutes Harry had found the sort of thing that we thought would be appropriate. It was a very attractive-looking bracelet. Mind you, he had to do a bit of haggling to get the price down to what he could afford, but that's something that Harry had always been good at. No one seems to do any haggling these days, which is rather a shame. Anyway, it was nothing like what you would find in one of those fancy jeweller's shops in Briggate because obviously it wasn't made of gold or silver or any other expensive metal but to me and Harry it looked just as good."

My grandfather's story brought to mind the pendant I had bought for Susan. I listened eagerly as he continued.

"Harry was very pleased with his purchase, and was convinced that it would do the trick."

"And did it work?" I asked, enthusiastically.

"Well it certainly did at first. Harry gave it to her on our next day back at school and he could see the positive result for himself as she immediately placed it onto her wrist with an encouraging smile on her face. Whether his gift alone, however, would have been enough to plant romantic thoughts into her mind that had not been there previously, I had my doubts. Anyway, within three days I knew with certainty that all hopes that she might have developed the same feelings for him that he had for her were totally dashed."

"Why, what happened, grandad?" I asked, intrigued by this turn of events.

"She threw it back at him. That's what happened. Her wrists had turned green. You see, if any form of jewellery that is worn on the body which has been made from cheap material that sort of thing could happen. I've known it happen with cheap necklaces."

"Could it happen with something like a pendant?" I asked.

"Of course it could if it was a very cheap one. It depends on what sort of metal it was made from. Anyway, Harry soon lost all interest in pursuing this girl, I'm pleased to say, and before long we were both once again enjoying the sort of escapades that we used to get up to. Now, I've finished the story. I'd appreciate it if you left me now to get on with the nap I came in for. I'm suddenly feeling very tired."

"What's the matter with you?" asked my father after I had returned to the kitchen. "You've gone very quiet. I hope you haven't been disturbing your grandad."

The reason I had gone quiet, as my father had put it, was because of the revelation made by my grandfather that cheap jewellery can make your skin turn green, which made me think again of the pendant that I was supposed to be giving to Susan. I decided to go out to see Billy. When I knocked on his door I was greeted by his mother.

"I'm afraid Billy's not coming out this afternoon," she informed me. "He was half an hour late coming home for his dinner. I had to warm it all up, so I've told him he'll have to stop in today."

She said it in such a way that I was left with the distinct impression that she was blaming me. I had wanted to discuss with him my dilemma regarding the pendant. How could I possibly find out whether or not it would make Susan's neck turn green?

Grandad Miller decided to accept my mother's invitation to stay for tea, which consisted of egg and chips, before leaving for home immediately afterwards, leaving me with the question of how to solve a problem that I hadn't known existed before his arrival.

CHAPTER NINETEEN

"What am I going to do about it, Billy?" I asked, after having told him about the story that my grandfather had related to me. We were just walking to school on the day following his visit.

"Do you know what I think, Neil?" he replied. "I bet he knows about the pendant and he's just trying to put the wind up you. You know he likes playing jokes on people. Are you sure you haven't told him about it?"

"No, Billy, I've never mentioned it. Why would I want to tell him that I've bought jewellery for a girl? He'd never stop reminding me of it."

"Well, if you want to know if it's going to turn her neck green there's only one thing you can do, isn't there?"

"What's that?" I asked, eagerly, hoping he might have found a worthwhile solution to my problem.

"You'll just have to wear it yourself."

"Don't be daft, Billy, I can't go around wearing a pendant round my neck. Grandad Miller said the bracelet took about three days to make the girl's wrist go green."

"Well I don't see how else you can find out."

"Can't you wear it, Billy? I'll lend it to you if you like."

"Get lost, Neil."

With the problem still unresolved we vaulted the low wall that led into the schoolyard and joined the line of boys that was just being formed. Almost immediately, I felt a tap on my shoulder.

"Are you two still wanting to join the scouts?" asked Johnny Jackson.

"You bet," said Billy, eagerly, but obviously avoiding any attempt to mention our previous attempt to do that very thing, "Were going down there tomorrow night."

"You won't be able to join if you do."

"Why?" I asked him, being keen not to repeat our earlier mistake. "It's the right day, isn't it?"

"Oh, yes, it's the right day, but our scoutmaster told us that we won't be taking any more new recruits until after Whitsuntide, because at the moment we're struggling to cope with the numbers we've got."

"Well, won't it be the same after Whitsuntide?" asked Billy.

"No, I don't think so, because they re-schedule everything after the holiday period and I know at least one person's leaving next week. If you wanted to join straight away I suppose you could always join another troop, but it would be better if you joined ours because as well as me, we've also got Ernie Peyton."

"I didn't know Ernie had joined. You haven't got Tucker Lane as well, have you?"

"No, and I think I'd probably leave if he became a member. He'd start taking over everything."

"If we wait until after Whitsuntide, would it mean that we'd miss a chance to go camping?" asked Billy.

"The scoutmaster told us that we will be going camping, but it won't be until the summer," replied Johnny Jackson.

"It must be during the school holidays then," I said, disappointedly, "And that's ages away."

"Yes, I think you're right, but it might not stop us going away for a weekend before then."

With that cheering thought, the school bell sounded and the two neatly formed lines, one of boys and one of girls, made its way behind Miss Hazlehurst into the school assembly hall.

After the headmaster's usual rambling address he indicated that Mr. Barnes had a few things to say.

"Now, on Saturday," he began, "The school rugby team will be playing it's final game and I would like to point out to everyone here and to the members of the team in particular that we are still entrenched at the foot of the league table. Now, when I began this venture in September I did not envision that we would find ourselves in this position but I am also aware of how much we have improved over the last few months having won two games quite recently. Now, if other results go our way, then one final victory may be enough to enable us not to finish in this position. I know the team members are ready to give their all but it would help enormously if they received as much support as possible from the other members of the school, especially as this is a home game which will be taking place on Bedford's Field at the top of Woodhouse Ridge which, after all, isn't very far away for anyone to travel."

He continued in a similar vein for a few more minutes before Mr. Rawcliffe called a halt to the proceedings and we all dispersed into our various classrooms. Billy and I followed the headmaster, being in the top class as we were due to move on to another school in September. Before long his history lesson was in full swing.

"Right then, you, Peter Rogers," he said rather forcefully, pointing to a boy on the back row who had apparently not been paying attention.

"Who, me Sir?" responded his startled victim.

"Yes boy, you; I want you to tell me everything you know about King Alfred."

"King Alfred, Sir?"

"Yes boy, that's what I said. What can you tell me about King Alfred?"

"He burnt some cakes, sir," was the reply.

The headmaster stared at him with an incredulous look on his face.

"I ask you a question about one of the greatest Englishmen that ever lived," he said, the tone of his voice beginning to sound angry, "And all you can tell me is that he burnt some cakes. Have I been wasting my time attempting to get some historical facts inside the heads of the pupils of this class?"

The object of his wrath was by this time looking very uncomfortable and attempting to make himself look as insignificant as possible. Mr. Rawcliffe, obviously noticing this, decided to change the direction of his questioning, and his manner became a little calmer.

"Now," he said, "I'm sure there must be someone in this room who can supply a better answer than the one we have just heard. Who can tell me anything more substantial about King Alfred?"

I was about to raise my hand as, I believe were several others but as the first person to raise her hand just happened to be Lorna Gale I think the rest of us realised that it would be much more entertaining to hear what she had to say.

"What! Is there no one at all?" said the headmaster trying really hard not to look in her direction. "Surely someone in the class must have been paying attention when I've been attempting to teach you about English History or am I simply wasting my time remaining in this profession? Very well, then I shall right a few facts on the blackboard to see if it jogs your memory."

I noticed, however, that Lorna hadn't put her hand down as I'm sure he expected her to but raised it even higher. When she started to prompt him by constantly repeating 'Sir, Sir' then it became obvious to him that he wasn't going to get away with his ploy.

"Very well, Miss Gale," he said, reluctantly, "I assume you have something you want to say on the subject."

"Yes, Sir," she replied.

"Very well, then, but let's make it brief, shall we?" What else do you have to tell us about King Alfred?"

Everyone else in the room visibly relaxed and eagerly looked forward to the forthcoming contest of wills.

"Well, Sir, you seemed to think that Peter ought to be able to tell you a lot more when he said that King Alfred bunt some cakes, but you see, Sir, I remember that lesson and no one told us what kind of cakes they were or how many of them. I mean if there were only one or two, then I think it was a bit unfair of the lady to shout at the king even if she didn't know who he was. Maybe she hadn't even told him how long they were supposed to be in the oven."

"Miss Gale," attempted the headmaster," noticeably aware of the sniggering going around the class but, as usual, he seemed unable to stop Lorna's verbal assault.

"My Auntie Jean tried to show me how to bake bread once, but I wasn't very good at it. I kept getting my hands covered in dough and had to keep washing it off. She never showed me how to make cakes though, but I think I can understand why it must have been so hard for the king to get it right."

"Thank you, I think you can sit down now."

Either Lorna hadn't heard the head's request or she chose to ignore it.

"I wonder if he had taken the cakes out of the oven before the lady came home whether he might have eaten any of them."

"Thank you, you may sit down now."

His victim finally gave some indication that she was being asked to do something.

"What did you say, sir?"

"Sit down now, please."

She finally did as directed but not without a puzzled expression on her face.

"I think we'll move onto something else now," said an exasperated Mr. Rawcliffe.

Before he had the chance to do so there was a knock on the door and Mr. Barnes entered the room. Walking over to him, he whispered something in his ear.

"Turn to page seventy-nine in your history books," said the headmaster and begin reading Chapter Eight. I shall be back in a few minutes."

"I wonder what that's all about," said Ernie Peyton from the row behind.

"I've no idea," I replied. "We'll just have to wait until he comes back, but there seems to be a lot of noise coming from Barnesy's class, doesn't there?"

There also seemed to a lot of footsteps rushing backwards and forwards outside the door. It was almost fifteen minutes after we had been left to our own devices that the door opened and everybody put their heads down pretending to read their history books.

Miss Hazlehurst entered the room. "The Headmaster," she began, "Wants me to tell you all to go into the school-yard. I know that it is not the normal time, but something has happened that we have to deal with and that means that there is no one available to take your class lesson at the moment."

Ken Stacey was the first to raise the question. "Why, what's happened Miss?"

She looked thoughtful for a moment before answering. "All I can tell you at the moment is that there has been an accident in Mr. Barnes's class. So can you all get off your seats and make your way outside immediately? I don't want to see anyone hanging around inside the premises. Is that understood? When we want you to return I will ring the bell."

We needed no more encouragement to accept what we were being offered, but I'm sure that all of us would have preferred to have had a little more information regarding what had occurred than what we had been given.

"I wonder who's had an accident?" said Billy. "It certainly can't be Barnesy because he looked all right when he came into the classroom, didn't he?"

Before I had a chance to say anything, an ambulance came hurtling along Jubilee Terrace from the direction of Woodhouse Street. After it had stopped right outside the school gates the driver and another man got out and rushed up the steps into the school, carrying a stretcher. A few minutes later, with every pupil in the schoolyard delighted to be outside but with a touch of apprehension at this change to routine, they re-appeared, only this time the stretcher had an occupant. Not being allowed to get close enough to see clearly we were unable to ascertain who the unfortunate pupil was.

"I wonder who it is, Neil. I can't see properly, can you?" said Billy.

"No, I can't even tell whether it's a boy or a girl."

We all watched as the patient was carefully placed in the back of the ambulance. Mr. Barnes climbed in with the unfortunate pupil and the ambulance set off towards Woodhouse Street. It was a further ten minutes before we were all summoned back into the building and told to gather in assembly with the rest of the school while the Headmaster made an announcement.

"No doubt you have all been wondering what has been happening during the last half hour," he began, "Well I have to tell you that one of your fellow pupils has met with a nasty accident when he tripped over a chair and injured his neck. Just how serious the injury is, we do not yet know, but Mr. Barnes has accompanied him to the hospital and I hope we may have more information before you leave school this afternoon."

"Who is it that's been injured, Sir?" asked Alan Bartle.

"The boy who had the accident is Nicholas Whitehead," replied the Headmaster.

Billy and I looked at each other in disbelief.

"Not Nicky," I said. "He's only just recovered from his broken arm."

Not knowing the extent of his injury was the worst part. Could it even be life-threatening? The remaining time that we spent in school was, for Billy and me in particular, a distressing time. By the time we were walking in the direction of home there had been no further news of his condition. The first thing we did after informing our parents about what had occurred was to go round to Nicky's house and see if we could get any more news. There was no answer, however, when we knocked on the door so we could only assume that either his mother or both of his parents were at the hospital. My mother and father, of course, were very concerned at the news and they allowed me to stay up until much later than I normally would have done. However, by the time that I did retire to bed I still had no knowledge whatsoever of how serious his condition might be.

CHAPTER TWENTY

It wasn't until late afternoon on the following day that we were able to ascertain the extent of Nicky's injury. We had called at his house immediately after leaving school and we were told by his mother that he had sprained his neck, but the damage was nowhere near as bad as it could have been. This left us feeling much relieved, though the fact that he had to wear a surgical collar until his next check-up at the hospital inevitably meant that he would not be joining us for any outdoor pursuits in the near future. He would also, of course, not be attending school for several weeks. This, as far as he was concerned, was the only thing he could find to be pleased about, his mother having allowed us to speak to him for a few minutes. He told us that he wasn't in much pain as long as he wore the collar, but he was finding it very uncomfortable.

On that same evening, after giving the matter much thought, I decided to sleep with the gypsy pendant around my neck. I was keen to see whether my neck turned green, but I suspected that I would have to wear it for more than an eight-hour period to give the experiment some validity. My remembrance of the bad luck I had experienced on the last occasion that it was in my possession for any reasonable length of time also gave me some anxious moments. The night passed reasonably well and when I awoke I felt considerably relieved. It was only when I attempted to get up and put my foot into the same chamber pot that I had half filled before retiring that my mood began to change. Up to a few days previously it had always resided under the bed. All that changed, however, when my mother heard on a radio programme that if it was kept in such a location then the steam rising from it would be likely to rust the springs. I immediately wondered if the curse of the pendant when worn by a male was manifesting itself again. Deep down I knew that it was an irrational thought but I just couldn't help myself. The thought, however, was about to grow stronger.

I decided to risk wearing the pendant again on the following evening after making sure that the chamber pot was not in a position where I would involuntarily step into it even though I had obeyed my mother's instructions about not placing it under the bed. Leaving the light on for a few minutes I sat up in bed reading a few pages from a Batman comic before pulling the switch above my head and letting the darkness engulf me. In the peaceful atmosphere of impending sleep I allowed my mind to be drawn into imagined situations, as I did on most nights, where I was instrumental in rescuing Susan Brown from whatever danger my state of drowsiness could summon up. When I awoke after a peaceful night's slumber the first thing I did was to reach out for the comic I had been reading before going to sleep, but in my haste to continue reading about the adventures of Batman and Robin I accidently knocked it off the bedside cabinet. It wasn't until I saw where it had landed that I realised that the curse of the gypsy pendant, at least in my mind, had struck again. I hastily retrieved it from its unfortunate resting place, took a sniff, then screwed it up and threw it into the waste bin in the corner of the room.

Before retiring on the following night I decided to ignore my grandfather's suggestion that the wearing of jewellery acquired for a price much lower than what one would expect to pay was not worth the misfortune that seemed to befall me every time I had this particular item in my possession, and as I returned it to its drawer I was no nearer to deciding what to do with it.

When I awoke on Friday morning my mind was immediately focussed on the trip to the Electra that same evening with Billy using the free tickets that we had been given earlier. However, my mother's announcement as I ate my breakfast took away the joyful feeling of anticipation and replaced it with one of dread.

"I'm taking you into town tomorrow morning," she said. "It's time we looked for your Whitsuntide clothes."

"Aw, mam, do I have to?" I pleaded, knowing that it would only fall on deaf ears. It was traditional, especially in the north of England, that on Whit Sunday, which occurred six weeks after Easter, that every child would be presented with a set of new clothes. This was particularly prevalent among the mill towns in the West Riding of Yorkshire. It's fair to say, I suppose, that some children actually enjoyed the occasion as the custom dictated that all the children visited close relatives such as aunts and uncles where they would be told how nice they looked in their smart, new clothes and be given a small amount of money to place in their pocket and, of course, the wider your circuit of relatives, the more you received. Billy and I, however, always hated it, and now that my mother had announced that I was about to be paraded around probably half the clothing shops in Leeds city centre my mood had changed completely.

"Have you been for your Whitsy clothes yet, Billy?" I asked as we made our way home from school.

"No, my mam hasn't said anything yet, but there's no chance that she's forgotten. Why do we have to do this every year?"

"I don't know, but the worst thing about it is that once you start wearing them they insist that you have to stay clean all the time, which just about rules out anything that's worth doing."

"I know. A few years ago I was just sitting on the causeway melting tar on the pavement by using the rays of the sun through a magnifying glass and my mam rushed out and played Hell with me just because I'd got a bit of tar on my new trousers."

As we passed the Electra we both walked over to peruse the poster.

"I've been thinking, Neil," said my companion. "If all those people who have a free ticket are going, plus a lot of people who haven't got a ticket, it could be full again."

"I hadn't thought of that, Billy, but surely they'll let all those who couldn't get in last week go in first, won't they?"

"I think we'd better get in the queue early anyway, just to be on the safe side."

I was about to enter the house when I noticed my Auntie Brenda just stepping out of hers. She was attired in a much more fashionable way than was usual and it made her look considerably younger than her fifty-something age. I caught up with her just before she reached the end of the street.

"Hello, Auntie Brenda," I said.

"Hello, young Neil," she replied. I couldn't quite make out whether the expression on her face was one of annoyance at her walk being interrupted or whether it was just my imagination.

"I was wondering if you'd like me to go round collecting jam jars for when you make some more jam," I suggested, hopefully.

Her answer wasn't what I had expected. "I'm afraid I don't really have much time to be making jam these days," she said, "So I doubt if I'll need any more jars. Still. It was nice of you to ask me, I suppose."

"Are you very busy now then, Auntie Brenda?" I asked.

"Well, let's just say that I've found something more interesting to do with my time."

"What's that then?" I persisted.

"Look, Neil, I'm in rather a hurry at the moment, so I must dash off. Give my regards to your mam and dad."

I watched her walk past Mrs. Ormond's sweet shop and turn the corner to walk down Speedwell Street.

I was puzzled with regard to her destination as she had given me no clue whatsoever. In fact, I had to admit that she had seemed rather secretive about it. As I retraced my steps along the street I couldn't help wondering what breakfasts would be like in the future without Auntie Brenda's jam to spread on my bread.

Before long, however, my mind had turned its attention to the evening's entertainment at the Electra with Billy. My mother hadn't been quite as gullible as I had expected after we had failed in our attempt to gain entrance on the previous Friday and my hope of holding on to the cinema money I had been given was never really an option. I even had to admit to her that Billy and I had received free passes for the re-scheduled performance. Nevertheless, I eagerly looked forward to the film. Realising that there would undoubtedly be another enormous queue bearing in mind that in addition to most of those that had attended previously and would be allowed to enter free of charge they would be joined by others who would be paying on the night.

The cinema was due to open its doors at seven o'clock and a queue was already forming when I called round for Billy at half past six.

"I think my Auntie Brenda might have got a fancy man, Billy," I told him as we walked towards the end of the queue.

"What makes you think that?" he replied.

"Well, she walked out of the house dressed in posh clothes and seemed to be in a hurry to go somewhere. She also told me that she's stopped making jam because she's got something much more interesting to do and that she just doesn't have the time anymore."

"That doesn't mean that she's got a fancy man though, does it?"

"Well why would she go out all posh-like? I was only two years old when my Uncle Arthur died. She might want to get married again."

"Well, what's wrong with that? A lot of women get married again and they don't always wait nine years. Look at those famous film stars. They seem to get married lots of times, and they don't always wait until their first husband has died."

I suddenly started laughing which got Billy rather puzzled. "What are you laughing for?" he asked.

"When you started talking about famous film stars I started to imagine myself sitting with you at the Electra when the big picture came on the screen announcing "THE WEDDING FEAST starring CLARK GABLE AND AUNTIE BRENDA.""

This time it was Billy's turn to laugh.

"I usually hate these sloppy love films, Billy," I said, "But if my Auntie Brenda was in it I'd probably give it a go."

We were about to attach ourselves to the end of the queue when we were joined by a familiar figure.

"Hiya, you two," announced Tucker Lane. "I've got a free pass for tonight, have you?"

I don't think either of us was very pleased about his joining us but there wasn't very much we could do about it.

"Yes," said Billy in answer to his question. "We came last week when the picture broke down."

I was glad that he didn't mention the fact that we never actually managed to gain entrance in case he came to the conclusion that we had come by them by subterfuge and were not really entitled to them, in which case he would probably state that he might have a better use for them and expect us to hand them over.

"It should be good," said our companion. "I like cowboy pictures."

The queue began to move and I realised that Tucker had already latched himself onto us and that we would probably all be sitting together which I wasn't very happy about. I didn't have to wait long for my supposition to be proved correct.

"Look, we'll sit here," he said, indicating a row of seats towards the rear of the stalls.

"We usually sit nearer the front," suggested Billy.

"No, that's no good," replied Tucker. "This row's just right. We can have a lot more fun here. It's a lot darker than at the front, so if we decided to stamp our feet if anything goes wrong with the projector or if we wanted to make a bit of noise it's not as easy to be seen. It's no good sitting on the back row though, because all the courting couples go there and they're all kissing and cuddling all the time. No we're better here."

As neither Billy nor I dared to suggest that the two of us sat somewhere else we unfortunately had to reluctantly accept the situation. We made our way to the centre of the row, which at that point was unoccupied by anyone else as, with the exception of two young couples who made their way onto the back row thus proving the validity of Tucker's statement, most of the other patrons headed for the front area of the stalls. It was fairly obvious, though, given the amount of free passes that had been handed out that eventually just about all of the remaining seats would be taken.

"Sitting in the middle," I suggested, "Might make it harder for us to get an ice cream before the big picture starts."

"Not to me," replied Tucker. "I'd just kick their legs out of the way. You just watch me."

It was at that point that I realised that his reasons for visiting the cinema were in no way the same as ours, and that there was very little possibility that we could escape his dominance. We resigned ourselves to the prospect of a very difficult evening.

There were always two or three short films before the main attraction and the first turned out to be a comedy featuring a character called Joe McDoakes, whose head always appeared from behind a bowling ball as the titles appeared on the screen. Tucker had decided to seat himself between the two of us and immediately rendered any conversation between Billy and me virtually impossible. From the beginning he could only be described as extremely noisy. Whenever he laughed at what was taking place on the screen it could probably be heard in the front row. When he communicated with either of us it wasn't in the whispered tones that might have been acceptable to the other patrons but was extremely loud as if he was still in the school playground rather than in the confined space of a cinema. Before the first film had ended several people in front had already looked behind them with angry expressions on their faces. Tucker simply ignored them.

The second film consisted of several songs played by one of the popular dance bands which caused our annoying schoolmate to start tapping on the back of the seat in front, which fortunately was one of the few unoccupied, while simultaneously tapping his feet in time to the music. I was really beginning to feel extremely uncomfortable with all the attention that we seemed to be getting. By the time the ice cream girl made an appearance I was thoroughly miserable and I was sure that the same could be said for Billy.

Tucker, in his attempt to lead the stampede down the aisle to the front of the queue, barged into a lad of a similar age who was attempting the same thing. What struck us immediately was that he seemed to have even more muscles on his impressive frame than our companion. This fact did nothing whatsoever to prevent the angry scowl that appeared on our companion's face.

Billy and I decided to stay where we were while we waited to see how things would unroll.

By this time two other lads had appeared on the scene. "What's the matter, Jimmy?" asked one of them. "Is this lad giving you trouble?"

"This stupid idiot," screamed Tucker's unintended victim, "Barged right into me."

"Who are you calling an idiot?" said our classmate with a touch of menace in his voice.

"Let's sort him out then," said the first speaker.

"Better not try," snarled Tucker, pointing in our direction, "I've got the rest of my gang over there."

We looked behind us to see who he was pointing at and then the penny dropped. We had reluctantly been recruited as part of his gang.

"Neither of them look very tough to me," said the other lad, turning in our direction.

Just then one of the security officials decided that the situation was beginning to get out of hand.

"Right, you two," he bellowed. "I've just about had enough of this." He towered over the lad called Jimmy and effortlessly grabbed him by the scruff of the neck and marched him towards the exit, despite his protests that he was the innocent victim.

The smirk on Tucker's face, however, gave way to a scowl when the same security man, after successfully despatching his first captive, returned and completed the same manoeuvre on him. After having satisfied himself that he had dealt with those he considered to be the ringleaders he didn't bother with the other two lads or with Billy and me and we tried to look as inconspicuous as possible. We immediately abandoned any thoughts of joining the ice cream queue that was being re-formed. Instead we were able to turn our attention towards the main feature which we thoroughly enjoyed. Whether our schoolmate and his antagonist squared up to each other outside in the street we neither knew nor cared and fortunately our brief period as members of Tucker Lane's gang had passed without us having to prove our worth in that respect.

CHAPTER TWENTYONE

"I knew we'd win," declared Billy as we marched triumphantly down Woodhouse Street. "I knew as soon as I set eyes on the lads we'd be playing against. It's a pity Nicky couldn't have played though. His mother said he should be all right in a couple of weeks, but that was the last match of the season so he won't be playing in any more."

"I don't think we'd have won if Tucker hadn't been playing though. That was the best I've ever seen him play."

"Yes, he seemed to be all fired up, didn't he?" said my companion. "He nearly got himself sent off at one point though. The referee looked very angry. It's a good job they missed from that penalty otherwise we'd have been behind and things might have gone differently."

Just before the game had begun Tucker had told me that he and the other lad who had been ejected from the Electra had faced up to each other as soon as they were outside and that his adversary had chickened out when he realised that his two mates weren't there to assist him. However, the fact that my classmate had a cut lip led me to the conclusion that his version of the event might not be strictly correct, though when I thought more about it I felt fairly sure though that the contest would almost certainly have been a very close one.

"We won't know until Monday," continued Billy, "Whether we've finished bottom of the league or not."

When we arrived home, feeling in a triumphant mood, I asked him if he wanted to come out again after dinner and maybe run wild on Woodhouse Ridge for a while. His reply really brought me down to earth. "I thought you said you were going with your mam to get your Whitsy clothes."

"Oh, crikey, Billy," I said, feeling thoroughly deflated. "I'd forgotten all about that."

He looked at me and his face showed a distinct lack of sympathy. "I really hate it, Billy. I always lose count of the number of shops I've been dragged through and sometimes she ends up buying the clothes from the first place we went to."

"I think most women are like that, Neil, but my mam usually waits until the last minute and she doesn't have time to be shopping all over the place."

When I entered the house I knew immediately that there was no possibility that my mother had changed her mind.

"Good Heavens, just look at you," she chided. "How on earth did you get into that state? You'll have to have a good scrubbing down before you go out with me. You can't be trying clothes on in that condition."

If my father had been home he would have asked me how the game went but my mother had always shown little interest in my sporting activities. After two kettles full of hot water had been added to the cold water from the tap, I spent about twenty minutes at the side of the sink, virtually naked while hoping that my auntie Molly didn't pop in from next door, before my mother decided that I was clean enough to accompany her on the shopping expedition that I was dreading, in the town centre later that afternoon.

My father arrived shortly afterwards and seemed pleased that we had won our final game. I had grown so tired of having to try to explain to him why we had lost so many of our previous games. After a dinner that was rather spoiled for me by knowing that, instead of playing outside with Billy, I would have to endure a tedious shopping expedition with my mother with me being the one that would be having to try things on.

It was half past one by the time all the dinner things had been washed up and cleared away and just twenty minutes after that we were standing outside the Primrose pub in Meanwood Road waiting for the tram to take us into town.

"I think we'll call at Burton's in Briggate first," she said. "They always have some nice clothes for boys in there."

"Why can't I get long trousers, mam?" I asked, knowing that it wasn't a realistic option as just about every boy of my age in our locality always wore short ones. "When will I be old enough?"

"Look the tram's coming," she said, completely ignoring my question.

"Mam," I said, after we had taken our seats on the tram, "How many shops do you think we'll have to look in before you find the right clothes?"

"Now how should I know? We'll just have to keep looking until we find something that looks really smart on you."

That was not the answer I wanted, but it was the one I knew I would get.

We alighted from the tram outside the West Yorkshire Bus Station in Vicar Lane and began walking up the Headrow towards our first destination. As we reached the traffic lights on the corner of Briggate I happened to glance to the right. What I saw gave me something to think about.

"Look, mam," I said. "Isn't that Auntie Brenda standing outside the Odeon?"

Before she had time to look, the figure that I had seen had quickly disappeared.

"What are you talking about?" my mother said, visibly annoyed. "There's nobody there that looks remotely like your Auntie Brenda. You're just trying to waste as much time as you can before we go into the shop."

"It was definitely her, mam," I protested. "Do you know what I think? I think she's got a fancy man and she was waiting for him and that they're going to the pictures together."

"Now stop it. If you saw anyone it must have been someone who looked like your Auntie Brenda. She wouldn't be going with a fancy man or whatever else you might call him. I don't think she's been out with anyone since your Uncle Arthur died."

"Well, that's what I think anyway, and I bet that's why she's stopped making jam. I bet it's because she hasn't got time anymore."

My mother allowed me to have the last word and we entered Burton's store and made our way to the children's section. What followed was a long period of absolute boredom as we examined just about every item of clothing that she considered might be suitable for a child of my age before deciding, as I expected she would, that it would be best to try several other stores in order to get a more varied choice. The price of each item was, of course, also a major consideration. It was as we approached the third store, which was Schofield's that I spotted Auntie Brenda again.

"Look, mam," I shouted excitedly, keen to have my earlier sighting vindicated. "That's Auntie Brenda over there. She must not have gone to the pictures, and look, she's got a fancy man with her."

"I told you," she started to say, getting visibly annoyed before realisation set in. "Oh, it is your Auntie Brenda."

I knew straight away that no apology would be offered.

"I've no idea who he is," she continued, "But I know it's not some fancy man that she's taken up with. No, there must be some other explanation."

"Are you going to ask her who he is, mam?"

"Of course I'm not. It isn't anything to do with me who your Auntie Brenda is seen with."

I could see for myself though that she was dying to find out.

"Look, mam, they seem to be looking at something in that shop window. Why don't we just pretend that we're walking past and then just notice her accidentally?"

I could see that she was thinking this over.

"No," she decided. "It's your Auntie Brenda's business and nobody else's. After all, she's only looking in a shop window. The other man's probably got nothing to do with her at all."

I was disappointed with her decision but decided not to argue which might antagonize her further. I just wanted the wretched afternoon to be over so that

I could go back home and engage in something more interesting. However, her curiosity was about to get the better of her.

"Oh, look, they've both gone into the shop together," she said. "I don't know what they sell in there. It's too far away to see."

"Well, if they've both gone in together," I said, "Why don't we just walk past the shop and see what's in the window. Auntie Brenda won't even see us."

I could see she was pondering this suggestion.

"All right, we'll just go have a look then. It's not far from the arcade that goes down to Marks and Spencer's, and that's where I was going to take you next."

We walked towards the shop that the two of them seemed to find so interesting. It was only a small shop but they had been gazing at the window for quite some time.

"Now just walk straight past," demanded my mother and just give the window a glance. I don't want your Auntie Brenda to think we've been spying on her."

"It seems to be just a stationery shop, mam," I said. "Maybe she just went in to buy a fountain pen."

"It seems to be more than just a stationery shop. It looks more like the sort of shop that someone who was interested in painting would go into."

"I didn't notice any tins of paint, and usually those sorts of places sell wallpaper as well, and if there was anything like that I think we'd have seen it."

"I don't mean that kind of painting. I mean where they use an easel and canvas, the sort of paintings that you would find in an art gallery."

"Maybe it's her fancy man that's interested and she just decided to go inside with him."

"Look, I've already told you to stop calling him her fancy man or there'll be trouble. I'm sure there's a perfectly simple explanation."

We continued to Marks and Spencer's and two other stores before my mother was satisfied that the clothes she had selected for me to wear on Whit Sunday would be at least as smart as any others that would be on display by any of the other children in our local community. At least on this occasion she had not forced us to revisit any of the stores that we had already been in.

The situation regarding Auntie Brenda was not mentioned again as we made our way home, but to me the encounter had proved a welcome distraction to what otherwise would have been a wretched afternoon. Immediately that I arrived home I went straight out to see Billy. I just felt like doing something a little more interesting.

"Shall we go play in the schoolyard?" he asked. "We might see someone we know."

Because it was so accessible at any time of the day owing to the lack of a gate and the fact that the low wall was so easy to climb over, children were often seen there, kicking a ball around or playing at Hopscotch.

It seemed as good an idea as any that I could come up with. Before we arrived, however, we saw Alan Bartle walking up the ginnel opposite the Electra.

"Hiya, Alan," shouted Billy as he approached us."

"Hello, you two," he responded. "What did you think of the match this morning? It was great, wasn't it? I bet if we'd had another season we could have finished near the top of the league."

"We don't know if we've still finished bottom, yet though, do we?" I suggested.

"I do," he responded. "I met Ken Stacey this morning and he told me that the Headingley boys lost and also one of the other teams that was near the bottom and that meant that out of the twelve teams in the league we finished tenth, but I still don't know where he got the news from."

I wasn't bothered where he heard it from so long as it was true. Both Billy and I and every other member of the team had dreaded the prospect of finishing at the bottom.

"I'm sure that if we hadn't made such a rotten start," added Alan, "By losing thirty-six nil to Armley School we'd have done a lot better, because we've been playing quite well lately, and don't forget Armley did finish top of the whole league. Still, I might as well appreciate this Saturday because I'm not looking forward to the next one."

"Why, what's happening next Saturday?" asked Billy.

"My mam's threatening to take me into town to get my Whitsuntide clothes and I always hate it. It always takes about three hours before she gets something that she considers to be right."

Billy started laughing.

"What's so funny about that?" Asked Alan, visibly displeased that my companion found his statement so amusing. I decided to get in first.

"I'll tell you why. It's because that's exactly what I've been doing all afternoon, and it was just like you said."

"Girls seem to like it though, don't they?" observed Billy. "They always like dressing up. Why can't they just have the custom for girls instead of us being roped in as well? I know we collect money from aunts and uncles on Whit Sunday but it's all so embarrassing."

"I don't mind girls doing it though," I said, "Because they always want to show you their knickers as well as their ordinary clothes."

"Yes," agreed Alan," They should just have it for girls because, as Billy just said, they like nothing better than to be wearing new clothes and making sure that everybody notices."

Our school friend left us as he was visiting some relative on Meanwood Road and we continued to the school yard. There didn't seem to be much going on. There were just three other lads that we didn't really know who were having a kick-around. Anyway they invited us to join in. The time passed pleasantly enough, but after a while we got bored and, with teatime beckoning, decided to make our way back home.

I hadn't had much time to talk to my father after having arrived home from town. I had been so keen to dash outside to see Billy. As I opened the door and stepped inside I found him alone seated on his favourite armchair near the fire. There were two things I wanted to talk to him about and, in the temporary absence of my mother, I knew immediately which of the two subjects to discuss first.

"Dad, Auntie Brenda's got herself a ------"

"Stop that now," Yelled my mother, making a miraculous appearance from the other room. I decided that it would be in my best interests to let the matter drop, but I hoped to get the chance to eavesdrop at some point later in the evening when my mother was bound to discuss with him the subject of Auntie Brenda's escapade.

I knew that the opportunity would not present itself until after I had gone upstairs to bed. Deciding to retire a little earlier than usual, I waited at the top of the steps, knowing that my mother would be likely to broach the subject as soon as I was out of sight. I didn't have to wait long before I heard her say the name Brenda. She was speaking in a low voice and I knew that I would have to creep down a few steps to hear anything of what was being said.

"What if she is?" I heard my father say. "If she wants a bit of company while she's getting older, then good luck to her. After all, it must be eight or nine years since Arthur died, mustn't it?"

I couldn't quite catch my mother's reply as she was almost speaking in a whisper. I decided to descend to the bottom of the staircase, and would probably have got away with it too if I hadn't been horribly betrayed. Nell suddenly appeared from around the corner and, clearly suspecting that I was up to some kind of mischief began barking furiously despite my signals to her to keep quiet. I raced back up the stairs and made it into the bedroom just as I heard my father raise his voice and tell her to be quiet. So I didn't hear anything else about Auntie Brenda's supposed indiscretion, but I was still keen to find out what she was up to.

CHAPTER TWENTYTWO

It wasn't until the following Tuesday that I was able to solve the mystery surrounding Auntie Brenda's strange behaviour and it came from an unexpected source. The day had begun quite unremarkably. I got dressed, got washed, had breakfast and walked to school with Billy. There was no indication whatsoever that this particular day would prove to be such an eventful one. The weather was sunny but a typical April shower began before we entered the schoolyard. It ended, however, even before the bell sounded for us to enter the school.

"When are you going to give Susan Brown that pendant?" asked Billy, as we entered the assembly hall.

"I don't know," I replied. "I still can't make up my mind whether to give it to her or not." It still resided in my bedroom drawer and I was no nearer to making a decision, especially after my grandfather had planted the suggestion into my mind that it might make her neck turn green.

"Well, she already knows now that you've got her a present," continued Billy. "She's going to start to wonder why you're taking so long to give it to her."

"I don't know, Billy. Maybe she's forgotten."

"I don't think so, Neil."

By the time we were seated in the classroom the subject of the gypsy pendant had been relegated to the back of my mind. It stayed that way until the bell sounded for the start of the morning break, at which point I came to a sudden decision.

"I'm going to give her the pendant this afternoon," I announced to Billy, as we made our way into the schoolyard, while attempting to keep my voice as low as possible. "I'm fed up with trying to make my mind up. If it makes her neck turn green then I can't do anything about it, can I?"

"I want to see if it brings her good luck, like it's supposed to," said Billy, "But I don't really believe in all that stuff."

"I don't either, Billy, but I'm going to tell her what Danny's mother told us anyway. Susan might believe it."

I wasn't prepared, however, for what I was about to learn a few minutes later. As the bell sounded to summon us back into the classroom we found ourselves walking behind Wanda Aspinall and Norma Clayton who were deep in conversation. I was taking very little notice of the topic under discussion until I heard Susan's name mentioned at which time I began to listen intently.

"When will Susan be leaving then?" asked Norma.

"I don't know," replied Wanda. "I only heard it from somebody else. I haven't spoken to Susan about it yet."

Any thoughts of possible embarrassment did not enter my head. I just had to know.

"What were you just saying about Susan?" I asked. "She's not leaving, is she?"

"And why should you be interested, I wonder?" asked Norma Clayton.

"I know why," said Wanda Aspinall. "It's because you want her to be your girlfriend, isn't it?"

"Well, what if I do?" I replied, surprising myself by admitting to others what I had never dared to do before. My mind was in turmoil. I just couldn't bear the thought of not seeing her again.

"Please tell me what you know," I begged.

"Well," continued Wanda. "I hear that her father has been offered a transfer to a Post Office in Hull and that he and her mother are very keen to go. They told Susan that because they would be moving near the coast they would be able to visit the seaside on a lot of weekends in the summer period."

I was devastated. "Did Susan say that she wants to go?" I persisted.

"I don't know," she responded, "But it won't really be up to her will it?"

I realised that she wouldn't really have any say in the matter. I knew that it would be her parents who would be making the decision.

"Maybe it's all a mistake," suggested Billy, sensing my discomfort as we entered the classroom and split from the two girls. Wanda did say that she'd only heard the news from someone else and not directly from Susan, didn't she?"

"I've got to find out though, Billy."

"That means you'll have to ask her yourself then, doesn't it?"

"Can't you do it for me?"

"No, Neil, I think you should do it. Then you can give her that pendant at the same time, like you said you would."

I decided to give the matter some thought and make a decision when I returned to school in the afternoon. As it was a Thursday and my mother did some cleaning work for an elderly friend on that one day of the week I had dinner at my Auntie Molly's who lived next door. As soon as I had finished eating I asked for the key to my house as I needed to take something to school for the afternoon lesson. I immediately went next door and took the pendant from its location in the top drawer in my bedroom. As I walked back to school with Billy I tried hard not to think about all the bad luck that I had encountered when I had previously carried it in my pocket. Fortunately, I didn't find myself tripping over anything and nothing bad happened. I spotted Susan in the schoolyard as soon as I arrived, but I knew that I needed to catch her when she was alone which wouldn't be easy. In fact the occasion didn't arrive until I followed her into the cloakroom.

"Are you in a hurry, Susan?" I said. "I just want to ask you something before we go into the classroom. Is it true that you're leaving?"

"All I know, Neil, is that my dad has been offered a job in Hull and that my mother, in particular, wants to go because she thinks that we'll be able to get a house near the seaside, but I don't really want to leave because all my friends are here." I couldn't help noticing that she didn't especially mention me, but I decided not to worry about that unduly.

"I don't want you to go, Susan," I said, with as much feeling as I could muster. "I want you to stay here."

She didn't say anything and time seemed to stand still for several minutes as we just looked at each other and I knew that the time to hand over the pendant had finally arrived. "Do you remember Billy telling you that I had bought you a present?" I said. "Well here it is." I took the object from my pocket and held it out to her.

She looked at it, took it from the palm of my hand and held it up.

"It's lovely," she responded, "But why have you bought me a present? It's not as if it's my birthday or anything."

"I bought it for you because I like you, Susan. I really like you."

As I realised that she wasn't about to reject the gift a warm feeling swept all over me and I began to recite the story that the gypsy lady had related to me concerning the supposed magical properties of the pendant, and I strangely found myself for the first time half believing the story. It seemed to be a magical moment in time similar to the one just before Christmas when the two of us had sheltered in the Electra doorway during a fierce hailstorm. If she didn't really want to leave, then perhaps any extraordinary powers that it might possess might help in achieving that end. I certainly hoped that it would.

She immediately placed it around her neck and tucked it inside her blouse. I was pleased that she hadn't left it in full view so that she didn't have to answer questions all afternoon regarding where it had come from. I'm not sure I believe in leprechauns," she said, "But we'll have to wait and see what happens, won't we?"

I half anticipated a peck on the cheek but it wasn't forthcoming. Realising that if we waited any longer we would be disciplined for being late, we walked into the classroom together, which I couldn't help noticing was observed by every girl in the room. For the remainder of the afternoon I felt like I was living in a dream world. Had I really expressed my feelings towards her after all this time? I could scarcely believe it. At that point

I couldn't help wondering why it had taken me so long, but I knew that fear of rejection was the chief cause, with fear of embarrassment a secondary one. As the bell sounded to signal the end of the school day I hoped that I might get the chance to walk back along the street with her but it didn't happen. As I left the building she was already attached and chatting to Valerie Trainer and Wanda Aspinall so I allowed Billy to catch me up.

"I thought you might have been walking back with Susan," he said.

"I would have liked to Billy but she was already chatting to Wanda and Valerie so I let them carry on walking."

"Girls are always chatting to each other, but it never seems to be about anything interesting, does it? I bet in a day they use three times as many words as we do."

"I think Lorna Gale, though, must use ten times as many."

Billy laughed at that. "Are you coming out again after tea, Neil?" he asked.

"I don't know yet, Billy. I don't really know what I want to do."

Normally I would have answered yes straight away, but my encounter with Susan and its successful conclusion dominated my mind. I could still see the trio as we left the schoolyard. Wanda Aspinall turned down the ginnel opposite the Electra while Susan and Valerie Trainer continued walking along the street. I watched them go as far as Ormond's sweet shop at which point Valerie turned right and headed down the hill.

"If I'm coming out again, Billy, I'll call round for you after tea."

I was still in what could only be described as a dreamy sort of mood when I entered the house and it was immediately noticed by my mother. "What's the matter with you?" she asked. "You look miles away as if you've been hypnotised. Are you all right?"

Nell walked over to investigate this new phenomenon that had invaded her space.

"Yes, of course I'm all right, mam. I was just thinking about something that happened at school, that's all."

Nell, deciding that there was really nothing out of the ordinary to investigate, returned to her comfort zone on the clip rug in front of the fire.

"Well, it must have been something really important to put you in that state. That's all I've got to say."

"No, it wasn't anything much," I lied, knowing that to me it was the most important event of the year so far.

I decided not to go out again before my father arrived home and we sat round the table for our evening meal. Immediately afterwards, however, I decided to pop round next door and have a chat with my Cousin Raymond. My conversations with him were always interesting and he always seemed to have a lot of time for me even though he was six years older than me. I found him as I often did with his face stuck into a magazine. On this occasion it was entitled WILDLIFE ILLUSTRATED.

"Hello young Neil," he greeted. "You should see some of the photographs and artwork in this magazine. They're absolutely superb. Just look at this full page picture of three lion cubs. The detail and clarity is amazing." He held the appropriate page in front of me and I had to admit that it was really impressive.

"Crikey!" I said. "How did the photographer get close enough to take that?"

"That's why it's regarded as a good picture," he explained, because not many can do that. They aren't all photographs in the magazine though, a lot of them are paintings and you never know, you might even find one of your Auntie Brenda's in a magazine sometime now that she's started going to art classes, that's if she's good enough of course."

"Auntie Brenda's going to art classes?" I repeated, my interest being immediately aroused.

"That's right," she's been going for a few weeks now, though I think she only goes once a week."

"I thought she'd got herself a fancy man," I said. I went on to explain to him about what I had witnessed when I went into town with my mother.

Raymond immediately started laughing. "A fancy man, that's a laugh, that is. No, I don't think I can see your Auntie Brenda doing that."

"She stopped making jam you know and I'd been wondering why ever since. I even thought it might have been because she'd run out of jam jars."

"I suppose now that she's got a new hobby she'll be practising a lot, so she won't have as much time to make jam, will she?" declared Raymond. "It's a pity though, because she does make it very well."

Having now found the answer to why she had been behaving so mysteriously I found myself rather disappointed that it wasn't something more interesting. "So what does she do at these art classes? What will she be painting while she's there? There won't be very much of interest inside a classroom."

"The teacher will probably bring something in for the class to paint. It might be a vase of flowers or a statuette. Sometimes they will paint real people. He might hire a model to pose for them. In fact I have heard that they sometimes hire people who are prepared to pose without any clothes on."

"Crikey, I wonder if Auntie Brenda's had to paint anybody like that."

"Now don't you go spreading any stories," suggested my cousin. "I think it would be very unlikely for that to happen."

So did I, when I thought seriously about it, but Raymond's latter statement had just made the reason for my aunt's behaviour sound that little bit more interesting. By the time I went to bed, however, the single issue that dominated my mind was the probability that Susan would be moving to the coast and that when that day arrived I might never see her again.

CHAPTER TWENTY THREE

During the next few days I noticed that Susan continued to wear the pendant though our relationship did not seem to have developed any further. As far as I knew she had not acquired any particular good fortune, but at least she hadn't complained that her neck had turned green.

On the Friday morning my mother had announced that we would all be going to the Jubilee Working Men's Club in the evening. This would be only the third time that I'd been given the opportunity to accompany them instead of spending most of the evening at my Auntie Molly's next door. I assumed that on this occasion they had decided that what was on offer would be suitable to a child of my age. I delayed mentioning it to Billy until we were walking home after school as I knew that he would be expecting us to go to the Electra, though we had both declared earlier that we didn't really fancy the film that was being shown.

"I thought we might have been going to the Astra or the Royal," he said, disappointment plainly showing on his face.

"I'm sorry, Billy, but there isn't really much I can do about it. If I tell them that I don't want to go, then they'll probably never take me again, and I do want to go, Billy, because It's something that's a bit different, and I know I enjoyed going last time even if it was ages ago. It's not like the children's Christmas party that they have. I always hate that."

"Will we be able to go to the pictures next week then?"

"I think so. They already told me that they wouldn't be able to take me every time, and they don't go every week, anyway. I think they're only taking me tonight because my Auntie Molly won't be able to look after me."

That was the best I could offer him and, although obviously disappointed, he seemed reasonably at ease with my explanation. The truth was that I was keen to visit the club again. It seemed a much more exciting prospect attending at night and it made me feel more grown-up.

"You don't have to have your tea early, do you?" asked my companion.

"No," I replied. "We don't need to be there until half past seven."

"Well, why don't we stay out a bit longer?"

Agreeing to his request was the least I could do. "I'd better see if my mother wants me to go on any errands first," I told him. "Then I'll call round for you."

My mother didn't have any errands for me, but she did tell me to ask if Mr. Senior needed anything bringing as he didn't get out of the house as much as he used to do. As he opened the door the always welcoming smell of tobacco smoke engulfed me.

"Come on in, lad. Come on in," he said. "What can I do for you? Are you wanting to hear another story from the days I was in the Merchant Navy?"

I would have loved to have heard another story but I knew I didn't have time. "No, it's not that today. My mam just wanted to know if you wanted anything bringing from the shop."

"That's very kind of her. As a matter of fact there's only one thing. I didn't get my morning newspaper delivered today. Could you possibly call and let them know. It's the newsagent at the end of Melville Road, do you see? If they've still got a copy left, could you get it for me? I'll give you sixpence and you can keep the change. It's the Daily Express by the way."

I left his house and called round immediately to see Billy.

"We won't be able to do much," he said, "If we have to carry a newspaper round all the time. I'll wait till you get back. Then we can play out."

I had no other option but to agree to his suggestion. I hurried up the street at the side of the Electra, but slowed down when I recognised the two ladies who were walking along Melville Road. They were heading in the opposite direction to the one in which I wanted to go but I followed them anyway and realised that it was possible that Billy might have been a little too hasty in deciding not to accompany me. Their conversation at first was nothing remarkable until they began to discuss church issues.

"I know this new vicar's been at St. Michael's for a few months now, Phyllis," exclaimed the larger of the two ladies, "But he hasn't earned the same respect for me as the previous one."

"I know what you mean, Edna. I remember him telling us at one sermon that when Jesus was born there was no room at the inn and that he had to be born in the stable."

"Well, what was wrong with that, Phyllis?"

"Well, he didn't say why there was no room at the inn, did he? I mean it's obvious, isn't it?"

"I don't see what's obvious about it."

They were now approaching the wrong end of Melville Road, but I wanted to hear the rest of the conversation. I continued to follow them as they turned down Speedwell Street.

"Well, didn't the vicar say that it was the first Christmas of all? Everybody knows you can't get a room at Christmas if you leave it until the last minute. They should have booked in advance."

Edna stopped in her tracks and turned sideways to face her companion, while I hung back. "Phyllis," she said, exasperatedly, "You've come out with some daft things in your life, but that's definitely the daftest."

"Why do you say that, Edna? He did say it was the first Christmas of all, didn't he?"

"I know he did, Phyllis. I know he did, but this was nearly two thousand years ago. It wouldn't have been any good looking for a phone box, would it, because the telephone hadn't even been invented, so perhaps you might be able to tell me how they could let the landlord of the inn know that they would be coming."

"Ooh sorry, Edna. I never thought of that."

"It's not only that anyway, Phyllis. I mean, Joseph wouldn't have had any way of knowing that the baby was going to be born on Christmas Day, would he? It could just as easily have been a couple of days later."

They set off walking again and, as I didn't think I would hear anything else worthwhile by following them, I decided to retrace my steps, realising that Billy had missed out on a very absorbing few minutes.

I acquired Mr. Senior's Daily Express and bought a comic for myself with the change. After I had given him the newspaper and been entertained with another of his sea stories, I realised that I didn't have time pay Billy a visit and went straight home.

We arrived at the Jubilee Working Men's Club just after seven o'clock and the first thing I noticed as we walked through the door was the cigarette smoke. It contaminated the entire room. Everything was as I remembered from the few other occasions that I had been allowed to accompany my parents. There was quite a wide stage, tables arranged in a haphazard fashion, each to accommodate four persons and a bar running almost the length of one of the walls. By far the most noticeable thing though was the noise. Even though the room was as yet only half full the sound was deafening despite the fact that nothing, at that particular moment, was happening on the stage. It was the sheer volume of everyone talking at once that was assaulting my eardrums. The room was occupied almost entirely by adults but I did spot a few children scattered here and there among them. The only one that I recognised was Ken Stacey, probably because he was head and shoulders higher than the others. However, as he was at the far side of the room, I had no chance of communicating with him for the time being.

My mother and I seated ourselves at one of the tables while my father walked to the bar. In fact every family that entered the club seemed to split up in this fashion. It was a ritual that had over the years become routine. The clubbers rarely seemed to vary the type of drink they would be supping, so the husband of each family didn't bother to ask any more. In our case my father would be bringing back a glass of Mackeson for my mother and a pint of Tetley's for himself. I hadn't been on many occasions but I knew he would be returning with a glass of lemonade.

"Who's going on the stage, dad?" I asked him after he arrived back from the bar. All I knew was that it would have to be an act that he considered suitable for me to watch.

"I think it's someone playing some sort of musical instrument," he replied, "But it won't be on until after they've done the Bingo. I've bought you a ticket at the bar so you can play along with us if you like."

"I thought children weren't allowed to play," said my mother. "It's encouraging them to gamble."

"I don't see any real harm in it. If he wins we'll just swap the card over and we can treat him afterwards."

That seemed a reasonable solution to me.

My father turned towards me and said "Don't get too excited, son. It's not going to be a hundred pounds, you know. Anyway, with all these players in the room it's very unlikely that you'll win anything at all."

My father's words were spot on. Four games were played and I never came close. I decided there and then that it was a stupid game, someone just calling numbers out while someone else marked them down on a card. There was no skill in the game whatsoever. Neither of my parents won anything either and I was glad when the whole thing came to an end.

Before the entertainment was due to be announced and while my father was at the bar ordering more drinks a woman approached us and it soon became obvious that she was known to my mother.

"Hello May," said the newcomer as she leaned across the table. "It's quite a while since I've seen you in here."

"Hello Kathleen," she replied. "It has been a week or two. Isn't Phil with you?"

"Yes, we've just come in, he's at the bar. Look he's talking to your Tom. He doesn't like playing Bingo, so we waited until it had finished."

I looked across at the bar and saw them engaged in conversation. Kathleen's husband looked vaguely familiar but I couldn't remember where I'd seen him before, so I decided I must be mistaken.

"Well," said my mother, "If you haven't found a seat yet why don't you come and join us? Neil, go and find another chair."

I did what she asked, which wasn't too difficult as there was a row of unused chairs at the wall opposite the bar. As the lady's husband turned round she indicated for him to come in our direction. Within minutes all five of us were seated at the table. Before a conversation could be started the announcer arrived on the stage.

"I'd like to introduce you," he began, "To someone who has kindly stepped in at the last minute to cover for the scheduled turn who has badly let us down. So please put your hands together for Mr. Arthur Atkins who is going to entertain you on the harmonica."

I stared hard as the new arrival approached from behind the curtain. "I know him, dad," I said, eagerly, but Arthur Atkins isn't his real name. His real name is Walter Zimmerman."

I explained to them about our encounter with him on Woodhouse Ridge a few weeks previously and how he was desperate to change his name.

He entertained us on the harmonica for about fifteen minutes and his efforts were well appreciated by the good-natured crowd. "He's going to do some comic patter now," I told them, revelling in the fact that I knew a little more than they did.

"Thank you very much," said the entertainer after the applause had died down. "Before continuing to play a few more popular tunes of the day I would like to share with you a few observations."

I eagerly waited for him to continue.

"This farmer was so good at his job that you could say he was outstanding in his own field, until it rained of course, and then he had to go back inside."

This statement was greeted by howls of laughter by everyone who was paying attention, including myself.

"This Scotsman married an Indian squaw. His wife said that she would like their first born son to be called Hawkeye out of respect to the Indian culture. Her husband wasn't too happy about this. Being Scottish he thought that the child's name should be representative of both cultures. So they compromised and decided to call him Hawkeye The Noo."

This one received even greater applause than the first. Even those who had earlier been deep in conversation stopped to listen and I couldn't help being impressed by his polished routine. He continued in a similar vein for a further few minutes. He then completed his act with some more harmonica playing.

We were now able to focus our attention on the couple who had recently joined us.

"I understand that you might be moving away soon, Phil," said my father.

"Aye, that's right, Tom, but I'm afraid our lass isn't so keen on the idea. That's so, isn't it, Kath?"

"It certainly is. She says that she doesn't want to lose all her school friends."

"Well, I suppose I can understand that, but you'll be moving a lot nearer to the coast, won't you? So I'm sure she'll come round."

It was obvious to me that they were referring to Susan and I realised that I had met her father when I went to the Astra cinema with my grandad. I became even more uncomfortable, however, with the next statement.

"The other day," said Susan's father, "She came home with a pendant round her neck. I asked her where she'd got it from but she just blushed and I couldn't get her to say any more. Maybe it's not just her school friends that she's bothered about missing. I reckon she's got herself a boyfriend and she's keeping quiet about it."

"Well I don't see anything wrong in it," said her mother. "I was very much like that when I was her age. I liked a particular boy at school, but I would have been too embarrassed to tell my parents about it."

It was at this point that I decided to go to the lavatory in the hope that the conversation would have moved on to something else by the time I got back. As I emerged from the Gent's I saw another way to delay my return to the table even further. Standing at the bar was the very person who had been entertaining us earlier. I decided to approach him. The only problem was that I wasn't sure what to call him. I took a chance.

"Hello Mr. Zimmerman," I said, "Or is it Mr. Atkins now?"

I could see straight away that he recognised me.

"Hello lad," he replied while lowering his voice at the same time. "I remember you. We had an interesting conversation on Woodhouse Ridge when you were with two other lads, didn't we?"

"That's right, so you managed to change your name then, did you?" The first time we had seen him he was extremely concerned that his name began with the letter 'Z' and told us a long story about the unfairness of a system which always seemed to favour those who had surnames beginning with a letter near the beginning of the alphabet.

"Well lad, not legally I'm afraid; but I discovered that anyone is entitled to have a stage name without the expense of a deed poll. The only condition is that you can't select a name that is used by someone else who is on the stage. I couldn't call myself Arthur Askey, for instance, because he's a well-known figure on the radio, but nobody on the stage seemed to be using the name Arthur Atkins, so I decided to choose that, and so far it's working quite well. In all other walks of life though I'll still be poor old Walter Zimmerman, but I've decided not to let it bother me as much as it used to, and I 'd like to thank you and your two friends for helping me out when you did."

I left him looking a lot more cheerful than on the two previous occasions that I had met him and returned to the table hoping that the previous topic of conversation had come to a conclusion. Unfortunately, my hopes were soon to be dashed.

"Ah, here he is now," said my father. "Mr. Brown was wondering, seeing that you are in the same class as their Susan, whether you might have seen anyone giving her a pendant."

I thought hard while trying at the same time not to look guilty. Would I be lying if I said that I hadn't seen anyone giving her a pendant? As I had given it to her myself I decided that it wouldn't be quite the same thing as seeing someone else give it to her. If Susan hadn't wanted her parents to know then there was no way that I was going to tell them.

"No, Mr. Brown, I never saw anyone hand it to her," I told him with as straight a face as I could manage.

We watched Arthur Atkins, alias Walter Zimmerman, entertain us with another performance before my father decided that we should head for home. Susan's parents decided to stay behind for a while longer, which I was pleased about as I didn't fancy being subjected to any more questions. I was just glad that, on this particular occasion that they hadn't brought her along with them.

CHAPTER TWENTYFOUR

Saturday was warm and sunny and I just couldn't wait to escape the confines of the house. Before I had time to finish breakfast, however, Billy was already knocking at the door. I assumed the same spirit of adventure was also in his thoughts. My mother insisted though that I would have to finish eating in what she termed a digni- fied and leisurely manner before being allowed to venture outside. I knew she would be catching the tram into town during the morning but as always on these occasions I knew that she would be back by dinnertime. My Auntie Molly, who lived next door, was the person she relied on to make sure that I behaved in what she classified as a sensible manner and didn't indulge in anything that would cause problems for any of our neighbours. I always did my best to adhere to my moth- er's demands and before long Billy and I were enjoying the freedom of the street.

"Do you know what I fancy doing today, Neil?" asked my companion. "I was thinking about it when I went to bed last night."

"What's that, Billy?"

"I want to walk along the Dammy in the other direction. We've never done it properly, have we?"

I knew what he meant. We always walked along the more scenic path at the bottom of Sugarwell Hill. On the other side of Buslingthorpe Lane the path at the side of the beck was a concrete one and the water seemed a great deal murkier which didn't make it ideal for either of the two pastimes we usually engaged in whenever we were in the area which were paddling or fishing for sticklebacks or other fish small enough to be caught in the sort of makeshift nets that were all that the local lads possessed. The beck totally lost its green environment as it meandered close to or under the streets of Woodhouse and Sheepscar before reaching the city centre and entering the river Aire.

Eventually, we found ourselves walking under the bridge and entering the more confined and much less pleasing environment but this was, we told ourselves, much more adventurous as just about anything could be lurking in the murky surroundings. With just a brick wall for company we continued our journey. The sun, having given way to shadow, made the atmosphere seem rather oppressive. Even the water in the beck was losing its sparkle. We were now entering the land of factories and back yards and we had not seen another soul.

"It's starting to pong a bit here, isn't it, Neil?" suggested Billy.

I didn't need to take a sniff to agree with his statement. It was a smell of dampness mixed with decaying matter. This was about as far as we had ever travelled in this direction and on that occasion it had begun to get dark which had prompted us to turn back. This time, however, we were both eager to continue.

"Look Billy," I said as we rounded a bend, "I think this is at the back of the leather factory where my dad works."

"Is he working there now?"

"Yes, he finishes at twelve o'clock, but he'll be working inside. I don't think he's likely to come into the yard. In fact I hope he doesn't. I don't think he would like me being on this part of the Dammy, especially with all these smells."

Fortunately, my supposition that my father would not make an appearance proved to be correct and we let the adventure continue. We seemed now to be in the Sheepscar area but the depressing nature of our surroundings remained unchanged. If anything the stench emanating from the beck had become even more obnoxious.

"I'm beginning to wish we hadn't come," said my companion, holding his nose. "I don't think I can stand much more of this."

As we rounded yet another bend we found ourselves at the back of a building with scaffolding around it.

"Oy," you two lads down there," said a gruff voice. "Come over here a minute, will you?"

We both looked up to see two men leaning over the rail of the top row of scaffolding before doing as they had asked.

"We know these two, don't we Gerry?" said one of the two men. "Aren't these the two lads that brought us some fish and chips when we were working on that last job?"

"Well, blow me, Alf," said the other man as he peered down at us. "I think you're right."

"You were mending the roof at the Electra," I shouted up, "And you wanted us to take a note to someone that worked there called Andrea, and you gave us some money for doing it."

"That's right," said the one called Gerry, smiling down at us. "I like these two lads, Alf I really do."

"Are you wanting us to take another message?" asked Billy because that fish and chip shop's a long way from here."

"Well, that's the situation exactly," he went on, "But it's not the fish and chip shop that I want you to take the message to. It's a different shop altogether."

"Is Andrea working somewhere else now then?" I asked him.

"Not as far as I know lad; no, this message is for somebody else. I think, if I remember rightly, I gave you sixpence each the last time. Well, I suppose it's only fair that you might have upped your rate by now, so I'll tell you what I'll do. If you deliver this message for me and bring back a reply there'll be ninepence each for you. Now, I can't say fairer than that, can I?"

Both Billy and I were only too eager to earn a bit of money for what we expected would be so simple a task and we both agreed to his terms.

"What shop is it, mister?" I asked him.

"It's called Jackson's and it's on the bottom end of North Street, but on the opposite side of the road to the Golden Cross Pub. The girl's name is Becky and I want you to hand it to her personally, do you understand?"

"You mean like we did to Andrea at the fish and chip shop." I said

"Yes, that's exactly what I mean," he replied while breaking into a laugh.

"I keep telling you Gerry. You'll get yourself into real bother one of these days," observed his companion.

"Aw, lay off, Alf, will you? You say that ever time." As his companion walked back along the scaffolding the one called Gerry addressed his next remarks to Billy and me. "Now, the message is in this envelope," he said, throwing it down to us; and don't forget that if you want to collect your money I expect you to bring me a reply. Now, the sooner you get yourselves off, lads the sooner you'll be back."

"What sort of shop is it, mister," I shouted, but he didn't hear as he had already retreated. However, one of the other workmen on the lower scaffolding who had obviously heard most of what had taken place called across to us.

"If I know Gerry," he said, "The type of shop you'll be looking for is a knocking shop."

"What's a knocking shop?" I asked. "Is it where they sell door knockers?"

He gave a hearty laugh. "Aye lad," he said. "You've hit the nail right on the head there. That's exactly what they sell and a lot more besides." He laughed again. "Door knockers, that's a good one that is."

"How do we get into North Street from here?" asked Billy.

"Come through the yard, lads. I'll open the gate for you."

We emerged into Sheepscar Street close to where it joined Chapeltown Road. From there we could see that it was just a short walk to the traffic lights where North Street joined Meanwood Road at the Golden Cross.

"I don't know many people in Woodhouse who have door knockers," said my companion. "Surely they must sell something else as well, Neil."

"Well, that's what the man said, isn't it? He said that they sold a lot of other things besides. Whatever else they sell they must specialise in door knockers, otherwise there wouldn't be any point in calling it a knocking shop, would there?"

We were just approaching the end of Meanwood Road when we noticed a woman crossing the road by the traffic lights.

"Excuse me, Mrs," said Billy as, as she approached. "Could you tell us where the knocking shop is in North Street?"

The lady gave an audible gasp and put her hand to her mouth. "I think you need to wash out your mouth with soap and water, young man" she admonished, gazing down at my companion with a frosty glare, before hurrying along the street.

"Why did she say that?" he muttered, dejectedly. "It's not as if I'd sworn or anything, is it?"

"I've no idea, Billy. I'm as surprised as you are."

We crossed over to the far side of North Street and began walking in the direction of the town centre. We located the shop almost immediately, though it looked nothing like what we had been led to believe. The name JACKSON'S above the window told us it had to be the right place.

"Oh, no," said Billy. "It's a woman's clothing shop. I don't want to go in there."

The window display, apart from such things as knitwear, also included several undergarments.

"Neither do I, Billy, but we haven't got much choice if we want to go back home with ninepence each."

"I wonder where they keep the door knockers," he said.

When we entered the shop we could see that they did also sell a few household items but not the type that we expected to see. As neither of us wanted to return home empty-handed we realised that there was no point in delaying the inevitable and stepped inside to discover that we were the only potential customers.

The middle-aged lady peered down at us over the counter. "Now, what can I do for you two lads? Are you looking for something nice and slinky for your girl friends?"

I immediately felt the blood rushing to my cheeks, and Billy seemed to be having the same problem.

"No," he said, "We haven't got girl friends; well, I haven't anyway, but Neil does."

"So, what sort of thing are you looking for?" asked the proprietor, turning towards me. Is it underwear that you want? I think you're probably a bit young to be buying that."

"We're not looking for anything, really," I said, desperate to change the way the conversation was heading and desperate to get out of the place as soon as our task had been performed. "We've just come to deliver a message for someone called Becky."

"I see," she said. "Just wait hear a minute, will you?" She disappeared behind a curtain into the back room.

"Why did you have to tell her that I had a girl friend, Billy? That was really embarrassing."

Before he had time to reply a younger lady appeared from behind the curtain.

"I'm Becky," she announced in a pleasant voice. "Were you asking for me?"

"Yes miss," said Billy. "We were told to give you this note." He handed the envelope to her.

"It's from someone called Gerry," I added, "And he wants us to take him a reply. He's working on a building site."

She opened the envelope and read the brief note. "I see," she said, after placing it back in the envelope. "Well, it's very good of you to bring it to me. If you'll just wait a few minutes I'll write something for you to take back to him."

We looked around that part of the shop that contained a few household and kitchen items but could see no sign of any door knockers. Two or three minutes later she produced a second envelope and handed it to us.

"There you are," she said. "I'd be very obliged if you'd take this reply back to him, and I think it's only fair that I give you sixpence each for your trouble." She took out her purse and handed us two silver coins. Neither of us had anticipated this new development, but we were extremely pleased that the morning was turning out to be quite a profitable one. Before leaving though there was one question I needed to know.

"Why can't we see your knockers, miss?" I asked.

She glared down at me. "What did you just say, young man?"

"He wanted to know where you kept your knockers," said Billy.

"They're covered up, of course. Where else would they be?" I can tell that you've been talking to Gerry because you sound just like him."

"Why don't you get them out when there are people in the shop?" I persisted. "Otherwise nobody will know what they look like, will they?"

"You two are going to be terrible men when you grow up. Now, I think you'd both better be on your way before I decide to take those sixpences back."

We needed no more encouragement to leave despite being rather puzzled by her attitude.

"How do they expect to sell any door knockers if they don't put them on display?" asked my companion.

"It beats me Billy. I mean aren't they supposed to specialise in them, or what?"

We soon forgot about what had occurred in the shop and concentrated on the fact that we would soon be on our way home with each of us being one shilling and threepence better off than when we had left. When we arrived at the yard Gerry and several of the other workers on the building site were sitting on the lower scaffolding with their legs dangling over the side and eating their lunch. I suddenly realised that I was supposed to be back home by dinnertime.

"Did you manage to collect a message from Becky?" asked Gerry.

We handed over the envelope, which he immediately opened and proceeded to read the contents.

"Don't forget to give the lads the money you promised them," urged one of his companions.

"Don't panic Ted," he replied. "I was just about to. In fact I'm so pleased with what she's written I think they deserve a shilling each for their trouble."

"Gee, thanks mister," responded Billy as he was handed a shilling piece.

"Could you tell me what time it is, please?" I asked him as he made the same gesture to me.

"Well, I make it ten minutes to twelve. Why, what's the hurry? Do you have somewhere urgent to go?"

"I told my mam I'd be back home by dinnertime, that's why."

"Well, better get off home then. There's no point getting yourself into trouble. I know what mothers can be like when they've been crossed."

"Where are you working next, mister?" I asked him.

"I don't know yet, lad," he said, laughing, "But maybe we'll see you again then, eh"

"We've got enough money to go back on the tram, Billy, if you want to."

"No, let's go back the same way we came," he replied. "I don't want to spend even a penny on tram fares. I think you've got plenty of time left to get back before your mother starts worrying."

We began to retrace our steps and soon passed the back of the building where my father worked. I listened intently for the sound of a hooter which my father had told me always indicated the end of the shift, but all was silent.

We continued on our way for several minutes before Billy took hold of my arm and stopped me.

"Look, Neil," he said, "What's that in the water?"

I looked to where he was pointing. "I'm not sure, Billy. It looks like a wooden box of some sort, but if it's floating there can't really be anything in it, can there otherwise it would sink?"

"I'm not sure about that, Neil. I mean it might have something quite light inside it. They could be bank notes or something like that. Maybe somebody robbed that bank at the end of Meanwood Road and had to throw away the evidence because the police were chasing him."

It was obvious that Billy's imagination was running riot again.

"That doesn't make any sense, Billy. What's the point in robbing a bank and then throwing the money away?"

"Well, it's because it's better than going to prison; that's why. Anyway, I'm going to see if I can reach it."

As we stood right on the edge of the concrete path the smell coming from the beck was overpowering.

"How are you going to reach it, Billy? You don't want to be paddling in there. The water's filthy."

"Look, there's a metal pole in that yard. I bet I can pull it nearer with that."

He walked into the deserted yard and returned with the said object. The level of the water was about eighteen inches below the path. Billy walked back to the edge and leaned over as far as he could. The pole just reached the edge of the box but in trying to pull it nearer to the bank he leaned over just a little too far and did a lovely belly flop into the murky water. I began to laugh as he started to fall, a laugh which abruptly ended as the foul contents of the beck splashed all over me. Fortunately for Billy the water was no more than three feet deep and he quickly climbed back onto the bank, but the stench was almost unbearable. The state I was in was bad enough and I knew I would have a lot of explaining to do when I faced my mother, but his situation was much worse.

"Cor, Billy," I said while holding my nose, "You stink something rotten."

Whether he was unaware of the likely consequences he would have to face when he arrived home I had no idea, but his only concern seemed to be the wooden box which he was proudly holding in front of him.

"I managed to get the box though," he beamed. "If there's money in it from a bank robbery we could get a reward from the police."

I thought that Billy's supposition regarding its contents was very unlikely, but I had to admit to a growing desire to see what it contained.

"I can't see any way to open it, Billy," I observed.

Undeterred, he went back into the yard and returned with a heavy stone. "This should smash it," he declared triumphantly.

"What if there's something inside that's breakable?" I asked.

"I think if there was it would have to have been heavy enough to sink, don't you?"

I realised that he was right and watched as he dropped the stone onto the box. It had the desired effect but we were totally unprepared for the overwhelming stench that again assaulted our nostrils. What it contained was rotting fish that, by the look of it, had probably been floating around for weeks.

"Cor, it stinks horrible," said Billy as he gave an almighty kick to send the offending article back where it came from. On this occasion we were pleased to note, it sank to the bottom.

We both decided that we had had more than enough adventure for one day and couldn't wait to reach the comfort of home. The only problem, however, was the explaining we would have to do because of the state we were in and Billy's problem was even bigger than mine.

When I entered the house my mother was in the other room, but before I had the chance to try to make myself look a little more presentable, if indeed that were possible, Nell walked over to me, sniffed at my clothes and with a look of disgust began to bark, thus fulfilling what she considered to be her duty in alerting my mother to the fact that some abominable apparition had invaded their space. I had to explain to her in the best way that I could how I had got into that state but her reaction was not as bad as it could have been.

"Get yourself upstairs," she snapped, "And get out of those disgusting things. Your father will be here any minute."

I was grateful that she had given me the opportunity to get changed before he arrived. I didn't go round to see how Billy had fared and as it rained after dinner I didn't see him again for the remainder of the day. When I went to bed I decided that I would stick to the scenic part of the Dammy in future

CHAPTER TWENTYFIVE

"There's a match on at Bus Vale this afternoon, May," said my father. "If you fancy going we can take Neil as well."

"I thought that tournament was on next month," replied my mother.

Every May a competition was organised at the Buslingthorpe Vale rugby ground in Meanwood Road involving local pub and factory teams in the area and we usually attended.

"It is next month," responded my father, "But this is a friendly game between our shop and a factory in Sheepscar Street."

My father used to play rugby on a regular basis until he had a cartilage accident just before I was born.

"It starts at three o'clock," he went on. "So we'll have to leave about half an hour before then."

My mother agreed to his suggestion which prompted a question from me. "Why don't we take Nell with us?" I asked. "We could let her have a run on Woodhouse Ridge before we got to the ground."

"What do you think, May?" he asked.

Nell put her head to one side and gazed up at my mother with the most pleading expression that she could muster.

"Oh, I'm not so sure, Tom. She caused quite a few problems when we took her to Roundhay Park, didn't she?"

"I don't think any of that was really her fault," I chipped in, "Apart from when she chased the geese and then she was only being playful. Don't forget how she managed to get all those people out of the maze. I don't really think she'll be any problem. Anyway, I'll look after her."

The object of the discussion walked over to me and licked my hand.

"All right then, we'll all go," decided my father, "But you'd better keep your promise and make sure that she doesn't get into any mischief."

I wasn't quite sure that I would be able to do that but I had no alternative but to accept his terms. We had just completed breakfast and I knew that the first thing I would have to do would be to call on Billy in case he had any plans that would have involved the two of us in the afternoon. When I knocked on the door he looked very forlorn as he opened it and stepped outside.

"What's the matter, Billy?" I asked him. "You don't look very happy."

"My mam was so annoyed when she saw the state I was in when I came home yesterday that she told me that I wouldn't be allowed to play out today," he replied.

"That's not fair, Billy. Look, the sun's shining and it's quite warm."

"I can't help it, Neil, and it's much worse than that she's insisting that I have to go to Sunday school today."

"Aw. That's rotten, Billy. I'm glad it's not me." It was only recently that my mother had become less insistent that I went. "I can't see much point in going there because we already have bible lessons in ordinary school."

"I was hoping you might come with me, Neil. I think she's only making me go as a punishment for getting my clothes dirty yesterday, so I don't think it will be every week."

"I don't want to go down there, Billy. It's dead boring. Hardly anybody from our class at school still goes."

I felt really sorry for him and as soon as I had made the remark I considered whether it would be really that bad if I just accompanied him for the one day.

"Aw, please Neil," he pleaded. "It'll be ten times worse if I have to go on my own."

I pondered the situation again before giving him my answer.

"I'll come on condition that it's only once and I don't want my mother to know that I've been. Otherwise she might want me to keep going."

"I promise I won't tell her anything. You can just let her think that we've been playing out. It starts at two o'clock."

I suddenly realised that I had the perfect get-out. "I won't be able to go, Billy. It always used to be in the morning and we're going out this afternoon. Why did they change the time?"

My closest friend looked thoroughly dejected. "I think they changed the time because a lot of people go to church during the morning."

"I'm sorry, Billy," was the best comment I could come up with. "We'll just have to hope that it's just the one time."

So I had no option but to find my own amusements up to the time that we had to leave. The weather remained fine, though perhaps a little cooler than an hour or two earlier as we descended the steps onto Woodhouse Ridge with me holding Nell on the lead. In her mind whenever we reached any terrain that was more interesting than the boring cobbled streets of Woodhouse it was time for her to be allowed to run free and to enjoy the diverse sights and smells that she only experienced occasionally. My father, however, had made it quite clear that I had to take responsibility for her and ensure that she did not get herself into the sort of mischief that she had indulged in at Roundhay Park a few weeks earlier. At least she was unlikely to encounter any geese in our current environment.

"Is it all right if I let Nell off the lead now, dad?" I asked him.

"Aye, lad, I suppose so," he grudgingly acknowledged, "But keep your eyes on her and if she looks like she's about to disappear then call her back."

The minute I unhooked her from the lead she ran along the path for about fifty or so yards before sitting down and berating us for being such slowcoaches.

"Do you think we've done right, Tom, bringing Nell with us?" suggested my mother. "We might have quite a bit of trouble hanging onto her once the game starts, especially if there are other dogs about."

"Well, there's not a lot we can do about it now is there, short of taking her back home?" replied my father. "We'll have to put her back on the lead before we go onto Grove Lane anyway, so let's see if we can tire her out a bit before then. Can't you find something to throw for her?" he asked, addressing his latter remarks to me.

"I can probably find a stick," I told him, "But what's the point? You know she never drops it even if she brings it back to you."

Nell had never cottoned on to the fact that there was a standard set of rules to this particular game and found it much more enjoyable to invent her own, part of the enjoyment no doubt being the look of frustration on the faces of the other participants.

"Well, just make sure that she doesn't disappear from sight," he said.

We continued our journey while I kept Nell in view as best I could. The only time she showed any inclination to wander off was when we were passing the area of dense vegetation known locally as Death Valley. She suddenly darted quickly to the left and I raced after her finding her at the foot of a tree barking furiously at an unconcerned squirrel sitting nonchalantly on a branch tucking into an acorn. She rather surprisingly came to me when I called. It was as though she was embarrassed by the fact that I had witnessed how ineffective she had been while attempting to demonstrate her imagined power over the local woodland creatures.

When we arrived at the spot where Billy and I had experienced our embarrassing encounter with Peggy Wiggins my father decided that it was time to regain control of our canine companion as we were about to leave the green environment of Woodhouse Ridge and enter Grove Lane, which was a busy bus route. From there it was a short walk to the Melbourne Arms before turning right onto Meanwood Road and then turning right again onto a ginnel which took us onto Buslingthorpe Vale Rugby League ground.

It wasn't a massive crowd that was gathered there, perhaps a hundred and fifty to two hundred would-be spectators, but I could see that Nell could sense that, in her eyes, something exciting was about to take place.

"Look, there's Phil and Kath over there, May," observed my father, "You know, the ones we were talking to at the club on Friday and if I'm not mistaken they've brought their daughter with them this time. She goes to your school, Neil so you might have someone to chat to if we make our way over there."

I immediately looked in the direction he was pointing at the far side of the pitch and immediately spotted Susan, though I knew that she and her parents hadn't noticed us yet. Before we had time to move, however, the two teams that were about to engage each other ran onto the pitch.

"Come on, Harry," shouted my father, immediately forgetting his earlier comment and concentrating on the event that was about to take place.

"Which one is Harry, dad?" I asked him.

"Why, he's the one leading the team onto the field, the ones in the red and black shirts. Harry Bassett is the captain of Tommy Wright's, which is the factory I work for."

"Don't you wish you were still playing, dad?"

"Not really, lad. I'm much too old for it now even if I hadn't had that cartilage operation. No, leave it for the younger ones, I say."

The crowd was starting to build up and there was plenty of shouting when the match began and Nell barked excitedly whenever the ball came anywhere near her. If we hadn't kept her on the lead I'm sure she would have joined in immediately.

"Hello, Tommy, love." said two attractive young ladies who had suddenly appeared at the side of my father. "Is this lady your wife then?"

My mother glared at them. The only people who I heard refer to him as Tommy, rather than Tom, were my Grandma Cawson and a couple of aunties.

"These two ladies are Rita and Stephanie." He explained to her. "They both work in the office."

The pair to whom he was referring had by this time disappeared into the crowd, giggling as they went.

"They seem to know you pretty well," said my mother, still looking a little annoyed.

"I don't see them very often, love," explained my father. "They rarely come out of the office. They're just two silly little girls really."

"They don't look very much like little girls to me."

"Who's that fat one that's playing on your side, dad? He doesn't look much like a rugby player to me."

It was a fairly reasonable statement to make, but my only purpose in making it was to defuse what promised to develop into a full blown argument.

"That's Jimmy Boyd, son," he said, grateful for a change to the way the conversation had been progressing. "Aye, he has put quite a bit of weight on lately and he doesn't do a great deal of running, but if you're ever tackled by him then you certainly know about it."

My father's words were soon to be validated as one of the players from the opposing team was running towards the try line when, in trying to avoid a tackle, he swerved and immediately ran straight into the person who we had just been discussing. He just sort of bounced off him and fell to the floor.

"There you are," uttered my father, "That's just what I was telling you about."

The game was halted temporarily as it took the lad from the opposing side a couple of minutes to get back to his feet. The game eventually restarted with a scrum down as he had been over the touch line when he fell.

By the time the whistle sounded to indicate the end of the first half Tommy Wright's Leather Factory were leading by ten points to eight which pleased my father no end. Even my mother had got lost in the excitement of the game and her earlier displeasure had been pushed to the back of her mind, though I suspected it might re-appear when we got back home.

"Shall we walk round to the other side of the pitch, May, and have a word with Phil and Kath before the second half starts?" asked my father.

"Yes, we can if you like. We don't really know anyone to chat to round this side, do we?" she replied, before adding, with a different tone to her voice, "Well, at least I don't anyway."

He chose to ignore the rather barbed second sentence and we began to make our way through the crowd. I was feeling quite excited at the possibility of coming face to face with Susan in surroundings other than the school classroom. Before we could reach our destination, however, we got ourselves boxed in where there was a particularly dense section of the crowd and, to make matters worse, Nell chose that particular moment to tug on the lead causing it to come loose from my hand.

"Where has she gone, Tom?" shouted my mother in a panic. "We'll never find her again in this crowd."

"Don't worry too much, love," he responded. Somebody's bound to stand on the lead, that's if she doesn't trip someone up first."

"I'll go see if I can find her, dad?" I told him.

"No, don't do that. If you disappear we'll have to come looking for you as well."

Although I heard his words they were to no avail as I was already out of his sight. I pushed through the crowd in the best way that I could, shouting Nell's name as I went. I thought I heard a faint bark but I couldn't be too sure as a cheer went up at the same time announcing the re-emergence of the two teams onto the pitch. Anyway, if it was a bark that I had heard I was quite unable to detect where it was coming from. I also heard my father shouting for me to come back. I was reluctant, however, to lose Nell. Within seconds a much louder cheer went up along with a lot of laughter.

"Look, there's a dog on the pitch," shouted someone close by. My canine companion had obviously decided that any hazard that she might face on the battlefield was less of an ordeal than the ones that she faced if she remained where she was.

I somehow managed to force my way to the front of the crowd just in time to see Nell avoid several tackles as she raced across the pitch with the lead still attached to her neck. The referee had already blown his whistle to halt play, but it was obvious that the spectators were enjoying every minute of the enforced interlude. Each failed attempt to apprehend the offender was greeted by an enormous cheer. I spotted Susan just opposite from where I was observing the proceedings and it was obvious from the expression on her face that she was finding the unscheduled entertainment hilarious, though she still seemed to be unaware of my presence.

Nell's adventure was eventually brought to a close when she attempted to evade the clutches of that same Jimmy Boyd that my father had been extolling the virtues of earlier. He planted his foot firmly on the dangling lead which not only stopped her in her tracks but also pulled her off her feet. My father immediately dashed onto the field of play and took her back into the crowd where my mother checked her over to make sure she was all right. By this time I had rejoined them.

We gave up all thoughts of joining Susan's parents on the other side of the ground and settled down to watch the remainder of the game. I wondered whether they would be returning home by tram or whether they would be walking back along the ridge. As they didn't have a dog in tow I assumed it would be the former. The second half did not provide many scoring attempts and my father's side eventually ran out winners by a score of sixteen points to thirteen.

We followed the crowd back along the ginnel into Meanwood Road. "Let's get the tram home, Tom," suggested my mother, rather forcefully. "My feet are hurting too much to walk back along the ridge."

"I was just going to suggest the same thing," he replied, "But we'll have to walk as far as the terminus to be sure of getting on. The tram stop outside the Melbourne will be heaving with people, what with everybody leaving at the same time."

My father's comment made perfect sense as we had been near the back of the crowd when everyone had made the rush to the exit. When we emerged into Meanwood Road it became obvious that not all of those in the queue would be able to get on board when the tram arrived. At least at the terminus all the seats both upstairs and downstairs would be unoccupied.

It took us five minutes to reach our destination and we were fortunate to see that our intended transport had already arrived but it was obvious that several other people had the same idea as a sizeable queue had already formed. That did not worry me, however, because part of it included Susan along with her mother and father. We were unable to speak to them, however, until we were all seated on the tram. My father decided that Nell would be less trouble if we went upstairs as it was obvious that by the time we reached the stop outside the Melbourne there would be passengers standing in the aisle downstairs. He was no doubt thinking of the havoc she had caused on the journey to Roundhay Park earlier. As soon as we had been recognised, my parents and Mr. And Mrs. Brown sat opposite each other so they could have a chat and it was suggested that Susan and I sit together on the front seats. They couldn't have known just how much I welcomed that suggestion and I hoped that she felt the same way.

"Are you and your family still moving to Hull, Susan?"

"They haven't said anything different to me, Neil," she replied, "But I get the impression lately that my mother's not too happy about leaving either, but my brother Peter is all for it."

"Nothing will be the same if you go. I might never see you again. I was hoping that pendant might make them change their minds. Are you still wearing it?"

"Yes, but I'm not sure I believe all that stuff about leprechauns and magical powers. The thing is, my dad is still very keen to go."

The short journey to our destination outside the Primrose Public House was over all too quickly. Nell, I was pleased to notice, behaved impeccably and gratefully accepted all the pets and strokes that came her way. I didn't speak a great deal to Susan as we made our way back home as I don't think either of us wanted to draw attention to the fact that we might be any other than casual school friends. When we arrived I immediately dashed round to see how Billy had got on at his enforced Sunday school attendance.

"It wasn't as bad as I expected Neil, but it was still a bit boring. Anyway, It'll be Whit Sunday next week so I'm pretty sure I won't be asked to go."

I knew what he meant. He would be expected to visit just about every relative in the vicinity to show off his new clothes and I knew that exactly the same ordeal would be forced onto me.

"There's one thing though, Neil," he continued. "I was told that the Boy Scout group will be recruiting at the first meeting after Whitsuntide."

At least that was one thing to cheer me up as I lay in bed that night, but it didn't prevent my mind from being dominated by the thought that Susan Brown would almost certainly be leaving our school forever and going to live about fifty miles away.

CHAPTER TWENTYSIX

It was Wednesday before I received the news that I was expecting but didn't want to hear.

"I'm afraid that Susan Brown will be leaving us at the end of the week when we break up for the half-term holiday at Whitsuntide," announced the headmaster during the morning assembly. "So I am sure all of us here would like to wish her the very best when she goes to her new school in Hull."

No one seemed surprised by his announcement, especially me, but I had certainly been hopeful of a different outcome and now it all seemed so final. I managed to speak to Susan during the mid-morning break and she confirmed everything that had been said.

"There's nothing I can do about it, Neil," she said. "It's all been confirmed and my dad will be accepting the new job at the end of the week. We will then be moving over to Hull and looking for a new place to stay while we live in digs. We will still have relatives in Woodhouse though, so we will have to keep coming back for visits."

So it seemed that that was the best I could look forward to.

During the remainder of the school day I have to confess to having little or no interest in the things I was being taught. I was imagining what it would be like sitting in the classroom day after day with the one girl that I had any real feelings for being absent for the whole time. I didn't speak to Susan again before I found myself walking home with Billy. His attempts to lighten my mood did little to help.

"Are you coming out again after tea, Neil?" he asked. "It's daylight until nearly nine o'clock now and I won't have to go to bed until ten o'clock. We can see if Nicky wants to come as well."

He fully understood why I was in this depressing mood and I decided it would be totally unfair to take it out on him. It was a warm and sunny day and surely being outside and doing something interesting would be better than sitting at home feeling miserable. I made an immediate attempt to lighten up a little.

"Okay, Billy, I'll call for you straight after tea and we can go round to see Nicky." Nicky had fully recovered from his injury and was due to return to school immediately after the Whitsuntide holiday.

I tried hard not to think about Susan's impending departure, but by the time Billy and I, having persuaded Nicky to join us which hadn't taken very much effort on our part, were walking up the hill towards the entrance to Woodhouse Ridge, it must have been obvious that she was still on my mind.

"Susan Brown's leaving on Friday, Nicky," I told him. "She's going to live in Hull."

"I know," he replied. "Johnny Jackson told me as he was going past our house on his way home from school. You liked her a lot, didn't you; but you can always get another girl friend, can't you?"

"She wasn't really my girl friend. We just liked each other, that's all, but she's the only girl I've ever been really interested in."

We paused at the entrance to the ridge and leaned on the rail taking in the vista before us that was so familiar: Sugarwell Hill at the other side of Meanwood Road, at the bottom of which the Dammy swiftly flowed towards its inevitable encounter with the River Aire in the city centre; the Destructor chimney owned by the council refuse department standing majestically by the roadside, the tallest construction of any kind in the city of Leeds and nearer to hand; on the ridge itself was the long abandoned bandstand and what remained of the terracing which before the war would have been occupied by ladies and gentlemen clad in their finest attire for the Sunday concert. We could just make out what the local kids had always called the Indian War Path, a very narrow path that hugged the contours of the hillside as it twisted and turned in various directions and which was much more interesting than the two more conventional wider paths above and beyond it.

"It's a lot hotter than I thought it was going to be," observed Billy as we made our way down the steps and onto the concrete path. "It seems more like July or August than the beginning of May."

"Yes, and it doesn't get dark for ages at this time of the year."

"Let's go play in Death Valley and Table Top," suggested Nicky, excitedly.

It seemed as good a place as any and we were all in agreement. We had travelled no more than a few yards before we encountered an elderly couple approaching us.

"I wish I'd known it was going to be as hot as this, Clara," said the man as they walked past us. "If I had I'd have worn something a lot cooler. I'm fair clemmed and that's a fact."

I looked at my two companions. "I've got to find out what 'clemmed' means," I said. "It's been driving me mad for weeks. Everybody seems to have a different meaning for it. Haven't either of you two any idea?"

"It's the first time I've heard it," responded Nicky, "But it must be something you say when you're too warm, mustn't it? At least that man that just passed us thinks so."

"I've no idea, Nicky, but I'm going to find out."

Before long we arrived at our intended destination. Death Valley was the name given to the area by all the local kids. It was so densely overgrown that imaginative minds could liken it to a jungle, an ideal place for boys of our age to act out some adventure. A few yards away was the area known as Table Top, a plateau which could only be reached by climbing a steep path. We decided to leave that for later and remain in the area which was most suitable for a game of Tarzan of the Apes. We were spoilt for choice with regard to suitable trees for climbing. We decided to take it in turns to see who could do the best Tarzan yell in the style of Johnny Wiesmuller who always played the part in the films we had seen at the Electra. I suggested that it would be much more effective if we actually climbed a tree and performed it from there. I managed to persuade Billy and Nicky that I should attempt it first on the grounds that it was my idea. After a little bit of arguing they both gave way and I walked over to what I considered to be the best tree for climbing. It wasn't too difficult to reach the fourth branch but I decided not to risk going any higher. I took a really deep breath in order to fill my lungs and gave out what, in my view, was every bit as good as the man himself managed on the screen. In fact I could almost imagine that a herd of elephants, all trumpeting, would soon be charging through the undergrowth to answer my call. I was keen to know what my two companions, who were standing a few yards back from the base of the tree, thought of my prowess. With this in mind I started to climb back down. I was still about fifteen feet from the ground when the branch I attempted to stand on broke away causing me to plunge heavily to the ground.

I obviously must have passed out for a while because when I awoke everything looked totally different. To begin with neither of my companions was in sight and the weather appeared to have changed. Instead of the warm sunshine that I had experienced earlier a cold mist seemed to have settled in giving a much more menacing appearance to my immediate surroundings. Obviously I must still have been in the same area, but I could not understand why apparently both Billy and Nicky had wandered off. I called their names several times without receiving any reply. Suddenly I heard what sounded like a child's voice. "Over here, over here; you can't catch me. You can't catch me," it said. I looked around but couldn't see anything at first. Then a small figure about three feet in height stepped from behind a tree. Despite its diminutive size it wasn't a child that I had heard for it had quite clearly the face of an adult male. What struck me as most odd was the fact that he was wearing a bright green jacket and had a ridiculous-looking green hat perched on his head. Before I could move towards him he disappeared again, but he continued to call out. "Can't catch me," he cried; "Can't catch me." He was obviously inviting me to follow him. I knew where I was but everything seemed so strange and I found myself shivering in the cold mist. I moved towards the spot where he had been standing and looked around. I shouted once more for my two friends but there was still no reply. I was perplexed as to why they had deserted me and why the weather had so dramatically changed.

The sun's rays suddenly broke through the mist and I spotted him running towards the back of the undergrowth where a near perpendicular bank rose up towards Table Top about fifty feet above us. I felt now that I had him cornered. Before I could reach him, however, he simply disappeared.

"Up here," he cried; "Up here."

I looked up to find him sitting on the branch of a tree about ten feet above me and this time he had a clay pipe in his hand.

"How did you do that?" I shouted.

"You can't catch me," he said. "I'm too quick for you."

"Are you a leprechaun?" I asked this strange creature.

"That I am, that I am; have been for nigh on two hundred years, and I've come a-looking for you I have."

"Why are you looking for me?"

"To tell you that you're doing it all wrong of course."

"What am I doing all wrong?"

"I'll have to be going now. I'm only allowed a few minutes, you see."

"But you haven't told me what I'm doing wrong."

"Sorry, can't stay. You'll just have to sleep on it and that's all I'm saying."

With that final statement he just disappeared, but I was by this time hearing other voices.

"Are you all right, Neil? Are you all right?" The voice was unmistakeably Billy's.

I suddenly realised that I was lying on my back and gazing at the sky. My two friends peered at me with anxious looks on their faces.

"What happened?" I asked them. "Did you see where he went?"

"What did you say?" asked Nicky.

"I asked you where he went, the leprechaun wearing the green hat and the green jacket. He was here talking to me and then he just disappeared."

I realised that I must have knocked myself out when I fell from the tree and imagined everything, but it all seemed so real.

"How long did I pass out for? How long is it since I fell?"

"It just happened a few seconds ago," said Billy. "We came over to you straight away."

"That's not possible I must have been out for at least a quarter of an hour."

I explained to them everything that had happened to me since I fell but they were adamant that that event had only just occurred. Had my encounter with the leprechaun then happened in the blink of an eye? It just didn't make any kind of sense to me. As far as injuries were concerned I didn't seem to have anything worse that a bruised knee and a headache. Considering from where I fell, I felt rather fortunate. I decided I wanted to head for home despite the fact that the weather was just as warm as it was when we entered the ridge, which was something else that also puzzled me. My companions, rather surprisingly, agreed to walk back with me. They were obviously fascinated by what I had told them and by my attempts to understand exactly what had happened to me.

"I don't see how everything that you told us happened could have done," said Nicky as we made our way home, "You were on the ground with us all the time. So it's not really possible, is it?"

"I bet he's just making it all up," added Billy.

"I didn't make any of it up, Billy. It wasn't at all like a dream either. It seemed so real. I think the leprechaun was trying to tell me something important. He told me that I was doing it all wrong and I didn't know what he meant. I think he was about to tell me what he meant but he must have changed his mind because he said that I'd just have to sleep on it."

We left the ridge and entered the street. My knee was starting to hurt rather badly, but what concerned me the most was what my mother might say when she saw the huge gash in my trousers.

"Are you going to tell your mam that you've fallen out of a tree?" asked Billy. "You might get a good hiding for doing it."

"I haven't got much choice, have I? My trousers are all ripped."

"Do you think she'll let you stay off school, Neil, because of your bruised knee?" asked Nicky.

"Don't be daft, Nicky. I'd have to have something a lot more serious than that. Anyway, I'm not sure I want to be off school. Susan's leaving at the end of the week, so I haven't got much time left to see her have I?"

By the time we entered our street I was beginning to feel really depressed, but uppermost in my mind was the fact that that brief period before I opened my eyes after falling seemed like ten or fifteen minutes but both of my friends still insisted that it was only a matter of a few seconds. Much to my dismay I was now having difficulty recalling exactly what had taken place. I knew that the leprechaun was trying to tell me something, but just as he was about to reveal exactly what, he just said that he would have to go and that he couldn't say any more.

"Look," said Nicky, "There's your girl friend over there."

I looked over to where he was pointing and spotted her and another girl that I didn't recognise, each with a skipping rope trying to jump in synchronised fashion. I decided not to disturb them as we hadn't been noticed.

However, just before we entered our street a sudden thought struck me.

"I'll have to go back up the hill to see Susan," I told my companions. "I think I know what the leprechaun was trying to tell me."

I didn't give them time to tell me that I was being stupid and that I had imagined it all. I began running towards the spot where I had last seen her. The two of them were still there.

"Susan," I called, "Can I talk to you for a minute?"

She stopped skipping and walked towards me. I attempted to explain what had happened to me after I fell out of the tree, but it all sounded so silly.

"Susan," I said, "I forgot to tell you that for the pendant to work you have to sleep on it. So when you go to bed tonight put it under your pillow."

"I don't really believe in all that Neil," she replied, "And my dad insists that we are all leaving after Whitsuntide."

"I'm not sure I do either but you've nothing else to lose, have you? What if it does have magical powers?

You might as well try it anyway. There's not much else you can do, is there?"

She agreed to give it a try. We both knew that we were clutching at straws, but when I went to bed I couldn't help but make a silent prayer.

CHAPTER TWENTYSEVEN

He looked a ridiculous figure standing at the bottom of the tree while wearing that silly green hat. Nevertheless, I was listening intently to what he had to say. "It's your own fault. It's your own fault, he chanted. "I wouldn't have let her get away like that. To be sure, I would not."

I assumed he was referring to Susan. "But I did tell her to sleep on it," I explained.

I knew that I was dreaming but once again everything seemed so real.

"Leave me alone," I eventually managed to say. "I need to wake up now."

I immediately opened my eyes and the image disappeared to be replaced by a new one. I turned onto my left side and gazed at the bedroom window. Despite the curtains being drawn together I could tell immediately that it was a glorious, sunny morning. The fact, however, that this particular Friday could well be the last time that I would ever set eyes on Susan Brown, thoroughly dampened my spirits. I was morose all through breakfast and when I found myself walking to school with Billy I couldn't help but inflict my mood onto him.

"Going to school's going to be terrible after Whitsuntide, Billy, with Susan not being there. I'll probably never see her again. I think I'll tell my mam that I've got a pain in my stomach and it hurts all the time. Then I won't have to go."

"You're getting all soppy again, Neil," he said. Don't forget that we might be joining the scouts next week"

"I know, Billy, but I just don't think I can face being in school anymore."

"If you pretend that you've got pains in your stomach I think Doctor Dunlop would send you to the Infirmary for them to do some tests. That's what happened with one of my uncles and they had to stick a tube up his bum to check it out. Anyway, if you were telling lies about it I bet your dad would find out and you'd probably get a good hiding."

What my closest friend was telling me made perfect sense, but it in no way helped to change my mood. When we entered the Assembly Hall, my first thought was to look for Susan. It did not take long for me to realise that she was not there. Had she and her family set off for Hull early? Was I to be deprived of even seeing her for what would probably be the last time? I could not bear the thought. The headmaster had already informed everybody that she would be leaving when we broke up for Whitsuntide and he offered no explanation for her absence on this particular day. As the Assembly period came to a close we all dispersed into our respective classrooms.

"Why hasn't Susan come, Billy?" I whispered to him before we took up our seats.

"I've no idea, Neil," he replied. I'm just as puzzled as you are. "Maybe she has left already."

I wondered if one of the girls might have more information, but didn't have time to ask as the headmaster was already taking command of his class. I wasn't expecting to pay much attention to his lesson in my current state of anxiety regarding the non-appearance of Susan, but from the moment he started speaking I was hooked from his very first sentence.

"Now," he began, "Is there anyone in this room apart from myself who is aware that Leeds was once an independent kingdom?"

His remark was greeted at first by total silence before Ken Stacey found the courage to speak. "I don't see how that can be true, sir," he said. "I mean Leeds is a city isn't it?"

"That's perfectly true, lad, and it has remained a city ever since King John granted it that status in the thirteenth century. However, I still maintain that it was indeed a kingdom in its own right long before that time."

I'm ashamed to admit that all thoughts of Susan had been temporarily banished from my mind. History had always been my favourite lesson and I waited eagerly for the headmaster to elaborate on his statement.

"If you have remembered anything at all from my history lessons over the past few months I'm sure you will recall that after the Romans left this island at the beginning of the fifth century small kingdoms sprang up all over Britain. In the main they consisted of various tribes each under the control of a tribal chieftain. One of these kingdoms was called Leodis but was probably, even then, pronounced as Leeds, though in the Anglo-Saxon tongue it was known as Elmet and that is how the village of Barwick-In-Elmet, which lies just off the road between Leeds and Tadcaster got its name."

It was obvious as I gazed across the classroom that the boys in particular were paying far more attention to this particular lesson than was normal. The headmaster continued.

"When King Edwin took the throne of Northumbria in the year 617, which then stretched throughout Yorkshire and into the south of what is now Scotland one of the first things he did was to stifle any perceived threats to his throne. This meant that he had to conquer any small British kingdom which dared to call itself independent and this of course included the kingdom of Leodis, which he succeeded in doing with very little difficulty having a much larger army available. The last king of Leodis, by the way, was called Ceretic."

He paused to allow this further information to be fully digested by his listeners.

"Now," he resumed, Are there any questions on this subject."

I was hoping that on this occasion Lorna Gale remained silent, yet I had no real need to worry as I had seen her yawning on at least two occasions. If the headmaster had noticed he had obviously chosen to ignore the fact and thereby save himself from having to extend his lesson by several minutes. No hands had been raised before I decided to raise my own.

"Yes, lad," he said, pointing in my direction, "What is your question?" He never addressed anyone by their personal name unless it was to bring them to the front of the class because of some breach of discipline.

"Why wasn't this included in the history book that we all read in class, sir?" I asked.

"That's right, sir," interrupted Alan Bartle. "I never saw it in the book either."

"The reason for that is quite simple. School history books deal with subjects of events that are of national importance only. Conquering the tiny kingdom of Leodis would not come into that category, though it is mentioned in either the Anglo-Saxon Chronicle or Bede's Eclesiastical History Of The English Nation, though I can't remember which. If you remember, when I was teaching you this period of history, I mentioned both of them as an excellent reference source."

I found it one of the most interesting morning lessons of the term and it kept my mind off Susan's non-appearance, but it dominated my thoughts again as soon as we entered the playground for the morning break. I looked for one of her friends who might have some explanation and spotted Wanda Aspinall chatting to Violet Pemberton.

"I'm walking over to talk to Wanda and Violet, Billy, "I told him.

"Aw, do you have to?" he replied. "There are three of the lads kicking a ball about over by the wall."

"Yes, I do Billy. I've got to find out why she isn't here."

"Well, you can please yourself, but I'm going for a kick about."

I wanted to join him, but thoughts of Susan were too strong.

I walked across to join the two girls. "Have you any idea why Susan hasn't come in today?" I asked.

"I suppose she must have already left for her new home in Hull," said Violet.

"And why would you want to know, I, wonder?" added Wanda.

I started to feel uncomfortable and hoped that my face wasn't turning crimson. "No real reason," I said, in what I hoped was a nonchalant manner. "I just wondered. That's all."

"We all know that you're sweet on her," laughed Wanda. "What are you going to do now that she's not here anymore?"

"Sophie Morton's always looking for a boy friend," suggested Violet, mischievously. "I'll put a good word in for you if you like."

As I left them and walked towards where Billy and the other lads were busy enjoying themselves both girls were giggling hysterically.

I joined in the kick-about for a while before we returned to the classroom. The remainder of the morning's lesson was, compared to what we had experienced earlier, considerably boring, and I was relieved to hear the school bell sound which signalled the end of it. My mood as Billy and I walked home together was not a good one.

"Well, that's it then, Billy," I said. "I'm never going to see Susan again, am I?"

"You don't know that for sure, Neil."

"Yes I do. She's already gone to live in Hull. I just know it."

"I bet you've got over it by the time we go back to school after the Whitsuntide holiday."

"I don't want to ever go back again, Billy."

"Well, I don't think there's very much you can do about that, Neil."

I knew that what he said was right but by the time we were walking back to school for the afternoon period my feeling of depression was even worse. What I didn't realise was that things were going to get infinitely better. Mr. Rawcliffe was about five minutes into his first lesson when there was a knock on the classroom door and Miss Hazlehurst walked in and whispered something in his ear.

"I want everyone in the room to remain silent while I attend to a small matter," he said. As soon as he had left the room the silence lasted for about thirty seconds before the constant muttering began. Everyone was aware that the last occasion upon which something like this occurred was when Nicky had an accident which led to him having to be taken to hospital. I hoped that no one else had suffered the same fate. The headmaster was away for more than ten minutes and his pupils were beginning to get agitated. He began to address the class as soon as he returned.

"I am delighted to inform you," he said, "That Susan Brown will be returning to this school immediately after the Whitsuntide holiday. The lady I have just been speaking to is Susan's mother and the family has decided after all not to relocate to Hull at the present time. Now, I suggest that you all get down to some work."

For the remainder of the afternoon I was feeling very pleased with myself, though a little disappointed that Susan herself had not made an appearance. Nevertheless, my mind was not altogether on the geography lesson. I was soon awakened from my musings by the headmaster's powerful voice.

"I'm sorry to interrupt your thoughts, Master Cawson," he boomed, "But perhaps you can tell us all why you are just sitting there with a silly grin on your face."

"Sorry, sir," I said, visibly startled.

"Well then, boy, I'm still waiting for an explanation."

Before I had chance to speak, I heard Wanda Aspinall's voice. "He wants Susan Brown to be his girl-friend, sir."

This statement was followed by girly giggles all around the classroom. I should have been feeling really embarrassed by this latest development, but I still felt elated with the realisation that Susan might not be leaving after all.

"I see," said the headmaster, with a smile on his face. "I think we'll leave the matter there then, but I expect you to be paying attention for the remainder of the afternoon's lesson. Is that understood?"

"Yes, sir," I replied.

I tried to give him the attention he asked for, and In the end I found out that it didn't prove too difficult because of my vastly improved state of mind and when the bell signalled the end of lessons I just couldn't wait to get myself outside. As Billy and I stepped outside the door we were greeted by an extremely impressive warm and sunny afternoon, one that matched my mood perfectly.

"We'll have to come out again after we get home, Billy," I said as we made our way along the street. "I can't stay cooped up inside right up to tea time."

"Right," said my companion, "I'll call round for you in five minutes."

I entered the house hoping that my mother would not have any errands that she wanted me to perform. Fortunately, she seemed glad to get me from under her feet as she was still performing one or two household chores, but she made me promise to be back inside by the time my father got home from work. As that was usually just after six o'clock it gave Billy and me just short of two hours to engage in whatever took our fancy.

"What do you fancy doing, Neil?" asked my closest friend as we stood in the street just a few minutes later.

"Well, it's such a warm, sunny afternoon, Billy," I replied. "Why don't we go onto the ridge?" I was hoping that I might encounter Susan once we were in her locality. However, as we walked across Melville Road and began walking up the hill there was no sign of her.

We reached the entrance to the ridge and leaned over the iron rail at the top of the few steps leading down to the concrete path. We often did this as it was one of our favourite vantage points and an excellent place for reflecting on times past.

"I wonder what caused Susan's dad to change his mind about going to Hull" I asked my companion.

"I've no idea, Neil," he replied, "But don't forget that Old Rawscliffe only said that they wouldn't be leaving at the present time. They might still be going later on."

I hadn't really taken much notice of that part of the headmaster's announcement, but at least the situation had improved from a few hours earlier.

We both stayed silent for a while as we gazed across the peaceful Meanwood valley with the ridge on one side and Sugarwell Hill on the other before Billy spoke again. "We've got a whole week to ourselves now, Neil, but I'm not really looking forward to Whit Sunday, are you?"

"No, I know we might collect a bit of money by showing people our Whitsuntide clothes, but it takes ages to get round all my aunts and uncles and my mam makes me keep them on all day and tells me that I mustn't play out in case I get them dirty. I always look forward to Whit Monday though. If it's a sunny day we often walk to that tea place in Adel Woods."

"What, do you mean you walk all the way? Don't you get the tram first as far as Meanwood terminus? I wouldn't want to walk that far."

"It's not really that bad, Billy. You hardly know that you're walking because you're in the countryside all the time. When you get to the end of the ridge you just cross over Grove Lane, and then walk along a ginnel to Monkbridge Road. You then follow another series of paths, one of which is where we saw that fox after the rugby game, that take you into Meanwood Woods. That's where you carry on walking by the side of the beck until you come to the Ring Road. After crossing that you find yourself on another path leading to a high bridge across the beck called the Seven Arches, which is deep in Adel Woods. After about ten or fifteen minutes you arrive at the tea place I mentioned and everybody sits on the banking with a tray of tea. Some people are eating sandwiches that they have brought with them. The best thing is realising that you've only had to cross three roads from the time you stepped onto Woodhouse Ridge. I've been told that you can go even further by crossing a golf course and ending up at Golden Acre Park, but we've never actually been that far."

"I have been as far as Adel Woods," indicated Billy, "But we never walked all the way. Anyway, I can't see me doing that on Whit Monday. I'm looking forward to having the week off school though, aren't you?"

"You bet, Billy; and I hope the weather stays like this."

"Don't forget, Neil, that we'll probably be able to join the scouts next week as well."

"Oh, I'd forgotten about that. I suppose there are a lot of things to look forward to, especially now that I know that Susan's coming back to school, even if it does turn out to be only temporary. I just wish I knew something for sure."

We never actually stepped onto the ridge, being contented to remain leaning against the iron rail while contemplating some of the activities we might be getting up to over the coming weeks, the warmth of the sun putting us in a lazy, relaxed mood. In my case, however, I was soon to be snapped out of it.

"Look," remarked Billy, "There's Susan over there."

I looked in the direction he was pointing and my heart leaped as it always did on those rare occasions when I met her unexpectedly. I stopped myself from running towards her and allowed her to approach me in a sedate manner.

"Did you hear the news, Neil?" she asked.

I was pleased that she still seemed to be wearing the pendant.

"Yes, Susan," I replied. "I heard that you will be coming back to school after Whitsuntide."

"Yes, but it's not all good news, because it seems that my dad's move to Hull has only been delayed."

"It's still better than it was before," suggested Billy. "I mean, something might still happen to stop him going."

"I don't think so, Billy," she replied before turning to face me. "It isn't that he's changed his mind about going. It's just that things aren't ready for him to step into the job yet."

"So, do you know when you're likely to be moving, Susan?"

"Not really, but I think it'll just be a matter of a few weeks. I still don't want to leave here, Neil, but my brother Peter and both of my parents think it would be a good thing to live near the sea, so I can't see my dad changing his mind."

After she had left I informed my constant companion that I fancied going back home. Realising that we had already used up much of the time we had allowed ourselves by just leaning on the rail at the top of the steps that led onto the ridge, he accompanied me back down the hill.

"You've gone very quiet, Neil," he said, acknowledging my lack of conversation. "Are you in a bad mood again?"

I thought hard about that, balancing in my mind the fact that Susan would be back at school for a few more weeks alongside the fact that it was still likely that she would then be moving away permanently.

I don't know, Billy," I answered. "I suppose you could just say that I'm fair clemmed, if I knew what it meant, that is."

About the Author

The author, born in 1939 at the beginning of the Second World War, has lived in Leeds all his life and has never seen any reason to leave. He was educated at Woodhouse Junior School up to the age of eleven before moving on to Leeds Central High School. He married in 1975 and most of his working life has been spent in the service of British Telecom. He has always possessed a desire to write, but it was not until reaching retirement age that he found he had the time to do so. 'The Woodhouse Pendant' is his third book.

9 781786 232458